Face Down in the Gene Pool

A Brooke Roberts Mystery

Novels by Nancy Labs

Wishing You Harm

Undead All over

Face Down in the Gene Pool

A Brooke Roberts Mystery

Nancy Labs

Doylestown, PA

PARAMETER
PUBLISHING

Cover

Cover design/layout: Wayne Labs

Face Down in the Gene Pool

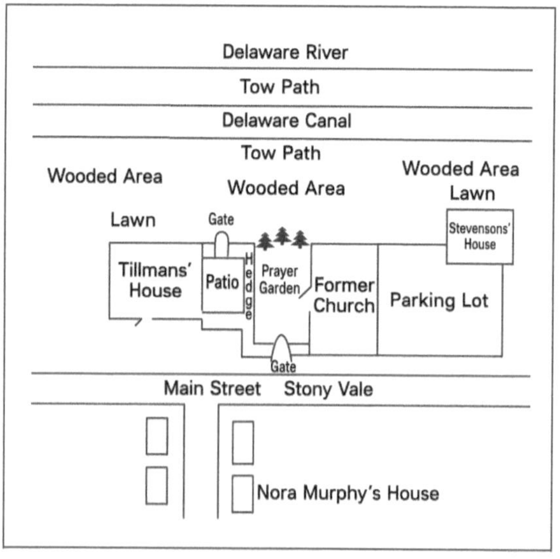

Partial map of Stony Vale shows Tillmans' house and patio, prayer garden, Stevensons' house, and the former church.

Prologue

The gate in the privet hedge opened easily, but no one was waiting on the patio when Jenna arrived. It wasn't her fault she was late. Had her contact given up and left?

Crossing the flagstones she knelt beside a pond and gazed at the goldfish flitting in and out among the lily pads. They seemed at peace with the world. No headaches. No stress. No fear. She scrunched her shoulders to relieve the tension and rubbed her arm, still stinging from Malcolm's possessive grasp. She shuddered at the thought that he might follow her here.

She looked down at her reflection in the water, stirred by the flutter of golden fins. To the world, she was a stunning twenty-nine-year-old with blue eyes, blond hair and a smile that drew men like a magnet. Friends told her she should have been a model—she had the looks, poise and personality. Instead, she'd followed a different path, one whose twists and turns had brought her here.

Footsteps approached from behind. It wasn't too late after all. She looked over her shoulder, but before she could speak, searing pain burrowed into her skull. And then blood. On her jacket. In her mouth. Dripping from her hair and onto the patio. She struggled to stand but the ground heaved beneath her, and the bright spring day faded to black.

One

D r. Prescott Tillman's home was the oldest and most distinguished dwelling in the tiny village of Stony Vale. Built two-and-a-quarter centuries ago, only those with the surname Tillman had ever lived beneath its roof. When his elder brother passed away, Dr. Tillman retired to his ancestral home with his wife, noted author, Eleanor Lawrence Tillman.

The Federal-era brick house sat well back from Main Street in Stony Vale on a property that sloped gently downhill to the Delaware Canal and River. A prayer garden enclosed by a hedge separated the house from the building next door—a former Methodist Church shared now by the Stony Vale Center for Alternative Spirituality and the Stony Vale Historical Society. The latter was hosting today's genealogy conference.

"It doesn't make sense," Brooke said as she and her 83-year-old great-uncle left the conference at noon on a bright day in late March. "A power couple like Dr. Tillman and his wife could have retired anywhere in the world—New Zealand, Portugal, Tuscany—anywhere. After such exciting careers, it must be tough adjusting to life in a little backwater like Stony Vale."

"I'm sure they're doing just fine," Uncle Nelson said as they passed the enclosed prayer garden. "I grew up in Stony Vale, and I completely understand Prescott's attachment to his native soil. If you study the history of the region, you'll find the Tillman name popping up everywhere.

"And as far as Eleanor's concerned," he continued, "she appreciates the peace and quiet of life along the river while she works on her next book—a departure, I understand, from her usual treatises on the bloodlines of European royalty."

In Brooke's opinion, none of those factors explained why Dr. Tillman, an icon in the field of transhumanism, had traded the global spotlight for a sleepy village along the Delaware just south of Easton. Perhaps, like Uncle Nelson, he had warm childhood memories of exploring the riverbanks and the rocky hillsides that gave the village its name. Perhaps he saw Stony Vale as idyllic, peaceful and charming—a land that time forgot, and a place to quiet his soul as he prepared to meet his Maker. Whatever the case, Brooke decided it was none of her business.

"I'm looking forward to meeting him," she said. "It was nice of him to invite you to lunch and to let me tag along."

"Indeed," her uncle agreed. "The meal promises to be a lot tastier than the box lunches they're handing out at the conference. But more importantly, Prescott's a colorful character, and I'm sure you'll enjoy his company."

They followed a walkway to the sprawling residence—not a mansion exactly, but approaching that in scale. Uncle Nelson rang the bell and seconds later, a tall, wiry individual with black-framed glasses and a mop of unkempt silver hair welcomed them inside. He was dressed casually in a herringbone tweed jacket, black tee-shirt and jeans, a distinct contrast to Uncle Nelson's signature dark suit, thin white hair and wire-rimmed glasses.

In the foyer, a trio of Welsh Corgis crowded around

Brooke, begging for attention. "I'm happy to meet you, Dr. Tillman," she said as cold, wet noses tickled her ankles. "Uncle Nelson speaks highly of you."

"Hah!" the scientist laughed. "You can't believe a word that old rascal says. And I'll have none of that doctor stuff. I dispensed with those formalities the day I retired. Call me Prescott—or Tillman, if you prefer. But don't let the word 'doctor' escape your lips."

That said, he led them down the hallway with the Corgis scuffling and scurrying behind him. "I call them my happy little mutants," he called over his shoulder. "Thanks to mutations in the FGF4 gene, they're doomed to a lifetime of waddling on legs too short and stubby for the rest of their bodies. But it doesn't seem to faze them. Look at their faces—have you ever seen such joy?"

In the kitchen, he removed some paninis from the fridge and was placing them in the microwave when the doorbell rang and set the Corgis scampering.

"I hope you don't mind," he said. "I've taken the liberty of inviting today's keynote speaker to join us."

Uncle Nelson seemed pleased by the news. "Mind? Not at all."

Here we go again, Brooke told herself. Since her husband's death nearly two years ago, her uncle had been trying to throw her into the arms of the handsome director of the Tri-County Historical Conservancy. Uncle Nelson's intentions were good— he wanted to see her settled in a stable relationship. But couldn't he understand that no one could ever take Karl's place?

Tillman returned a moment later with David Price. Uncle Nelson shook David's hand, but Brooke's greeting was less cordial—a quick hello and a polite smile before turning her attention to a Corgi who seemed to have developed an affection for her.

"While I'm finishing up here," Tillman said as he dodged the Corgis in his path, "go out to the patio and take a look at the fishpond my children gave me for my birthday last fall. They named it 'the gene pool'—the sort of gag you'd expect when dear old dad happens to be a geneticist. It's a private oasis out there with the privet hedge screening us from view. You'll have to come back later this spring and see the perennials when they start blooming."

David seemed keen to take a look, but instead of joining them, Uncle Nelson stayed behind to chat with their host. His scheme was painfully obvious. He was giving David an opportunity to cozy up to Brooke and work his magic. But there was no magic—just idle chatter about nothing at all as they walked through the sunroom toward the patio. Midsentence, David fell silent, his hand on the doorknob and his eyes fixed on something in the distance.

Brooke followed his gaze and saw beds of rich brown earth where flowers would soon blossom. Off to one side, plastic sheeting protected patio furniture and next to it…?

A woman floating face down in Prescott Tillman's gene pool.

Two

A scream rose in Brooke's throat but she swallowed it and raced to the pond. Was the woman still alive? Kneeling down, she struggled to turn the body over. It took a few tries, and when she finally succeeded, the woman slithered from her hand, splashed beneath the water and bobbed to the surface. She gasped when a familiar face came into view. Jenna Henley, her forehead split open and the skin surrounding the wound white and puckered like fungus on a rotting log.

"Stand back," David said from over Brooke's shoulder. But she didn't stand back. Instead, she helped him drag Jenna out of the pond and onto the flagstones, her blue eyes staring blindly at the vast, azure sky while one fragile white hand trailed in the water.

Kneeling beside her, David pried her mouth open and pressed his lips against hers. Out goes the bad air; in goes the good. But the good air did no good—it was too late for that.

Footsteps approached from the rear. "How ghastly," Brooke heard Uncle Nelson say. Seconds later, he was on his phone, describing the scene to a 9-1-1 dispatcher.

"What is it?" Tillman shouted from the sunroom. Soon he too was at their side, his jaw slack as he stared at the lifeless creature sprawled on the flagstones. "This is terrible," he moaned. "A nightmare. A disaster." He reached for his phone. "I've got to tell my wife."

David stood up and peeled off his wet blazer. "Is that wise? The fewer people who know about this, the better. At least until the police get here."

"I agree with David," Uncle Nelson said. "Best to keep chaos at a minimum." He glanced at Brooke. "Are you all right, my dear?"

She barely heard the question, caught up as she was in reliving her last moments with Jenna. They'd been chatting in the registration line when Jenna fell silent, her eyes on a swarthy, dark-haired guy in jeans and a leather jacket.

"I can't believe Malcolm followed me here," she'd whispered. *"He's been stalking me because he thinks I'm seeing my old boyfriend. I'd better talk to him before he makes a scene. Save me a seat, will you?"*

Brooke had saved a seat, but Jenna never came back.

A siren wailed in the distance, growing louder and falling silent in front of the house. Seconds later, a team of EMTs barreled through the gate in the hedge, followed by two uniformed officers. As they went about their business, voices swelled in the background.

"Just what we don't need," Tillman groaned. "The folks at the conference heard the siren and came running."

"Prescott!" a woman's voice shouted over the din. "Are you alright?" She elbowed her way through the crowd that blocked the gate in the hedge. When she saw Jenna, she gasped and clutched at her heart.

"This is a crime scene, ma'am," a cop said. "I'll have to ask you to leave the area—same as everyone else."

"She's my wife," Tillman spoke up. "This is our home."

The officer paused to consider the situation. "Okay then. But the rest of you—stay back beyond the hedge."

Mrs. Tillman drew close to her husband and touched his arm. When he didn't respond, she stepped away and watched in silence as one cop took pictures and the other stood guard at the gate.

Moments later, a pair of familiar faces appeared—Homicide Detective James Burleigh and his sidekick, Detective Jason Radley. They looked the same as when Brooke had last seen them six months ago. Burleigh was still about thirty pounds overweight, still wearing a charcoal-gray suit that should have been replaced two seasons ago and still scowling from beneath a pair of bushy gray eyebrows. His younger sidekick also looked the same—tall and lanky with a longish face that radiated perpetual cynicism.

The detectives knelt to examine the body, and after conferring with the EMTs, they walked to the opening in the hedge and gazed out over the lawn leading eastward toward the canal and the river. It was easy to read their thoughts. The stampede from the genealogy conference had obliterated the killer's footprints. Not only that, but Brooke's attempts at rescue and David's attempt at resuscitation probably destroyed traces of evidence near the pond.

Burleigh's eyes came to rest on Brooke. "What puts you at the crime scene?"

She nodded toward her host. "Dr. Tillman invited us to lunch. David Price and I were on our way to look at the fishpond, and then…"

Her gaze shifted to Jenna who lay like a discarded rag doll on the flagstones.

"We were at a genealogy conference," Dr. Tillman managed to explain. "A daylong event at the building next door."

Burleigh nodded. "And you are…?"

"Dr. Prescott Tillman. This is my home."

"And your relationship to the deceased?"

"I never saw her before." He hesitated, his eyes probing Jenna's face. "That I can recall with any certainty."

"But you may have seen her before?"

"Possibly. I travel in wide circles."

His wife frowned at those words and looked away, her silvery hair glimmering in the sunlight. If Burleigh noticed Mrs. Tillman's reaction, he didn't let on. Instead, he turned to David Price and reached out his hand. "Good to see you again, Mr. Price. But not under these circumstances."

"No, sir."

"And your relationship to the deceased?"

"We've never met."

Burleigh turned to Uncle Nelson. "Well, Dr. Roberts, it's been some time since our paths crossed. I trust you've been well since we last saw you? No more close calls?"

Uncle Nelson assured him that life had quieted down considerably—until this moment.

That settled, Burleigh asked Tillman for permission to conduct interviews in the sunroom while the team went about their business on the patio. When Tillman agreed to the plan, Burleigh said he'd begin with Brooke while the others waited in the living room until needed.

The questioning was pretty straightforward and so were Brooke's answers. She explained that she and Jenna were neighbors in the Beacon Arms Apartments in Easton, several miles north of Stony Vale. In addition, Jenna was a vendor in the Artisans' Emporium, a co-op where vendors rented space to sell high-end merchandise. She also worked parttime in a veterinary clinic, and she was writing a book that she wanted Brooke to edit. They'd been discussing it in the registration line when Jenna excused herself to talk to Malcolm, a guy she'd been seeing who showed up unexpectedly. He followed her, Jenna said, because he suspected her of seeing her old boyfriend. They left together, and she never came back.

"Malcolm's last name?" Burleigh asked.

"She didn't say."

"The old boyfriend's name?"

Brooke shrugged. "I have no idea. To tell you the truth, I didn't know Jenna very well. We were acquaintances, not friends. She wanted me to edit her book—something about the harmful effects of inbreeding in dogs."

After a few more questions, Burleigh fixed Brooke in a familiar stare. "I know how your mind works," he said. "You like solving puzzles—in fact it's second nature with you. I can't stop you from playing armchair detective, but I can and will insist that you leave the heavy lifting to us. Do you understand?"

"I never intended to solve those other two cases," she reminded him. "It just turned out that way."

He drew in his breath and it seemed to her that his face reddened. "I want you to listen to me, and listen good. You're lucky to be alive after those two incidents. Third times the charm, so don't push your luck."

He dismissed her with a wave of his hand and a request that she send her uncle for questioning. In the living room, she took a seat directly across from the Tillmans who sat silently at either end of the sofa, the three Corgis wedged in between them. David Price occupied a chair to Brooke's left, and she noticed him trying to make eye contact, just like he'd done during the keynote. Several times she'd caught him gazing at her from the podium, and each time she'd looked away. Ignoring him, she leaned back in the chair and reflected on the day's events.

It was easy to figure out what happened. Jenna and this Malcolm guy got into an argument about Jenna seeing her old boyfriend. For some reason they moved the argument to the Tillman's patio where Malcolm killed her in a fit of jealousy and threw her body in the pond. The case would be closed by the end of the day. And yet…

She recalled the way Tillman responded to Burleigh's questions on the patio. After saying he didn't know Jenna, he walked back the remark a second later. His wife had noticed it too—Brooke could tell by the way she'd looked at him. Did he know more about Jenna than he was willing to say, and was that the reason he and Eleanor were on opposite ends of the sofa?

These thoughts occupied her mind until Uncle Nelson returned from the sunroom and announced that he and Brooke were free to go. Shaking off his silence, Tillman suggested they leave by a side door to avoid the crowd on the opposite lawn, and his wife spoke up to say that under the circumstances, the afternoon sessions at the conference were cancelled.

On the way home, Uncle Nelson suggested they pick up something for lunch—something easy to digest, given what they'd been through. Brooke agreed and once that was settled, the drive proceeded in silence.

Three

Ted Roslyn stretched his legs beneath his favorite table at his favorite coffeeshop. It was good to be back in the Lehigh Valley after three weeks of speaking engagements across the country. His talks had been well received, and his podcast, *Dispelling the Darkness*, was gaining subscribers daily. Judging from the comments, people liked what he had to say.

But as much as it felt good to be home after a three-week trek, he'd felt a hollow emptiness when he'd unlocked the door last night with no wife, no kids and no pets waiting to greet him. But maybe—just maybe—that was about to change.

Picking up his phone, he scrolled to a photo he'd received earlier that morning. Ashley sure was easy on the eyes, Long, blond hair swept back in a ponytail. Blue eyes smiling at him from behind glasses with bulky, black frames. The scholarly look, she'd told him. He agreed—the glasses made her appear bookish and smart—which she was. But she was another person altogether when she swapped the glasses for contacts. Scholarly or drop-dead gorgeous. Both were winners.

Sometimes though, he wondered what she saw in him. He wasn't bad looking in an uncombed, casual sort of way. With deep-set brown eyes, a broad forehead and a square jaw, he projected a strong, confident image in his twice weekly video podcasts. His deficits weren't in the looks department—they were in the wealth department. Years ago, he quit his job at a respected newspaper and had gone independent. His audience was growing, but his finances had yet to catch up.

So far, Ashley didn't seem to mind that he wasn't rolling in the green stuff. They'd met over the Christmas holidays at a lecture about archaeology in the Holy Lands. When he learned that this lovely creature shared his Christian faith, he'd begun to wonder if they had a future together. Hints she'd dropped had led him to think that she was wondering the same thing.

Even so, something seemed to be holding him back. Was it the scars of his first marriage? Was he afraid of making another mistake? And what about children? He was thirty-eight; Ashley just turned thirty-two. Would she want a family or would that interfere with her plans for graduate school and a university position teaching ancient Middle Eastern history?

But he was getting ahead of himself. Ashley currently taught world history in a Pittsburgh high school. She'd be back in the area a week from now to visit her parents for spring break. He'd cleared his calendar to allow time for them to be together, and he expected his doubts to vanish by the time the week was over. In the meanwhile, he had work to do. Podcast scripts didn't write themselves.

He entered the word *transhumanism* into his laptop and brought up a definition. *Transhumanism*, it said, *is the belief that humans can transcend their physical limitations through the use of neurotech, biotech, nanotech and* AI.

Sounds good on the surface. The impulse to transcend human limitations is the engine that drives exploration and invention. But transhumanists had bigger goals than that. They sought to direct human evolution toward a posthuman future. What would being posthuman look like? That was a question Ted intended to explore.

He took a sip of coffee and glanced out the window at the vehicles lined up in the parking lot. In the distance he saw a woman get out of a car. Something about her seemed familiar, and as she drew closer, the details came into focus. Chestnut hair cut just about chin length. Well-defined cheek bones, a slender figure and an oval face that tapered to a graceful chin. The reason he was having trouble committing to Ashley—the real reason—the one he hated to admit to himself—had just opened the door.

As she approached, he scrambled to his feet and stared without speaking.

"Ted?" Brooke began. It sounded like a question—like she'd forgotten his name. But there was no way she could forget—not after all they'd been through together.

"Hey," he said. "Good to see you. How're things going?"

Her response came slowly. "It's been a rough day. Other than that…"

The rough part he could believe. She looked frazzled and unsettled. He thought of their earlier encounters and the things that followed. Just seeing her was a warning that danger was near, but she didn't seem particularly dangerous at the moment. If anything, she seemed forlorn. Bewildered. Needy in a way that brought back memories of the day they'd first met. He'd given her a name that autumn afternoon—the Sad-Eyed Woman of Mystery. And here she was, still sad-eyed and still mysterious.

"I was invited to lunch this afternoon," she told him. "At the home of a man named Prescott Tillman."

The name sent Ted's mind reeling. "THE Prescott Tillman? The guy who pitches transhumanism at conferences all over the world?"

She nodded. "He's a friend of my uncle's. He and his wife moved to Stony Vale a while back. He sent us outside to see his fishpond. There was a body in the water."

"Wow," Ted said, and then he said it again. That's how it was with Brooke. Her news was never normal. It was the sort of news that rattled a person to his core. That was part of the fascination.

"Ted—I knew her," she continued. "We'd spoken just a few hours earlier, and there she was. Dead. Murdered. And it happened during a genealogy conference. Genealogy, of all things. How dangerous can that be?"

He turned the question over in his mind. "Pretty dangerous," he concluded. "Contested wills. Paternity suits. Monarchies overthrown. Civil wars. And then there's eugenics and transhumanism. The human gene pool's swimming with sharks."

A weak smile faded as quickly as it had come. "I'd like to talk more," she said. "But not now. My uncle's waiting in the car."

She excused herself and made her purchase at the counter. As she was leaving, her eyes met his, and just like that, the old electricity was back.

Four

The chocolate-chip scone should have been melt-in-your-mouth luscious, but at the moment it tasted like cardboard. Brooke had no appetite—finding a dead body has that effect on a person. And she didn't feel much like talking as she sat at Uncle Nelson's kitchen table. But there was a story to be told, and since he wanted to hear it, she forced herself to talk.

"Seems cut and dried, doesn't it?" he said once she'd provided the details. "I suspect the detectives will have this Malcolm individual behind bars before the day's over. But if they don't…" He fixed her in a stern gaze, one she'd seen many times before. "Promise me you'll let the experts handle the investigation. We don't need you getting tangled up in the things like you did after Karl's death and after the murder last fall at Sussex Academy."

Brooke put down her mug of tea. "It's not like I wanted to get involved in those cases. I was in the center of the first one—it involved my husband, in case you've forgotten. And as far as Sussex Academy is concerned, I got dragged into that mess whether I wanted to be involved or not."

"I realize that. But in each case, you allowed your analytical mind to steer you into straight into trouble." He laid a hand gently across hers. "Promise you won't let it happen again."

She gazed at his blue-veined hand resting on hers. Her great-uncle was the sweetest, dearest thing in the world, and her only living relative. "Assuming I have an analytical mind," she said, "Who helped me develop it? Who read Sherlock Holmes stories to me when I was little, and who watched TV mysteries with me and challenged me to beat the detectives to a solution? And who gave me books of brain teasers for my birthday and coached me in chess strategies? If I have an analytical mind, it's because of you."

He raised both hands in surrender. "Guilty as charged. But to be fair, I challenged you to be an armchair detective, not a practicing one."

She eyed him critically. "Detective Burleigh used that same phrase. Did he put you up to this?"

Her uncle shrugged. "He may have mentioned something along those lines—only because he's concerned for your well-being. But that's beside the point. The truth is, my dear, I don't want to lose you."

The expression on his elderly face tugged at Brooke's heart. "I'll make you a deal. I'll promise to stay out of the investigation if you'll promise to stop setting me up with…"

The intercom buzzed, announcing a visitor. David Price, of course. The last person Brooke wanted to see. Soon he was with them at the table, slathering cream cheese on a cinnamon-raisin bagel. Apparently finding a dead body had no effect on his appetite.

"Wrong, wrong, wrong," he smirked when Brooke retold her story. "Malcolm Mackenzie didn't follow Jenna to the conference—he stopped by to hear my keynote address."

Uncle Nelson placed the scone he was eating back on his

plate. "Did you say 'Malcolm Mackenzie'? The contractor who specializes in historic restoration? The one the Historical Conservancy keeps recommending?"

"That's right," David said. "I've known him for years. We met at a preservation conference seven years ago when I was curating a museum in Brooklyn."

Brooke found the news astonishing. David was the director of the Historical Conservancy and Uncle Nelson sat on the board. Both men had high standards for the contractors and speakers they recommended.

"Are we talking about the same person?" she asked. "Six feet or thereabouts. Swarthy. Good-looking with dark hair."

David nodded. "That's the guy."

She let out a laugh. "I hate to burst your bubble, but your friend left the conference with Jenna, and a few hours later, she showed up in the Tillmans' fishpond. It's pretty obvious what happened."

David dismissed the idea with a laugh. "There's nothing obvious about it."

"Of course, there is. Malcolm had the opportunity and the motive."

"And the motive was…?"

"Jealousy. He was upset that Jenna was seeing her old boyfriend again."

The comment earned a dismissive frown. "Even if that were true," David argued, "Mac wouldn't bash a woman over the head and throw her in a pond."

"Such things have been known to happen."

"Not in this case. I'd stake my life on it."

"I'm inclined to agree with David," Uncle Nelson said. "Malcolm Mackenzie is a skilled craftsman with a reputation for excellence."

"That's right," David agreed. "When it comes to his work, Mac's a perfectionist."

Brooke scoffed at the remark. "Did you ever think that perfectionists might not like their girlfriends seeing other guys? The situation drove him crazy, and he killed her in a fit of rage. Or at least that's what the evidence suggests."

David gave her a look that showed just how deeply he disagreed with her so-called evidence. She glanced at her uncle for support, but his brow was furrowed, his eyes downcast and he appeared to be recalibrating.

She took a sip of tea. Without Malcolm as a suspect, who would have killed Jenna and tossed her, face down, in Prescott Tillman's gene pool?

If not Malcolm, then who?

Five

The question was still foremost in Brooke's mind when she woke up on Sunday morning. *If not Malcolm, then who?* She was tempted to linger beneath the covers and ponder the matter, but there was work to be done.

Outside, an icy drizzle fell from sky, and spring, having made a brief appearance the day before, was nowhere to be seen. She forced herself out of bed, and once she'd turned it back into a sofa, she brewed coffee and sat down in front of her laptop. Her editing business had picked up recently, and she welcomed the increased workload. And not just for the income. She and Karl had invested wisely, and while she wasn't rolling in cash, she wasn't needy either. Her real reason for taking on new clients was more nuanced than that. She glanced at her wedding ring. Work was a distraction that kept her from thinking about the life she and Karl had shared.

She entered her password into her laptop and opened the file for a bi-monthly newsletter she was editing for the Hewitt Gallery in Bethlehem. The headline story spoke of an upcoming exhibit featuring a series of abstract paintings—a departure from the easier-to-sell impressionist pieces the gallery was known for. Other articles discussed an installation of Tiffany windows at the Allentown Art Museum and highlighted current exhibits at the many colleges and university galleries dotting the Lehigh Valley.

The material was interesting, but Brooke's mind was elsewhere. She kept picturing Jenna's reaction to seeing Malcolm in the open doorway in the foyer at the genealogy conference. There were many ways a woman might respond to being followed by a man she considered overly possessive. She might be furious at him for crowding her. She might see him as a neurotic loser, worthy of contempt. Conversely, she might find him adorable—an affectionate puppy who wanted nothing more than to be in her presence. Instead, Jenna seemed to see him as a threat. Her reaction spoke volumes, and so did the timing of the crime. And while Uncle Nelson and David saw Malcolm's perfectionistic nature as an asset, Brooke had a different slant on the matter.

She pictured a crowded courtroom and a hardnosed prosecutor pacing back and forth before a jury. *"We've heard the defendant described as a 'perfectionist,'"* the prosector would say. *"But perfectionism sometimes walks hand in hand with a mental condition known as pathological narcissism. Individuals with this personality disorder are determined to maintain control at all costs. I would argue that Malcolm Mackenzie was more than a jealous lover—he was a narcissistic control freak who micromanaged every aspect of his love affair with Jenna. When a rival threatened his control, he snapped and killed her in a fit of narcissistic rage."*

Another picture sprang to mind—Prescott Tillman with his wild, white hair and a look of utter bewilderment on his face. He'd told the detectives he'd never seen Jenna before, but no sooner had he made that statement than he walked it back by saying he traveled in wide circles.

Was Tillman being hypervigilant by answering that way, or

was he struggling to keep a lid on details he didn't want to reveal? The look on his wife's face suggested the latter, and that made Tillman a possible answer to the question—*if not Malcolm, then who?*

Curious to learn more, Brooke went online and watched news videos about the murder. One source said Jenna sustained a blow to the head from a rock found at the bottom of the Tillmans' pond. But according to the Tillmans, there'd been no rocks on the patio or in the flowerbeds. That meant, they insisted, that the killer brought it there from somewhere else. But it wasn't the head injury that killed Jenna. Instead, she'd died from drowning.

Another story focused on Jenna's family in Utah. Her dad was a professor at Brigham Young University. Her mom worked parttime at the Provo Public Library. They had nine kids—Jenna was the oldest.

"We haven't seen her in years," the distraught mother sobbed. "There'd been a misunderstanding, and while we begged her to reconcile, she refused. And now…" The woman turned her face away and buried it in her husband's shoulder.

"This is not the reunion we'd hoped for," Jenna's father said, his stalwart posture failing to mask his grief. "In just a few days, she'll return to us in a coffin."

Another report named Brooke as the individual who'd found Jenna's body. So much for anonymity. Before long, complete strangers would be after her with questions. The thought was unsettling. She was a private person, and she didn't want people scaling the walls of the fortress she'd built for herself.

And that included Ted Roslyn. Eighteen months ago, he'd saved her life and the lives of two other people. She was indebted to him, but the interest he'd shown in her seemed to go beyond friendship. She'd maintained her distance for that reason and for one other reason as well. God. With Ted, God was always in the picture.

She heard a knock at the door. "Open up," a voice called out. "It's me, Maggie."

Brooke braced herself for an emotional encounter. Her high-maintenance neighbor was the manager of the Artisans' Emporium where Jenna rented retail space. More than that, Maggie and Jenna were friends, and they often hung out together at each other's apartments.

When Brooke opened the door, Maggie stumbled across the threshold and threw herself in Brooke's arms.

I can't believe it," she said, her tall, lanky body quivering as she sobbed. "Jenna—murdered—how is it possible?"

Brooke held her that way until the tears subsided. After that, she settled Maggie at the kitchen table and poured coffee for both of them.

"Look at me," Maggie said. "I'm a mess." She ran a hand through her spiky yellow hair—not blond, but yellow—as in daffodils, taxis and children's raincoats. She pointed to her plaid, flannel pajama bottoms and baggy gray hoodie. "I cried myself to sleep last night, and I woke up too upset to get dressed and go to work. It took me almost an hour to find someone to cover for me."

She paused to dab at her eyes with a tissue. "You were at the genealogy conference yesterday—tell me what happened." When Brooke finished, Maggie took a sip of coffee and sat in thought.

"It could be Malcolm," she finally said. "But in my opinion, the cops should be talking to Jenna's business partner, Nora Murphy."

Brooke's ears perked up at that statement. Here was another possible answer to the *if-not-Malcolm-then-who* question. She listened attentively as Maggie described an incident that took place in the Emporium a week or so ago. Nora stormed into the store, shouting and yelling and accusing Jenna of hitting on her boyfriend, a guy named Seth Walker. "*Malcolm isn't good enough for you?"* Nora had screamed. *"You have to get your hands on Seth as well?"*

"The whole thing took place in front of vendors and customers," Maggie said. "It was a huge mess and when Nora started acting aggressive, I threatened to call the police if she didn't leave."

"Wow—you really thought she might get violent?"

"That's right. And if you could have heard her language…" Maggie rolled her eyes at the thought. "I guess you can see now why I think Nora should be considered a suspect. But there's more to it than just that. She lives in Stony Vale—just a block from where Jenna died."

She let out a sigh and stared morosely at her half-empty coffee mug. "Up until that day, Jenna was happy and bubbly and excited about an agency finally locating her birthmother. The fight with Nora put a damper on all that."

Brooke thought of the heartbroken parents she'd seen on the news. "I didn't know Jenna was adopted."

"She was, and she spent a ton of money trying to find her real mom. She and her birthmother were planning a reunion in a few weeks. I have no idea who she is or where she lives, and the poor woman probably has no idea what happened."

Sighing, Maggie reached into her pocket, pulled out a key and laid it on the table. "Jenna asked me to feed her kittens while she visits her mom. And now that Jenna's dead, I keep wondering what will happen to them."

"Kittens?" Brooke said. "We can't have pets in this building. It says so in the lease."

Maggie waved off the comment. "No one in this dump cares about the rules. But that's beside the point. Now that Jenna's gone, someone has to look after Donnie and Marie."

Brooke smiled at the names. Donnie and Marie were a Mormon brother-and-sister act from a long time ago. Their names probably reflected Jenna's Mormon upbringing.

"You'll probably think I'm crazy," Maggie said, "but I'm spooked about going up to her apartment by myself. What if I feel a cold chill against the back of my neck. What if I hear footsteps in the bedroom or a voice whispering in the shadows? You've heard of such things, haven't you?"

Brooke recalled those terrible days after Karl's death and the strange feeling she'd had that he was still with her in the house. An illusion, she'd told herself. A habit of mind, like the sensation of a phantom limb when the real one's gone.

"I can't shake the idea," Maggie said. "But the kittens will starve if I don't take care of them. Go up there with me—please?"

Brooke pictured two little kittens mewing for someone to feed them. "Sure, I'll go with you," she said. "We can't let them starve."

Six

Maggie unlocked the door to Jenna's fifth-floor apartment, and when she opened it, something small and beige raced past and into an adjacent room. Not a disembodied spirit—just a startled kitten. A second kitten with black fur and amber eyes watched Brooke from the opposite side of the room. Maggie introduced the kitten as Marie, and when she headed for the kitchen, Marie followed.

While they were gone, Brooke eyed her surroundings. For the most part, the furnishings represented the sorts of repurposed items Jenna sold at Artisans' Emporium. A coat of white paint had turned an out-of-date coffee table into a stylish piece with an upscale vibe. A layer of silver paint had converted an old French-provincial bureau into a trendy sideboard. And the focal point of the room, a faux fireplace with a faux-marble finish, provided a touch of elegance. Chic but cheap. Champagne taste on a beer budget.

A folder lay on the coffee table, its contents spilling out on the surface. Curious, Brooke glanced at the title page. *Birthing our Four-Legged Friends: The Dark History of Dog Breeding and Inbreeding.* The sight tugged at her heart—this was the manuscript Jenna had been telling her about when Malcolm showed up.

She turned her attention to a bookshelf next to the sofa with a photo of Jenna posed with a mob of people of various ages. Brooke was studying it when Maggie came out of the kitchen with a can of cat food.

"The Henley clan," Maggie said. "Jenna's adoptive parents thought they couldn't have kids, but once they adopted Jenna, the mom got pregnant and had one baby after another. Jenna grew up thinking this was her biological family, but when she turned twenty-one, her parents broke the news—she was adopted and they'd never told her. She was so upset about being lied to that she moved east and broke off contact with her family and with the Mormon church. A couple months ago she met some Mormon missionaries who were trying to get her to join up again, but I don't think she was interested."

"If she were estranged from her family," Brooke says, "why does she have this photo out where everybody can see it?"

"Sentimental, I guess," Maggie said as she scraped cat food into a bowl. "Or maybe she was thinking of getting in touch with them again. We never really talked about it."

"Anyway," she continued, "while I'm changing the litter box, do me a favor and look around for a photo album Jenna made for her birthmother. As soon as I can figure out the woman's name, I'll make sure she gets it."

"Wait a minute," Brooke said. "The police will want everything left as it is." She paused to think. "In fact, we probably shouldn't be here. Not until the police have had a chance to..."

She was cut short by the sound of a key rattling in the door. "That's funny," a raspy male voice said from the hall. "The apartment's unlocked. Suspicious, don't you think, considering the tenant was murdered?"

The door flew open, revealing Jake Miller, the building supervisor—a scrawny guy with a long, greasy, gray ponytail that fell against the collar of his denim shirt. Detective Burleigh was right behind him, followed by two forensics technicians suited up in white.

At the sight of intruders, Donnie hissed and dashed to the safety of the bedroom. Burleigh barely seemed to notice the cat's disappearing act. Instead, he fixed his eyes on Brooke. "What are you doing here?" he growled.

She knew what he was thinking. He thought he'd caught her meddling in the investigation, just one day after he'd told her not to.

"My neighbor was feeding Jenna's kittens," she explained. "She asked me to keep her company."

Before Burleigh could respond, Jake cut in. "Hah! Let me remind you ladies that there's a fine for keeping pets in this building. Two hundred dollars per animal per month. The tenant was here eight months, so that'll be…" He paused to do the math. "Thirty-two hundred dollars. And since it sounds like you gals were party to this arrangement, I'm holding you both accountable."

"Don't be an ass," Maggie scoffed. "The kittens are only a few weeks old. How could they have been here eight months when they weren't even born?"

Burleigh frowned at the exchange. "This is a homicide investigation," he told Jake. "Let's forget about the cats—at least for now."

"Easy for you to say 'forget about the cats.'" Jake shot back. "The moment I start forgetting about the cats, this place'll be crawling with animals. Cats. Dogs. Gerbils. Snakes. Lizards. Birds. All of them peeing and pooping and smelling things up."

"You can deal with that later," Burleigh said. "At the moment we've got more important issues to address."

"More important to you. Running this building is important to me."

Marie, who'd been sizing up the situation, toddled over to Detective Burleigh and rubbed up against his pant leg.

"Isn't that precious?" Maggie cooed. "I think she likes you."

"Well, I don't like her." He pointed toward the bedroom. "Put her in there with the other one."

"Fine, but you don't have to be nasty about it."

Maggie did as the detective instructed, and when she returned, Burleigh glared at her and then at Brooke.

"Are you ladies aware that tampering with evidence is a federal offense, punishable by fines, jail time or both?

Maggie laughed at the detective. "Are you saying that feeding kittens is a federal offense?"

He stared at her from beneath his bushy gray eyebrows. "What I'm saying is that there's an appropriate way to proceed in a situation like this one. If we'd known, we would have dispatched an officer to keep an eye on things while you went about your business. Instead, you barged in here and risked destroying evidence."

"Don't be absurd," Maggie countered. "How was I supposed to know there's a right way and a wrong way to feed kittens when their owner's been murdered? And if you wanted Jenna's friends to stay out of the apartment, you should have closed it off with police tape. Since you didn't, it's your fault if evidence is destroyed, not mine. And not Brooke's either."

She looked at Jake. "Donnie and Marie were Jenna's babies. She loved them and they loved her, and now they're all alone in the world. What's going to happen to them?"

"They can drop dead for all I care," Jake snapped. "And if you don't get them out of here by midnight, I'll dump them in a shelter first thing in the morning."

"You can't do that," Maggie gasped. "They'll be euthanized."

"You think I care? I just want them out of the building."

"But how? And when?" She looked at Brooke. "Where can

I take them?"

"How about Bernie's place?" Brooke said, referring to Maggie's significant other. "Maybe he could watch them for a few days."

"I suppose. But his Rottweilers won't be very happy about it."

"That settles it then," Burleigh said. "Problem solved."

"No, it isn't," Jake said. "We haven't decided on the fine."

"There is no fine," Burleigh shot back. "Clearly the cats don't belong to either of these ladies."

"Then who do I collect from?"

Burleigh ignored the question and instead took Maggie's name and phone number and ordered her not to leave the building until he questioned her.

Back in Brooke's apartment, Maggie flopped down on the sofa. "Could you believe that cop's attitude?"

"He's a homicide detective. You can't expect him to be the life of the party."

"No, but I expect him to be civil. Did you see how he treated Marie?"

"Maybe he doesn't like cats."

"Marie isn't a cat. She's a kitten. There's a big difference."

Maggie reached into her pocket and pulled out a small blue book and held it out for Brooke to see. "Jenna's photo album. I found it on the bedside table when I put Marie in the room with Donnie."

Brooke couldn't believe her eyes. "Didn't you hear what Burleigh said about tampering with evidence?"

"This isn't evidence. It's just a bunch of pictures of Jenna growing up."

Brooke had other opinions on the matter, but in spite of her misgivings, she looked over Maggie's shoulder at photos of a bright-eyed infant, a golden-haired toddler, a little girl kicking a soccer ball, a teenager ready for the prom, a high school graduate and on and on through the milestones of Jenna's short life.

"Now," said Maggie, "all I have to do is find out the name of Jenna's birthmother. Maybe somebody at work knows who she is."

Half-an-hour later, Burleigh phoned to tell Maggie to come to Jenna's apartment for questioning. She was back before long, standing in the hallway outside Brooke's door with a cat carrier in each hand.

"Can you believe it" she cried. "Jake said if I take Donnie and Marie into my apartment for even a second, he'll consider them my property and hit me with a fine. And he followed me from the fifth floor to make sure."

She gestured with one elbow, and when Brooke looked— there was Jake, lurking at the end of the corridor.

"This is harassment," Maggie shouted at him. "I should contact the owners of this building and get you fired."

"Try it and see what happens," he shouted back.

Maggie set the carriers down with a thud. "Bernie has no idea about any of this. How will he react when I show up at his door with a pair of kittens?"

Brooke pictured the six-foot-four, former wrestler turned tattoo artist. And then she pictured Bernie's Rottweilers licking their chops as the aroma of kittens filled the house. It wouldn't be a pretty sight, but there was no point in saying as much.

"I'm sure he'll understand," she told Maggie. "One look, and the kittens will win him over."

"Oh really? Bernie hates cats as much as Jake does. What if he takes Donnie and Marie to a shelter when I'm not looking? I won't have a moment's peace until I find them a home."

She picked up the cat carriers and headed toward the elevator. Halfway there she stopped and turned around. "I almost forgot. There's a memorial sort of thing for Jenna in the parking lot tonight. It starts around eight. If Bernie doesn't kill me, I'll see you there."

Seven

Ted hadn't worked a news beat in years, but the Jenna Henley murder called forth the investigative reporter instincts he'd honed back in the day. He rolled into Stony Vale around noon on Sunday, anxious to join the crowd in front of the Tillmans' house. As might be expected, news vans and other vehicles lined both sides of the street, forcing him to park a couple blocks away.

As he walked back, he passed the building that hosted yesterday's genealogy conference. Decades ago, this small, gothic-revival church was sold to an organization called the Stony Vale Center for Alternative Spirituality. In its glory days, the Center attracted mystics and gurus and shamans from around the country, but from what Ted understood, things had quieted down of late.

A thick hedge separated the Center from the Tillman's property, and a gate in the hedge beckoned visitors to enter a prayer garden. Ted hurried past it and soon was mingling with reporters, media tech people and curious onlookers, all of them waiting for a glimpse of the famous Dr. Prescott Tillman and his equally famous wife, Eleanor.

Ted noted the various press badges pinned to people's jackets. Among them were mainstream and independent outlets as well as tabloids like *The National Enquirer, People Magazine* and *Star*—sensational publications selling sensational stories about sensational people. No doubt about it, the Jenna Henley story was sensational. A jealous lover. An internationally acclaimed scientist. A beautiful young victim floating like Ophelia in the scientist's fishpond. They would eat up the headlines for weeks to come—or at least until the next scandal broke.

Soon Ted was mingling with the crowd and chatting up the locals who seemed quite happy to talk about Tillman, the hometown boy who made good.

"Prescott and Eleanor are regular folks," an old gentleman commented. "You'd expect them to be stuck on themselves, but they're not. They love Stony Vale and the people who live here."

A young, tattooed woman with pink hair talked about a summer festival the Tillmans were organizing. "There'll be pony rides and bouncy houses for the kids, and we'll have people in costumes for different stages of our history. I'm running the water ice stand, so stop by and say hi." She hesitated, her smile flirtatious. "If you're nice, I'll slip you a free one."

A wizened old woman was quick to state her opinion. "Folks blame Malcolm Mackenzie, but think about it—Jenna Henley died in the Tillmans' pond. Maybe people should stop praising Dr. Tillman and start asking questions about how in the devil she got there."

A tall, musclebound guy wearing a Harley jacket weighed in on Malcolm Mackenzie. "The guy's a smug so-and-so, and I wouldn't put anything past him. It's obvious he murdered Jenna. It's a mystery why they haven't arrested him."

"I think they should question Nora Murphy," said a petite,

middle-aged woman who seemed to have overheard. "I understand she was none too happy when she found out Jenna was hitting on her boyfriend. There's a story there—I'd bet my life on it."

Ted continued mixing with the neighbors, but when he asked about Tillman's transhumanist ideas, their eyes glazed over. Why talk about science and technology when gossip and speculation were way more exciting?

He fared better with members of the press, some of whom were well-informed about Tillman's participation in the Human Genome Project in the 1990s, his collaboration in the development of several gene-editing therapies and his contributions to an array of ground-breaking technologies. Others mentioned his books and academic papers as well as his time spent on the faculties of Stanford, Caltech and Princeton. The man was a hero, some proclaimed. A giant whose research was furthering the development of life-saving medical breakthroughs.

But not all members of the press saw Tillman as a hero. To some, he was a diabolical genius, working in secret to propel the human race into a transhumanist dystopia. When coupled with artificial intelligence, they argued, the technologies he championed had the potential to completely alter—and destroy—what it meant to be human.

Much of this Ted had already gleaned from his research into the man's background. After an hour, he'd grown bored with the repetitive stories and decided to call it quits. On the way back to his Jeep, he passed the prayer garden. A sign on the gate beckoned him to enter, and so he did.

The space where he found himself didn't hold much appeal on this cloudy, damp afternoon. Last autumn's decaying leaves lay underfoot and threatened to overwhelm the flowerbeds bordering the hedge. A plus was the clever arrangement of evergreens that created sequestered nooks for private prayer and meditation.

He glanced around to get a sense of the layout. There were three ways to access the garden. The first was the gate through which he'd entered. The second was a door on the north-facing wall of the former church building. The third was through the rear of the garden where what had once been open space had, over time, become a semipermeable wall of trees and shrubs. There was no fourth exit. Instead. a hedge created a barrier between the garden and the Tillmans' property.

He walked to the rear of the garden and looked to his right. Not far away he saw a house of the same vintage as the old church building—probably the parsonage years ago. To his left was the Tillman's house. It took only a few seconds to walk close enough to see the entrance to the patio, roped off now with police tape.

Back in the prayer garden, he scanned the tops of the trees for surveillance cameras. There didn't seem to be any, and while the stained-glass windows in the former church sanctuary looked down over the garden, the thick chunks of colored glass kept anyone from looking out. That meant that almost anything could take place in this sequestered spot. Lovers' trysts. Drug deals. Theft. Murder. No one would be the wiser.

Hearing a sound, he darted behind an evergreen and watched a fortyish guy with a thick but nicely trimmed beard and a short, dirty blond ponytail exit the building. His clothes were casual—jeans, a gray tee-shirt and a tweed blazer. After looking around as though making sure he was alone, he pulled a wad of paper out of his pocket and held a cigarette lighter to it. Suspicious behavior, Ted thought, coming one day after a murder. Was he burning evidence? The fragrance hit Ted's nose. No, he wasn't burning evidence. He was burning sage—an ancient shamanic trick designed to chase away negative energy and evil spirits.

Once the ritual played out, the man sat on a bench, his posture erect and his eyes closed. Ted was about to leave him to his meditations, but thought better of it. He'd come to Stony Vale to learn what he could about Prescott Tillman. He didn't like the idea of going home empty handed.

At the sound of Ted's approach, the man opened his eyes. "If you're a reporter," he said with a frown, "I've got nothing to say."

Ted extended his right hand. "Not to worry. I used to be a reporter, but not anymore. These days, I'm a praying man like yourself." He held out his hand. "Ted Roslyn."

"To clarify," the man said, "I was meditating, not praying." He shook Ted's hand, his expression wary and his grip tentative. "I'm the director of the Stony Vale Center for Alternative Spirituality. In case you're interested, I teach two meditation classes each week. You can sign up online."

"How about that," Ted said. "I happen to be in the ministry myself. But I don't think I caught your name."

"That's because I never said it. I'm Ryan Stevenson. In case you're wondering, this isn't a church—at least not in the traditional sense."

"And my ministry isn't traditional either, I'm a Christian podcaster and conference speaker." He reached into his pocket and handed Ryan a card that said: *Ted Roslyn: Dispelling the Darkness Ministries.* "Mind if I sit down?"

The question was greeted with a shrug. Hardly a warm invitation, but it would have to do.

"A podcaster, eh?" Ryan said as Ted took a seat next to him. "Mind if I ask what kind of following you've got?"

"Not half-a-million like some people I know. A hundred-thousand subscribers, give or take. But I'm still building my audience."

Ryan let out a cynical laugh. "A hundred-thousand? I'm lucky if I get two dozen people showing up on a Sunday morning. None today of course—the police are still finishing their investigation. My dad used to keep this place packed to the rafters, both on Sundays and through the week for classes and meetings. Membership started falling off when Dad…" Ryan hesitated, "when he fell ill. I was recruited to keep things going, but I don't seem to have his magic touch."

He looked at Ted, his eyes dark and brooding. "So, if you're not a reporter, what are you doing here?"

"Interestingly, my podcasts focus on alternative spiritualities," Ted explained. "But from a Christian slant. I discuss UFOs, occultism, Theosophy from—those sorts of things. Lately I've been digging into the darker side of transhumanism—animal-human hybrids, xenotransplantation, genetically-engineered super soldiers to name a few related issues. My curiosity was piqued when I heard about Prescott Tillman being dragged into the murder investigation. I've watched a few of his lectures and I'd like to know more about the guy."

"You're not the only one," Ryan commented. "These days, he's pretty tight-lipped about his past accomplishments. If you ask him, he'll tell you his days as an academic are over. He says he came back to his hometown to work on genealogy, tie up a few writing projects, launch a historical society and spearhead what he and his wife refer to as the Stony Vale Renaissance."

Ryan looked down at the ground. "I don't mean to be rude," he said, "but we're all pretty shaken up about the murder. My wife's away for the weekend and I'm trying to hold down the fort with three freaked-out kids and my elderly parents who can't believe such a thing happened in our quiet little community. I stepped out for a moment to collect my thoughts, so if you'll excuse me…"

"No problem," Ted said. He rose to his feet and shook Ryan's hand. "If you'd like to talk, you've got my card."

Driving home, Ted puzzled over the things he'd learned. He was having difficulty believing that someone as frighteningly brilliant and aggressively competitive as Prescott Tillman was willing to step out of the spotlight he'd dominated for years.

How could a guy like that spend his golden years digging into family history, organizing summer festivals with ponies and bouncy houses and running a historical society? Was it possible this new persona was a cover for something else? Did Tillman have a side gig he wasn't talking about, and if so, was it related to Jenna's murder?

Eight

Outside the Beacon Arms, a crowd had assembled on Sunday night for Jenna's memorial service. While Brooke wanted to join them, she dreaded the questions her neighbors would soon be asking. She decided to make a brief appearance to show her respects. After that, she'd beat a path back to her own apartment and lock the door behind her.

Out in the parking lot, candles flickered in the chilly night air, casting shadows across the faces of the mourners. Sticks of incense breathed a heady aroma into the gloom, and while an occasional note of laughter wafted into the sky, for the most part, people were subdued, their voices hushed.

Brooke turned her back on the crowd and at the mound of grocery-store flowers and stuffed animals people had brought to celebrate Jenna's life. There were photos as well. Jenna atop a ski slope. Jenna scuffling through leaves in autumn. Jenna laughing with friends outside a Broadway theater. Jenna's eyes gleaming in the light of paper lanterns at a garden party. But there'd be no more skiing. No more scuffling through leaves.

No more Broadway plays. No more garden parties with paper lanterns.

A hand touched her arm—not even three minutes out the door and already the questions were about to start. Looking around, she saw a weather-beaten face framed by a shock of gray curls.

"Chilly, isn't it?" the woman said as she pulled a paisley shawl tightly around the shoulders of her long black dress. She looked up, her eyes boring into Brooke's in a way that felt intrusive. "I'm Anita from the first floor. Someone said you found Jenna's body. Is it true?"

Brooke had no desire to participate in a Q and A with a complete stranger, but neither did she want to be rude. "That's true, but I'd rather not talk about it."

"Death is never a pleasant topic," Anita said. "Especially when it involves someone so young. And yet, I wasn't surprised to learn of Jenna's passing. Her aura was fading, and the remedies I suggested—herbal teas, aromatherapy, reiki—failed to help." She pushed back a strand of gray hair, revealing dangling, crescent-moon earrings. "The last time I saw Jenna, her aura was a pale, murky gray. I knew then that she wasn't long for this world."

Brooke choked back the remarks that sprang to her lips. She had no time for this sort of nonsense and no time for so-called psychics who preyed on people's emotions. "How interesting," she murmured as she edged back a step or two. "Now, if you'll excuse me…"

Anita clutched at her arm to keep her from leaving. "Don't go. Not yet. Not until I've told you my dream." She turned her gaze heavenward as though the dream were about to be displayed in technicolor on the clouds hovering overhead. "The night before Jenna died," she said, "I saw her beside a roaring sea, the wind tossing her hair and her dress billowing out around her legs. And in the sky—two moons. Do you know the meaning of two moons?"

"I don't put much stock in that sort of thing."

"Perhaps you should. Two moons always mean death."

A shiver traveled up Brooke's spine. The woman was a lunatic.

"As I watched," Anita continued, "a creature—half woman/half fish—burst out of the waves. The goddess Melusine. A water spirit who'd come to claim Jenna for her own."

Brooke knew the story of Melusine. As a child she'd been fascinated with the legends of this shape-shifting creature—a woman six days of the week and a mermaid the seventh. Melusine had hidden her dual nature from her husband, and when he spied on her and learned the truth, she fled, never to be seen again. As a result, scholars of mythology regarded Melusine as the guardian of women's secrets—the ones they kept from even their closest companions.

Anita fingered an eye-of-Horus necklace at her throat. "I must warn you my dear. Melusine has set her sights on you as well."

The words were ridiculous, but even so, goosebumps prickled up Brooke's arms.

"You must be careful," Anita continued. "Otherwise—"

Brooke shook herself loose and headed toward the building. Only one encounter with a neighbor and already she couldn't wait to get away.

In the distance, news vans lined the perimeter of the parking lot. Just outside the door, a youngish guy shoved a microphone in Brooke's face. "Brooke Roberts?" he began, his eyes eager behind his thick glasses. "I understand you found Jenna Henley's body. Would you mind telling our viewers what you saw?"

Brooke drew back in disgust. "Of course, I'd mind. This is a memorial service. We're Jenna's neighbors and we're grieving. Try showing some respect."

The reporter moved closer, so close that his microphone almost touched her nose. "Can you describe the pond? And the fish—were they the usual large goldfish or the smaller variety?"

"What an absurd question. What difference would it make?"

She didn't wait for an answer. Picking up her pace, she headed for the door with the reporter at her heels. Once inside, she boarded the elevator, pushed the button and breathed a grateful sigh when the door closed in the reporter's young, eager face.

Nine

The old house loomed dark and ominous over a barren stretch of road. Other than a faint, amber glow from a first-floor window, there were no lights to indicate that anyone was inside.

David Price sat in his Miata and stared at this Second Empire monstrosity. He recalled the day a couple of weeks ago when Malcolm Mackenzie, known to his friends as Mac, dropped by his office to brag about buying this rundown disaster. "Trust me," he'd said as he showed David a dozen or so photos. "It's a mess now, but it'll be a showplace by the time I'm ready to flip it. Just like the Victorian I unloaded in January."

As much as it pained David to admit it, there was a strong possibility that Mac's prediction would never be realized. Brooke wasn't the only person who'd seen him leave the genealogy conference with Jenna. There were plenty of others, and they'd been only too happy to talk to any reporter who cared to thrust a mic under their noses. According to their analyses, there was no need to prove Mac innocent when all the evidence said he was guilty. If a jury agreed, Mac's days of restoring old houses and flipping them for jaw-dropping prices would be over.

Getting out of his car, David dodged the reporters gathered outside the house and made his way to the weather-beaten front door. "Open up," he called as he pounded on the worn, oak surface. "It's me—David."

The door cracked open enough for him to slither into the darkened foyer and then closed behind him. Mac greeted him with a nod, his appearance nearly as bleak as the walls that loomed over them, stained and discolored from years of neglect. David followed him through a maze of tool boxes, stepladders, paint cans and brushes and into a cavernous room where a dying fire cast a feeble glow on spectral objects arranged at random. Not ghosts as they at first appeared, but furniture covered with drop cloths.

Mac took a seat on one end of a shrouded sofa while David sat on the other. In front of them was a coffee table and three objects—Mac's phone, an empty glass and a half-empty bottle of scotch. Was the bottle full when Mac started drinking? If so, he was in a bad way.

An eerie silence settled over the room, broken only by the sound of embers crackling in the fireplace. In the semi-darkness, David groped for words to express his concern. How are you didn't seem right—one look at Mac answered that question. How are you holding up, sounded better, but when he gave it a shot, Mac groaned and said nothing.

As the silence deepened, David chastised himself for not having rehearsed a speech beforehand—something comforting that would shatter the gloom and offer a glimmer of hope. But it was Mac, not David, who spoke up first.

"I can't believe she's gone," he murmured. "There she was, right next to me in the prayer garden. And just a few hours later..."

He choked back a sob and turned his head away. "What am I going to do? The cops are calling me 'a person of interest.'

At any minute they'll show up and drag me out of here in cuffs."

He slumped forward, his head in his hands. "If they knew how much I loved her, they'd realize I never could have hurt her. Not in a thousand years."

David leaned over and clamped a hand on his friend's shoulder. "I'm here for you buddy. I'll do whatever I can to get you out of this jam."

Silence descended again, interrupted by the snap of a falling ember. There was another sound as well—a strange shuffling noise approaching from the hall. To David's surprise, a Scottie puppy waddled into the room and nuzzled up against Mac's leg.

A trace of a smile teased at Mac's lips. "Meet Nessie," he said, his smile vanishing as quickly as it had come. "A birthday present from Jenna. The perfect gift, she said, for the Scotsman who has everything."

He reached for his phone, and after scrolling around, showed David a photo of a tiny black puppy poking its head out of a plaid gift bag. Subsequent photos showed Jenna romping with Nessie in the backyard. Jenna making a snow angel while Nessie licked her face. Jenna sleeping, her golden hair tumbling across her shoulders while the puppy snuggled up against her.

"She was so beautiful," Mac said when David returned the phone. "I used to look at her and think of a line from an old poem—something about a face that launched a thousand ships."

Setting the phone aside, he leaned back against the drop cloth, his shoulders slumped. "I had no idea she'd be at the genealogy conference on Saturday. I was amazed to see her, but instead of coming over to say hi like I expected, she accused me of stalking her. I could tell she was upset, so I suggested we go out to the prayer garden to talk. When we sat down, she kept checking her watch, like she expected to meet someone, and the next thing I knew she was crying. When I tried to calm her down, she got up and ran off—not to the conference, but to the open end of the prayer garden facing the canal and the river. When I caught up to her, she pushed me away and said she was upset and wanted to be left alone. She kept at it, so I got mad and said if that's the way she wanted it, that's the way it would be.

"By then, I was too heated to sit through your lecture, so I headed for my truck. I'd seen the conference schedule, and I knew Seth Walker was supposed to lead a session about Native American genealogy. And that's when it hit me. Jenna'd been checking her watch because she was hoping to meet up with Seth and she didn't want me knowing about it.

Fuming, Mac poured a couple fingers of Scotch, downed them in a single gulp and heaved the glass at the fireplace where it shattered into glimmering pieces before falling to the floor. "I'll do worse to Seth Walker if he crosses my path," he shouted. "If I catch sight of the bastard, I'll wring his neck until he can't breathe, and then I'll laugh while he dies."

While the outburst was distressing, David didn't take it seriously. Mac wasn't the type to wring people's necks, especially when the neck belonged to a rugged, outdoorsy guy like Seth Walker. Alcohol was the fuel behind this tantrum, and once Mac sobered up, the rage would abate.

Or would it? David's friendship with Mac was a collegial one, and other than a beer or two after a conference, they'd never actually hung out together. Did Mac have a dark side David knew nothing about?

"I spent the rest of the day on Saturday driving up one side of the Delaware and down the other," Mac continued. "I got home around five and found a bunch of cop cars outside the house. When I got out of the truck, a short detective with bushy eyebrows flashed an ID in my face and asked what I knew about Jenna's murder. The question made no sense. Jenna murdered? It wasn't possible. But it was possible. She's dead and before long, I'll be in prison for a murder I never would have dreamed of committing."

He looked over at David. "You believe me, don't you?"

"Of course, I believe you," David said, but his answer was less certain than it would have been the day before, and he hoped his voice didn't betray his doubts.

David glanced at the Scottie, its furry, black head tilted as though perplexed by its master's dark mood. Across the room, shards of glass glistened on the hearth. Would Mac think to sweep them up? Would he remember to feed Nessie and let him out now and then? Mac would eventually pull himself together, but what would happen in the interim? Would the dog be safe? Should David offer to dog sit for a few days? If so, what would that entail? He'd just moved back into his historic home after a devastating fire, and he could only imagine the havoc a puppy would wreak on the place. Messes left on antique rugs. Teeth marks on eighteenth century table legs. Scratches on hardwood floors.

And then he glanced again at the broken glass. No—he had to intervene. The little dog needed protection.

"I'd be happy to watch Nessie for a few days," he said. "One less thing for you to worry about until you're back on your feet."

After a long silence, Mac agreed. Picking Nessie up, David carried him to the door and then Mac locked the door behind them.

Ten

Monday brought steady rain as well as steady coverage of Jenna's murder. Brooke scanned the online news and picked a headline at random. The video showed reporters huddled beneath umbrellas outside the Tillmans' house. When Tillman emerged, they rushed at him, microphones raised. Frowning, he hurried to a silver Mercedes, and as he backed out of the driveway, his red backup lights gleamed like devil's eyes in the rain.

A second news site discussed Tillman's decision to leave academia and devote himself to genealogy and an exploration of regional history. Another addressed his scientific research into aspects of the transhumanist movement. *"Therapeutic enhancement employs emerging technologies to remediate injuries, disabilities and chronic illness,"* he said in a video clip. *"Alteration enhancement, on the other hand, uses these same technologies to guide human evolution toward Mankind 2.0—a posthuman race endowed with godlike knowledge and longevity. And that, my friends, is the end goal of transhumanism."*

Further stories leaned more heavily toward gossip. How

did a beautiful woman end up in Tillman's fishpond? Had he and Jenna Henley been lovers? If so, wouldn't a man of his extraordinary intellect have known that murdering his lover and tossing her into his backyard pond would garner unwanted attention? And what about his alibi? Would it hold up to scrutiny?

The majority of the news stories, however, zeroed in on Malcolm Mackenzie. He'd been named a person of interest, and it was only a matter of time, many believed, before he'd be charged in Jenna's murder.

The phone rang—it was Uncle Nelson calling to ask if she could give him a ride and attend tonight's meeting of the Stony Vale Historical Society. He'd been planning to go with David Price, but David phoned to say he was watching Malcolm's Scottie puppy until Malcolm was in better spirits. The puppy had been alone all day and David didn't feel right about leaving him alone in the evening.

Brooke pictured a tiny, black dog with large, wistful eyes. And then she thought of Donnie and Marie mewing from their cat carriers. Sad how our furry friends become victims of the tragedies that befall their owners.

"We'll be meeting in the house that was once the church parsonage," Uncle Nelson explained. "And just so you know, due to this terrible tragedy, we won't be following our usual meeting agenda this evening. Instead, we'll have a quiet meal and a time of sharing."

Brooke wasn't big on times of sharing. She preferred to keep her feelings to herself, but her uncle seemed eager to go, so she agreed to help him out.

At five Brooke turned off her laptop and locked her apartment door behind her. Outside, the rain fell in torrents on wilted flowers, soggy stuffed animals and ruined photos—the sad remnants of last night's memorial service.

Uncle Nelson was waiting in the entry to the senior living

center when she arrived. On the way to Stony Vale, he explained that their host, Ryan Stevenson, was the son of the former leader of the Center for Spiritual Transformation. When Ryan's father, Ralph Stevenson, was stricken with Alzheimer's, Ryan and his family moved back to the area to help his mother deal with his father's declining health. Ryan and his wife assumed leadership of the center, and with it, the privilege of living in the former parsonage that was part of the Center's property.

"I think I've got that straight," Brooke said as they pulled into the parking lot between the Center and the former parsonage.

"I'm sure it will become clear once you've meet everyone," her great-uncle assured her.

Getting out of the car, she and Uncle Nelson shared his oversized umbrella and hurried from the parking lot to a stone house of the same vintage as the former church. When they rang, a tall, fortyish guy with a neatly trimmed beard and a short, ash-blond ponytail opened the door. After greeting Uncle Nelson, he introduced himself to Brooke as Ryan Stevenson and welcomed them into the foyer where a life-size sculpture of a woman in a diaphanous gown stood on a wooden base, her arms reaching upward and her gaze fixed on the ceiling.

"Aurora, goddess of the dawn," he explained. "A gift to my dad on the twenty-fifth anniversary of his service to the Center for Spiritual Growth. Some people think she bears a strong resemblance to my mom."

Having said that, he deposited the umbrella and Brooke's rain jacket in a room to their left and escorted them into a living room furnished with a pale beige sofa and matching chairs accented with light gray throw pillows. Artwork with a metaphysical theme added a splash of color to the white walls.

Two Historical Society members were already there. Eleanor Tillman looked lovely tonight in black slacks and a loose-fitting white sweater accented with strands of silver that matched the highlights in her hair. Augusta Stoddard, on the other hand, was a sturdy woman with short, steel-gray hair. She remained seated, her greeting a mere nod, while Eleanor rose and welcomed Uncle Nelson with a smile and a hug.

Turning to Brooke, she extended a manicured hand. "We didn't have an opportunity to speak during that dreadful incident on Saturday, and yet I feel as though I already know you. Your uncle is always singing your praises."

"I'm afraid he's somewhat partial," Brooke said with a glance at the old gentleman who chatted amiably with the formidable Augusta Stoddard.

"Nonsense," said Eleanor. "He speaks highly of your abilities as an editor. Perhaps at some point, I'll have need of your services."

She was momentarily speechless. Eleanor Tillman was a best-selling author. Landing a client like that would be a huge boost to Brooke's career.

The doorbell rang, sending Ryan off to answer it. He returned moments later with a petite, bright-eyed woman with short, black hair cut in a pixie style. She greeted Uncle Nelson with a peck on the cheek, and turning her elfin smile toward Brooke, introduced herself as Nora Murphy.

Brooke regarded her with curiosity. Maggie had described Nora screaming at Jenna in front of customers and vendors at the Emporium. But tonight, there was nothing in Nora's friendly demeanor to suggest that she was capable of throwing a public temper tantrum. Instead, she seemed the soul of kindness as she praised Ryan for his part in hosting the genealogy conference and expressed sadness that it ended so tragically. He responded by thanking her for baking cookies for the breakroom and helping hand out boxed lunches at noon on Saturday. Nora's love fest continued as she hugged Eleanor and offered words of comfort for what she and Prescott had gone through on Saturday. Moving on to Augusta, Nora made a fuss over the Daughters of the American Revolution pin on the lapel of Augusta's navy-blue pantsuit, and praised her for the beginner's workshop she'd led following the keynote address.

But in spite of Nora's show of kindness, something seemed off. She was too friendly. Too chatty. Too quick to laugh in spite of the solemnity of the occasion.

Nora turned back to Eleanor. "Is Prescott skipping out on us tonight?"

"Not at all," Eleanor said with a glance at her watch. "In spite of the downpour, the stubborn old fool was determined to spend the day grave-digging. I expect him at any moment."

Uncle Nelson gave her a confused smile. "Grave digging? Did I hear you correctly?"

"I assumed you knew the term. In genealogy-speak, it means searching for the grave of a long-dead relative."

"A challenging endeavor," Augusta remarked with a sniff. "I've logged countless hours photographing tombstones and digging through dusty records in courthouses, churches, libraries and historical societies." She fingered the pin on her lapel. "The Daughters of the American Revolution are very particular about the research they'll accept. One's pedigree must be established beyond a shadow of a doubt."

Pedigree? Brooke found the word off-putting. What was this woman—a dog vying for best-in-show?

"Thanks to databases compiled by the Mormon Church," Augusta continued, "today's researchers have a much easier time than I ever did. You've all heard of the Granite Mountain Vault in Utah?"

When Brooke pleaded ignorance, Augusta launched into a description of this miracle of engineering, a repository of the world's genealogical data buried beneath 700 feet of solid rock and designed to withstand a thermonuclear blast.

"I recently met a missionary whose father is an archivist

at the facility," she continued. "The young man was supposed to speak at my workshop on Saturday, but he never showed up. It struck me as odd because Mormon missionaries are generally reliable. This fellow never even called to explain or to apologize, but it hardly mattered. When you've led genealogy workshops as long as I have, there's no shortage of material."

As she spoke, an older woman in a flowing, white pantsuit led an elderly gentleman into the room. Greeting Brooke, she introduced herself as Doris Stevenson, Ryan's mother and then introduced the gentleman as Ryan's father, Ralph Stevenson. She situated her husband in a seat next to her and placed a hand on his arm as though keeping him from wandering off.

They'd just gotten settled when three children bounded into the room and announced that the dinner table was set and the water glasses filled. Ryan introduced the oldest, a skinny girl who looked to be about ten, as his daughter, Tamara, and the younger kids as his sons, Jared and Justin.

With that, everyone headed to the dining room, a casual space with a rustic, country vibe. A spinach salad with strawberries and balsamic dressing was making its way around the table when the doorbell rang. Ryan rose to answer it and returned with Prescott Tillman, his bushy, white hair glistening with raindrops.

"Sorry I'm late," Tillman said. "At my age, driving at night is challenging enough. The storm made it even more so."

Once seated, he leaned back in his chair and gazed at each person in a way that felt warm and inclusive. "After what happened on Saturday, I can't tell you how much I've been looking forward to this gathering. The blessing of a shared meal in this house—a place that's offered spiritual sustenance to the Stony Vale community through the generations—is a healing experience for all of us."

Ryan lifted his wine glass in a toast. "Let's drink to that," he said, and the others followed suit.

Once the salads were done, Nora helped Doris clear the table and the two women returned from the kitchen with bowls of vegetables and a platter of roasted chicken garnished with herbs.

"Did you find the grave you were looking for?" Augusta asked Tillman as the food was passed around.

"Indeed, I did. There he was—smack in the middle of a Quaker Cemetery. Ezra Houck—my great, great, great grandfather."

"I'd love to see your photos," Augusta said. "I've got a scrapbook dedicated to nothing but ancestral gravestones, some dating back to the late 1600s in Barnstable, Massachusetts."

Tillman put down his fork. "Would you believe it? As anxious as I was to get away this morning, I went off without my camera."

Augusta seemed shocked by the news. "And you didn't take pictures with your phone?"

"I stupidly forgot to charge the darn thing, and somewhere along the way, the battery gave out. That's why I couldn't call to say I'd be late."

"Tsk, tsk," Augusta said, with a shake of an index finger. "You call yourself a research scientist and yet you couldn't be bothered to document your findings?"

Laughing, he raised both hands in surrender. "Guilty as charged."

Everyone seemed amused except Eleanor. She glared at her husband from across the table, her lips parted like she was about to speak. She closed her mouth when a woman's voice rang out from the rear of the house.

"Hey, everybody! I'm home!"

Ryan rose from the table to greet his wife who he introduced as Heather. She was tall and sturdy with lustrous, strawberry-blond hair pulled back in a ponytail. Her plaid flannel jacket, denim skirt and work boots gave her the appearance of a pioneer wife—an outdoorsy woman who could split logs, shoot varmints, break horses and give birth—all on the same day.

"I would have been back sooner," Heather explained, "but I had a once-in-a-lifetime opportunity to have lunch with the author of a book about the Doomsday Vault."

"The Doomsday Vault?" her older son echoed. "That sounds like a movie. Or a video game."

"It's neither," she replied. "It's a nickname for the Svalbard Global Seed Bank in Norway, 800 miles from the North Pole."

"The North Pole?" her younger son asked, his eyes bright and hopeful. "Near Santa's house?"

"It's pretty close to Santa's house," she acknowledged. "But it's not in the business of making toys. Instead, it's an underground vault that freezes and stores millions of varieties of seeds."

The boy's smile faded. "Seeds are no fun. I'd rather have toys."

Heather smiled at her youngest. "You wouldn't feel that way if the earth was struck by an asteroid or a deadly pandemic or a nuclear war. If that happens, you'll be grateful for a chance to reseed the ground and start over."

The child fell silent, his eyes fixed on his plate. He'd asked about Santa, and his mom responded with threats of global catastrophe.

"I'm familiar with the project," Tillman remarked. "It has a lot in common with the Global Genome Initiative that seeks to cryofreeze the DNA of every life form on Earth. In the event of a worldwide calamity, the survivors will be able to repopulate the planet.

"I've often wondered," he continued, a twinkle in his eyes, "if that's how Noah assembled two of every kind of creature on his ark. What's more efficient—storing DNA samples or maintaining an enormous floating zoo? That, of course, raises questions about advanced technologies lost in the sands of time, but that's a subject for another conversation."

Ryan shook his head and laughed. "I never know when to take you seriously, Prescott."

"A challenge many share, I assure you."

Doris wrapped her arms around herself and shuddered. "All this talk about doomsday is depressing. Life is challenging enough without allowing negative thoughts to color our thinking."

"Spoken like a true escapist," Heather remarked. She took a bite of chicken and as she chewed, her shoulders stiffened and she sat up a bit straighter. Turning her face away, she spit the food into her napkin and pivoted to glare at her mother-in-law. "Where did you get this?"

"The supermarket was out of organic chicken," Doris said, her gaze meeting Heather's. "There was no time to go elsewhere, so I bought what they had."

Heather laid down her fork. "You're joking, aren't you?"

"It was a challenging day. I was pressed for time."

"Do you have any idea about the deplorable conditions under which these creatures were raised?"

"Of course I do. You've told me a thousand times."

Heather jammed her fork into a slab of chicken and held it up for all to see. "This pitiful creature was penned up with thousands like it, each wallowing in its own filth while being cut off from fresh air, grass and sunshine. It was force-fed a diet of genetically modified grains until it was so bloated, its legs broke beneath its weight. Its entire existence was one of endless suffering in conditions no living entity should have to endure."

Pushing back her chair, she rose from the table. "If you'll excuse me, I've lost my appetite." With that, she marched out of the dining room and left the others staring at their plates.

The silence was broken moments later by Tamara. "How

could you do such a thing?" she asked her grandmother.

"There are times in life, my dear, when we have to be flexible."

"But it's wrong," Tamara persisted. "The farmers are mean to their animals, and that's why we always buy chicken from…"

"That will be enough," her father said. "You're being disrespectful."

Sinking back in her seat, Tamara folded her hands and fell silent, her lips quivering.

An awkward silence fell over the room, at least until Ralph Stevenson rose from his seat and began pacing back and forth. "Angry, angry, angry," he muttered, his hands flailing in the air. "Angry, angry—always angry."

Ryan rose from the table, but when he tried to steer his father back to his seat, the old man pushed him away. "Hands off," he shouted, and then he shuffled out of the room.

"I'm sorry, Mom," Ryan said as he headed after his father. "You know how Heather can be."

"I certainly do."

"She means well. And she's right—the things she described are true."

"I know they are," Doris countered, her gaze steely as she glared at her son. "But Heather stayed longer than expected at the agriculture conference and left me here alone with your father and the children. Do you know what it's like trying to oversee three different home-school curricula while watching out for an Alzheimer's patient? I couldn't leave for the grocery store until you got back."

"I'll explain that to Heather."

"I'd appreciate that."

Once Ryan was gone, Doris looked apologetically at those seated around the table. "This gathering was intended to be a time of healing," she said. "Not a time of rancor and animosity. Please accept my apology."

"Not to worry," Tillman spoke up. "We're all stressed by recent events. And by the way, Doris, the meal was delicious. Especially the chicken."

Eleven

fter dinner, everyone adjourned to the living room for dessert and coffee. By then Ryan and his father were elsewhere in the house, and when Brooke asked if she could use the powder room, Doris directed her to a bathroom on the second floor.

As Brooke made her way along the narrow upstairs hallway, voices erupted from behind a door to her left. She didn't mean to eavesdrop, but it was hard to miss the angry words flying back and forth.

"My mother treats you with respect," Ryan shouted. "She deserves the same in return—especially in front of our guests."

"You always take her side against mine," Heather responded. "If it wasn't for your sentimental loyalty to your parents, we'd be homesteading in Wyoming instead of wasting our lives trying to revitalize this godforsaken little village."

"Coming to Stony Vale was your idea—remember? You said that by living with my parents, we'd keep my folks out of assisted living and protect my inheritance."

"That was before your DNA results. And now..." her voice

broke, and it seemed like she was crying. "How are we supposed to live out our dreams now that we know what hangs over our heads? I can't even look at your father without thinking that you'll end up just like him."

Their voices fell silent, and afraid of being caught, Brooke darted into the bathroom. When she emerged, Nora Murphy was waiting at the door.

"Could I have a word with you?" Nora asked. "In private?"

Curious, Brook retreated into the bathroom to make room for Nora who hastily closed the door behind them.

"I'll just be a minute," Nora said, her voice lowered. "You and Jenna were friends—right?"

"Acquaintances. We lived in the same building, but…"

"But you knew each other. That's all that matters. Did she ever talk about me?"

Brooke shook her head. "She and I rarely spoke."

"What about other people in the building? Did she talk to them about me?"

Brooke had no intention of repeating the things Maggie had said about Nora screaming at Jenna in the Emporium. "I keep to myself," she answered instead. "Not much gossip comes my way."

Nora fell silent—but only for a moment. "Sooner or later you'll hear about an argument between me and Jenna at the Emporium. I didn't mean for it to get out of control, but I couldn't help myself. I caught her hitting on my boyfriend, and I let her know how upset I was. Unfortunately, lots of people were in the Emporium that day, and now I'm afraid…"

She bit her lower lip and looked away. It was easy to guess her thoughts. She was afraid the detectives would learn she was ticked off at Jenna and see it as a motive.

"The detectives haven't gotten around to me yet," Nora continued. "But Eleanor said their questions are brutal and they twist everything to make it seem like you're lying. But why are they so pushy when it's obvious Malcolm did it."

"Why are you so worried?" Brooke asked. "You've got wit-nesses who saw you at the genealogy conference."

"But I didn't stay the whole time. Once I signed in, I took the cookies to the breakroom and skipped the keynote so I could walk home and finish a sewing project for a client. I got back to the conference in time for Augusta's workshop, but I wasn't there at the time of Jenna's death. I didn't tell a soul what I was doing and I don't know if anyone saw me leave and come back."

Brooke didn't respond. Without a clear alibi, Nora's con-cerns were justified.

They left it at that and when Brooke returned to the living room, Ryan was there but his dad and Heather were nowhere in sight. Nora returned a few minutes later, and when Augusta Stoddard commented on the lateness of the hour, Nora echoed the remark. Ryan offered to get their coats from the study, but both women said not to bother—they'd show themselves out.

The Tillmans excused themselves after a few minutes, and once they'd left the room, Uncle Nelson got to his feet and an-nounced that he and Brooke would be leaving as well.

Ryan turned toward Brooke. "You had a rain jacket and an umbrella, didn't you?"

"Yes, but I can get them myself."

She walked ahead of Ryan and her uncle but stopped out-side the study when she heard Eleanor's voice.

"I don't believe for one second that your phone wasn't charged."

"I can't help what you believe or don't believe," her hus-band said. "I told you the battery died, and I meant it."

"Then show it to me, Prescott. Show me that the battery's dead."

There was no response.

"You weren't in any cemeteries today, were you?"

Again, no response.

"Where did you go?"

"Stop this, Eleanor. I went exactly where I said I went."

"Then prove it."

Uncle Nelson and Ryan chose that moment to enter the foyer.

"I thought you were getting your jacket," Brooke's uncle spoke up. "What's taking so long?"

Brooke glared at him. He'd just blown her cover and let the Tillmans know she'd been eavesdropping. It seemed that Eleanor heard him as well, judging from the frosty stare she gave Brooke when she entered the study. Tillman, on the other hand, turned his face away, his eyes fixed on a stained-glass window depicting the sun rising above a garden—a companion piece, Brooke assumed, to Aurora, goddess of the dawn.

She hastily retrieved her jacket and her uncle's umbrella. Back at home, she lay awake thinking about the things she'd overheard. The relationships in the Stevensons' household weren't nearly as loving and supportive as Uncle Nelson had portrayed them. And Nora Murphy, the petite, happy-go-lucky spirit who baked cookies and sewed slipcovers, was a likely suspect in Jenna's murder. And finally, there was the hometown hero. Why did Tillman lie about where he'd been all day, and why did he double down when his wife confronted him?

Twelve

Old houses creak and groan in the night, especially in a rainstorm like this one. But it wasn't the wind and the rain that were keeping Eleanor awake. It was the sounds she kept imagining. A door opening. Glass breaking. Footsteps on the stairs.

She glanced at Prescott sleeping next to her. She'd begged him to get a security system when they'd moved to Stony Vale a year ago. It was the sort of thing a person did these days. Common sense, she'd told him.

And his response? *Stony Vale isn't like that. It's an idyllic place where people leave their doors unlocked at night.*

But there was no such idyllic place—not in this day and age. And now, thanks to her husband's wishful thinking, there was no security footage to identify the person who killed Jenna. If there'd been a camera—just one—the crime would be solved by now. Or maybe it never would have happened.

Why haven't the police arrested Malcolm, she wondered. She thought back to late last fall when his construction crew ripped out the cabinets in the kitchen and installed custom-made replacements. Day after day they'd traipsed across the patio, past the fishpond and into the house. Malcolm knew the lay of the land, and he also knew that she and Prescott would be at the genealogy conference on Saturday, leaving the house and the patio unguarded. She'd told the detectives as much, so why wasn't Malcolm arrested? What more evidence did they need?

She closed her eyes, her ears tuned to the noises of the night. *Sleep*, she told herself, and when sleep refused to obey, she slipped out of bed and eased her feet into a pair of slippers. A cup of herbal tea might help her relax.

Being careful not to wake Prescott, Eleanor opened the bedroom door, closed it softly behind her and tiptoed down the stairs. The grandfather clock in the foyer added its tick-tock rhythm to the sounds of the night as did the refrigerator humming softly in the kitchen. She started when the ice maker ejected cubes into the bin. Normally the sound went unnoticed, but tonight it sent a frisson of fear up her spine. *Stop it*, she told herself as she put water on to boil. *There's nothing to be afraid of.*

Leaning against the counter, she turned her gaze to the sunroom. After the incident on Saturday, she'd closed the blinds to block out the memory of Jenna lying on the flagstones like a huge, bloated fish. But that wasn't all she was blocking out—she was terrified of looking through the plate glass and seeing someone looking in. And for that reason, the blinds would stay closed until the killer was behind bars.

The kettle squealed, causing her to jump. She'd never been jumpy before, but now every nerve was on edge and her imagination only made things worse. *Calm down*, she reminded herself. *Try to think pleasant thoughts.*

And then, to her surprise, a pleasant thought wafted in from the blue—one that hadn't occurred to her earlier. On Saturday, Prescott told the detectives he'd never met Jenna Henley, only to walk the remark back seconds later. It had bothered

Eleanor at the time, but now that she thought about it, at some point, he must have noticed Jenna working at Artisans' Emporium, and that's why she seemed familiar. That was it, plain and simple. There was nothing nefarious about it.

The positive thought faded as quickly as it came. Prescott lied to her tonight—she was sure of it. But why? *Don't be a dimwit,* she told herself. At seventy, Prescott was still handsome and dynamic, still the charismatic figure who'd basked in the attention of adoring, young grad students and female colleagues looking for his approval.

Eleanor had never questioned his frequent outings since their return to Stony Vale. This was his childhood home, and his explorations along Memory Lane took him in many directions. To be honest, she'd welcomed the hours of uninterrupted silence to work on her latest book—*Mergers and Acquisitions: Marriages of the Moneyed Elite.* The project was a departure from her usual investigations into the bloodlines of European royalty. Now, instead of diving into secrets of the royal bedchamber, she was diving into the ties that bind power couples in media, finance, politics and big tech. These prominent individuals with interlocking interests controlled the world, and she intended to let her readers know just how much power these elite figures wielded.

She recalled her editor's cautionary words. *"Your readers don't want this sort of stuff. They want love affairs. Divorces. Glitz and glamor. And that's what your publisher wants as well—do I make myself clear or do I need to elucidate further?"*

She'd felt brave for ignoring the warning and for vowing to publish the book herself if it came to that. But since the murder, she'd felt her resolve weakening, and tonight a frightening thought had taken hold. She could name several authors and journalists who'd died in mysterious circumstances while writing tell-alls about powerful people. Their deaths sent a warning to those of an investigative bent—watch what you say or you'll meet the same fate.

And now she couldn't help but wonder if she was in danger. Had someone hoped to silence her, only to silence Jenna by mistake? Not that Eleanor looked like a 29-year-old beauty. But what if someone realized only too late that they'd assaulted the wrong person?

The soft padding of bare feet in the hallway warned her of Prescott's approach.

"You okay?" he asked as he entered the kitchen, his white hair in disarray.

She shrugged. "Bad nerves. I was restless and thought a cup of tea might help. Go back to bed. I'll be up in a few minutes."

Instead of complying, he reached out to her and held her at arm's length, his eyes probing her face. She could only imagine what he saw when he gazed at her. Not the rosy glow of an adoring grad student but the faded glory of an anxious, aging wife.

"It'll be all right, Eleanor," he said softly. "Once the police find the murderer, we'll put this behind us like it never happened. But first, I have a confession to make. You were right. I didn't go to the cemetery today."

She felt her stomach drop. She'd been worrying about another woman. Was he about to confirm those fears?

"Instead of looking for tombstones," he said, "I went to the Jersey shore. Ocean Grove. Belmar. Spring Lake. The usual spots."

Eleanor tried not to react. Those beaches were some of their favorite daytrips. "Who went with you?" she asked, not sure if she wanted an answer.

"No one went with me. After the murder, I needed to get away. You know how the sound of the waves settles my mind."

She scoffed at his explanation. "You expect me to believe that in all this rain, you went for a walk in the sand with the wind in your hair as you pondered the meaning of life?"

He let out a sigh. "It wasn't much of a beach day, that's for sure, but there were moments when the rain lightened up. In between, I found a restaurant or a bar with a view."

She pictured a window table overlooking the beach. Candlelight. Wine. And in the distance, rain pounding the dunes while the ocean roared and foamed.

"Did it ever occur to you," she said, "that I might have enjoyed getting away for the day? Instead, I was alone in this house, nervous and frightened when the wind rattled the shutters or a reporter knocked on the door."

"There was a method to my madness, Eleanor. I'm in a bit of a trouble, and I was trying to figure a way out." He gestured toward the stools at the breakfast bar. "Maybe we should sit down and talk about it."

"I'm a big girl, Prescott. Just tell me and stop the theatrics."

"All right then. I misled the detectives on Saturday."

A wave of relief rushed over her. He was concerned that the detectives had misunderstood his confusion about recognizing or not recognizing Jenna. With that on his mind, he needed comfort, not criticism.

"If that's all you're worried about," she said, "maybe I can help you. You probably recognized Jenna from the Artisans' Emporium but didn't remember where you'd seen her. Once you explain that to the detectives, everything will be all right."

He shrugged off the remark. "I wish it were that simple. While waiting for the detectives to question me on Saturday, I kept thinking how things must look to them. A young woman was found dead in our pond. Did they think I killed her? The thought had me flustered, and when the detectives asked where I was at the time of Jenna's death, I said I was at the conference."

"That's true," she told him. "You were in the lecture hall, listening to David Price's keynote address, while I stayed at the registration table in the vestibule to welcome latecomers. You didn't leave the building until a little before noon."

He shook his head. "I bagged the keynote and came back home to transcribe some notes. I intended to tell you as much, but you weren't in the vestibule when I left the building. I walked back along Main Street, entered the house through the front door and went straight to my study. Once the headphones were on, thirty people could have been murdered on the patio and I wouldn't have heard a thing."

"That's not possible," Eleanor said, confused by his announcement. "I was at the registration table the whole…" She hesitated as the moment came back to her. "I ran to the powder room just as the keynote began. That must have been when you left."

He fixed her in a stern stare. "Did you tell the detectives you went to the powder room?"

She shook her head. "I told them I was registering latecomers at the time of Jenna's death. It never occurred to me to mention the few minutes when I was away from the table." She fell silent as the reality of the situation came home to her. "That means you don't have an alibi."

He ran a hand through his silvery hair. "It's worse than that, Eleanor. You told the detectives you were at the registration table and didn't see anyone leaving the building. If the truth comes out, they'll think you lied to cover up for me. They'll conclude that I murdered Jenna Henley and that…"

Eleanor's knees went weak. "And that I aided and abetted her murder."

Thirteen

Family Friends Veterinary Clinic was jumping when Detective Radley and his boss strolled through the door on Tuesday morning. A quick head count revealed two cats, a rabbit, a collie, a long-haired dachshund and a chihuahua with the personality of a rat. Jenna Henley had worked here parttime, and while the detectives had no reason to think a coworker had a hand in her death, sometimes a remark made in passing opened up a new line of inquiry. But that wasn't the only reason they were stopping by. They'd learned that Jenna had recently located her birthmother. The woman needed to be notified of Jenna's passing, but so far, no one seemed to know who she was. Perhaps a coworker could provide the information.

A receptionist greeted them, and when they showed their IDs and introduced themselves, she hastily arranged for them to speak to staff members.

"We loved Jenna and so did the animals and their owners," a senior vet told them. "She left in January to expand her home décor business, and then contacted us a few weeks ago to say her funding fell though. When she asked if she could have her old job back, we were happy to grant her request."

Radley made a note of that. Jenna thought she had enough start-up cash to quit her job, but somehow the money disappeared. Where did it come from, and why did it vanish? Was it connected to her death?

A second vet talked about a book Jenna was writing about the devastating effects of dog inbreeding. Hip dysplasia. Heart problems. Shortened lifespans. Abnormal body proportions. The list of genetic issues goes on and on.

"Jenna was fascinated with genetics," the vet said. "Partly because she was adopted and knew nothing about her own biological heritage."

When asked, everyone on the staff claimed to have an alibi for Saturday morning. Those alibis needed to be confirmed, but they were likely to hold up. When asked about Jenna's birthmother, no one had a clue who she was.

The next stop was Artisans' Emporium, the multivendor establishment where Jenna rented retail space. The business was located in an old barn that had been converted into upscale retail space by Mackenzie Restoration, the company owned by person of interest, Malcolm Mackenzie. Radley and the boss wanted to follow up on stories of a confrontation between Jenna and her business partner from the perspective of her fellow vendors.

Entering the building, Radley got a nose hit of assorted gift-shop fragrances. Incense. Soap. Candles. Potpourri. The place smelled like a French whore house. Not that he'd ever visited a French whore house, but the comparison seemed apt.

At the checkout counter, the boss introduced him to store manager Maggie Jenkins whom he'd interviewed on Sunday. She was a tall, lanky woman with short, spiky yellow hair that erupted from her skull like the crest of an exotic bird. The fluorescent-green pantsuit that flapped loosely around her arms and legs added to the illusion.

A brief tour of the place ended at the booth where Nora Murphy sold fabric items and Jenna sold repurposed stuff—a step ladder turned into a bookcase, a sofa concocted from the wreckage of a claw-foot tub, a minibar made from a discarded kitchen cabinet—those sorts of things.

After that, Maggie excused herself and went back to tend to the register on the first floor while the detectives made the rounds of the other vendors to find out what they knew about Nora's altercation with Jenna. Without exception, the vendors spoke highly of Jenna, but a few remarked that she hadn't been herself for the last month or so. Instead, she'd seemed moody and nervous and not as likely to engage in conversation. In addition, she'd complained of headaches and fatigue.

Radley made a note of that. Was Jenna's malaise connected to the loss of the start-up money for her business, or was it due to a deteriorating relationship with Malcolm Mackenzie, or did she have a physical condition that wasn't being treated?

When asked about Malcolm Mackenzie, the vendors praised his work in remodeling the barn, but some hinted at a dark side as well. Like most perfectionists, he could be a tad self-absorbed.

"A tad self-absorbed?" said an older woman with lip, nose and eyebrow piercings. "The man's an egotistical, control freak. I never understood how Jenna put up with him."

She showed the detectives her merchandise—strange, freakish sculptures made from what she called *found objects.* "Malcolm had the nerve to call my work garbage—can you believe it?"

Garbage seemed an apt description, but Radley refrained from saying so.

When asked about Nora Murphy, the vendors' remarks were more colorful. Nora was arrogant! Rude! A drama queen! They described a nuclear meltdown with Nora calling Jenna a slut and accusing her of stealing Seth Walker and shouting that her partnership with Jenna was over and so was their friendship. It went on for at least fifteen minutes—in full view of the customers with Jenna fighting back tears and begging Nora to listen to her side of things. Instead, Nora swore at her and stormed out of the store when the manager—Maggie—threated to call the police.

As to the question of Jenna's birthmother, no one knew who she was.

Back on the first floor, Maggie beckoned them over to the checkout counter. "There's something I need to tell you," she whispered. "Something I forgot to mention on Sunday. We'll talk in my office." Glancing around, she waved at a clerk who was arranging merchandise. "Watch the register for a few minutes. I won't be long."

The office was barely large enough for a filing cabinet, two chairs and a desk. When Radley offered to stand, she said not to bother—she'd sit on the desk. But first, she locked the door. "That's to keep people from barging in without knocking," she explained.

Radley sat down next to Detective Burleigh and prepared to do his usual schtick—taking notes, asking an occasional question and studying the subject's body language which in this case was highly animated. He watched Maggie hop up on the desk, her eyes bright and her fluorescent-green sleeves flapping like wings.

"At the time we spoke on Sunday," she said to Burleigh, "I was upset about the murder and the kittens, and that's why I forgot to mention something that might be important. It came back to me last night."

"No harm done." Burleigh said. "People often remember things after an initial interview. That's why we like to follow up with a second. So, please continue."

She nodded and resumed her story. "The night before

Jenna's murder, I was at a friend's apartment on the fifth floor until around two in the morning. As I was leaving, a man in a hoodie sneaked out of Jenna's apartment. The moment he saw me, he pulled up the hood, looked down at the floor and raced to the elevator. I asked him to hold the door, but he let it close before I got there."

"Any idea who he was?"

She shook her head. "It wasn't Malcolm—I'd recognize him anywhere. The same for Seth Walker, Jenna's old boyfriend."

"What about security cameras?" Radley spoke up.

Maggie shrugged off the question. "Half the cameras in the Beacon Arms don't work."

There was a knock at the door. "Maggie?" a woman's voice said. "Sorry to interrupt, but I need to talk to you about what to do with Jenna's stuff."

Maggie rolled her eyes. "Nora," she whispered. "Can you believe it? Two days since Jenna's death, and already she wants to get her stuff out of the booth."

"We'd like to speak to her," Burleigh said. "Send her in when you're done."

Nodding, Maggie hopped off the desk and fluttered out of the office.

Radley got out of his seat and approached the closed door. The words were muffled, but it seemed that Nora wanted Maggie to contact Jenna's next of kin—her birthmother—to find out what she wanted done with Jenna's unsold inventory.

A discussion ensued, but the gist of it was that Maggie had no clue who Jenna's birthmother was so how could she contact her. It sounded like Nora knew the woman's identity, but her voice was lowered and Radley didn't catch the name.

The conversation ended shortly after that, and he returned to his seat just as Nora opened the door. Her eyes widened when the detectives stood up and flashed their IDs, and for a moment it looked like she might make a run for it. She didn't, but it took a few seconds for her to pull herself together and take the seat Radley offered.

"You've saved us a trip," Burleigh said. "We were planning to stop by your house later today."

She nodded and looked away. "I can only imagine what people have told you," she said. "They think I killed Jenna, don't they?"

The boss took his time answering. "We understand there was an unpleasant exchange between you and the deceased, but there's no reason to assume it led to murder. Having said that, we're interviewing everyone who was at the genealogy conference on Saturday as well as Jenna's coworkers. You fit in both categories, so let's begin with your business partnership."

Nora bit her lip and fidgeted with a ring on her right hand, twisting it this way and that. Why the long hesitation? Was she cooking up a story—one she hoped they'd buy?

"Jenna and I met through mutual friends," she finally said. "Last summer we decided to pool our talents and start a home decorating business. She was seeing a guy named Seth Walker at the time, and when she dumped him for Malcolm, Seth and I started hanging out together. About a month ago, I started worrying that he might be seeing someone else, so I followed him from his video studio to a coffeeshop. When I looked through the window, there they were—Seth and Jenna leaning across a table, their heads almost touching. I was stunned. How could Jenna—the person I trusted most in the world—be hitting on my boyfriend?"

She sniffed back a tear. "The argument about Seth wasn't supposed to get out of control like it did. I never should have carried on that way, and if Jenna was still here, I'd tell her as much."

"So, you don't think she was hitting on your boyfriend?" Radley asked.

"I didn't say that. Malcolm makes a ton of money and Jenna thought she hit the jackpot when she hooked up with him. Once she realized he was an egotistical jerk, she wanted Seth back and she wasn't going to let me stand in her way."

Radley made a note of that. With Jenna out of the way, Nora's problem was solved.

"According to the registration list at the genealogy conference," Burleigh said, "you were one of the first to sign in. What happened after that?"

Nora got a tissue from her pocket and dabbed at her eyes. "I dropped off cookies for the breakroom. After that, I skipped the keynote and walked home to work on a sewing project for a client. I returned at ten-thirty for Augusta Stoddard's beginner's workshop, and at noon, I helped Doris Stevenson hand out box lunches. We'd just started eating when we heard the sirens outside the Tillman's house."

"Can anyone confirm your whereabouts when you left the conference?"

The ring twisting continued, a bit more violently this time. "I didn't tell anyone, if that's what you mean. But a neighbor might have seen me walking back and forth."

"Have you ever been on the Tillmans' patio?"

She drew in her breath. "Plenty of times. But not on Saturday morning."

"But you knew the patio was a private space?"
She nodded.

"And you knew the Tillmans would be at the conference."

"Of course. I was on the committee that planned it. And I knew Dr. Tillman was skipping the box lunches to have lunch at home with some friends. His wife and I teased him about it."

With that, she sat up straighter, her posture no longer slouched and defensive. "Speaking of Prescott Tillman," she said, "last Christmas I was with some friends at the casino in Bethlehem. I happened to look up from the slot machine and I saw him near one of the exits chatting with someone who looked like Jenna. They left together, and when I asked Jenna about it later, she said I was mistaken because she was in her apartment that night, watching a movie. But I'm sure of it, and I'm sure Jenna lied."

Radley made a note of the remark. On Saturday morning, Tillman had denied knowing Jenna, only to couch his comment in uncertainty. Was he really uncertain, or had something gone on between the two of them that December night?

"One last question," Radley said. "Would you happen to know the identity of Jenna's birthmother?"

Nora nodded. "She's Kathryn Gilbert Strauss from Wellsboro, a few hours northwest of here."

"And how did you find that out if you and Jenna weren't speaking?"

"Jenna was always sending texts trying to patch things up between us. She told me the good news, but I didn't respond. I regret that now."

That seemed to wrap it up. The boss dismissed Nora, and after thanking Maggie for the use of her office, they exited the Emporium.

"So," Radley said as they got in the car. "Do you think we should get a warrant for Nora's phone to check out the texts between her and Jenna."

The boss thought for a moment. "Let's put that on the backburner for now, at least until we've finished up our initial interviews. At the moment, I'd like you to contact the authorities in Wellsboro and let them know they need to tell Kathryn Strauss about Jenna's death."

"Will do," Radley said, and with that the conversation shifted back to Nora. She had a motive—jealousy over Jenna and Seth Walker. And unless there were witnesses to corroborate Nora's story about going home to work on a sewing project, she had the opportunity as well.

Back at headquarters, the detectives parted company—Burleigh to his office and Radley to his cubicle. The assignment he was about to hand the cops in Wellsboro—notifying a person of a loved one's death—was the toughest part of an officer's job. Or nearly the toughest part. Being shot at, smacked in the head with baseball bats and blasted with pepper spray weren't much fun either.

The cop who answered in Wellsboro listened to Radley's story and put him on hold for what seemed an eternity. When someone finally picked up, it wasn't the officer who'd taken the information. It was the chief of police, and the things he told Radley sent him rocketing out of his chair.

With the phone pressed to his ear, he raced down the hall, barged into Burleigh's office and thrust the phone in his face. "Boss," he said. "You are so not going to believe this."

Fourteen

"So that's the story," Maggie told Brooke. "The night before Jenna was murdered, a guy in a hoodie sneaked out of her apartment."

Brooke stared at her in disbelief. "And you're only telling me that now? He could have been the murderer. How could you forget something so important?"

"You think I forgot on purpose? I only remembered last night. But I've got more important news. Today at work, Nora Murphy coughed up the name of Jenna's birthmother. She's Kathryn Gilbert Strauss and she lives in Wellsboro, just a few hours from here. The detectives were there at the time and they got it straight from the horse's mouth."

She fell silent, thinking. "They've probably contacted her by now to tell her about Jenna."

Brooke thought about that terrible morning when a cop knocked on her door and said they'd recovered Karl's body from a stream at the bottom of a steep embankment. They needed her to come with them to the station to identify the remains.

"I keep thinking about how devastated Kathryn must be,"

Maggie said. "And that's why I decided to go to Wellsboro and deliver Jenna's photo album in person."

Brooke tried not to laugh. "You can't barge in on a complete stranger like that. Not when she's mourning the death of a daughter she never met. Mail her the album with a note saying how wonderful Jenna was."

"No—something this sensitive needs to be handled in person. And that's why I want you to come with me. You won't have to do anything. I'll book a room and pay for it myself. Two nights, that's it. All you have to do is keep me company on the drive out and back. We'll leave tomorrow morning at eight."

"I'm busy tomorrow."

"The next day then."

"I have a better idea. Ask Bernie to go with you."

"I can't. People want fresh tattoos to show off when the weather warms up. He's booked solid, but more than that, he's got two Rottweilers plus Donnie and Marie to think about. If tomorrow's not good for you, we can leave first thing Thursday morning."

"Sorry, but I've got work to do."

"You work for yourself," Maggie said. "You can set your own schedule."

Brooke held her ground, and after fifteen minutes of arm twisting, Maggie gave up and stomped out of the apartment.

▾ ▾ ▾

Someone pounded on the door early the next morning. Maggie, Brooke told herself, coming back for more arm twisting. But it wasn't Maggie. It was Jake the building supervisor, a clipboard in his hand and a smirk on his face.

"You attended a memorial service in the parking lot on Sunday night?" he asked.

"That's right. I stopped by to pay my respects to Jenna."

"And did paying your respects include littering the area with flowers, coffee cups, cigarette butts, empty beer cans and stuffed animals?"

"I had nothing to do with that. I went there empty-handed and left a few minutes later."

"Minutes. Hours. The time doesn't matter. What matters," Jake said, "is that I've identified every resident who showed up at that shindig. By participating in an unauthorized gathering on the premises, you violated the terms of your lease and forfeited your security deposit. If you'll sign here…" He shoved the clipboard at her.

"I'm not signing anything."

His eyes narrowed. "You'd better watch yourself, missy. It's bad enough that you and your friend pulled a fast one with those cats. I let you off easy then, but this time you'd better straighten up and fly right."

"I already told you I had nothing to do with—"

It was too late. Jake was already marching down the hall, his greasy, gray pony tail hanging against the back of his denim shirt. "You'll be hearing from the landlord's attorneys," he called over his shoulder.

Brooke slammed the door. She was sick of apartment life and sick of people barging in unannounced and making demands on her time and energy. Maybe it was time to get serious about buying a house.

She glanced at her phone. Should she call the agent who'd sold the house she and Karl once shared? She pictured the timber frame in the woods. The Adirondack chairs on the deck. Her laptop open to an editing project. Karl's students arriving for a morning class in the studio above the barn. Later she'd join Karl, her easel directly across from his. She imagined a brush in her hand, a canvas in front of her and her palette loaded with the colors she loved. Alizarin crimson. Phthalo blue. Viridian. Yellow ochre. Burnt sienna. Titanium white.

She'd chosen a tiny cramped unit in the Beacon Arms as motivation to get serious about buying a house. Another factor was a month-to-month lease that would allow her to move whenever it suited her. But those weren't the only reasons she'd opted for a shoe-box sized apartment. There was no room for an easel. If she couldn't look up from her painting and see Karl smiling at her from behind his easel, she wouldn't paint at all.

Grief and Self-pity arose from the shadows to whisper in her ear, but she shouted them down. Work, she told herself as she opened her laptop. Work would hold her grief at bay.

She finished three short pieces, sent them to the client and left to run a few errands. Afterward, she decided to pay a visit to Uncle Nelson. They'd have a cup of tea and compare notes—one armchair detective to another.

When she arrived, she buzzed his apartment from the vestibule, but when he answered, he seemed less than happy to hear her voice.

"Don't be silly," he said when she questioned him. "Of course I'm glad you stopped by."

His tone of voice troubled her. Was something wrong. Was he sick? She fretted about it on the elevator, and when he welcomed her to his apartment, the worried look on his face did nothing to allay her fears. "We've got company," he whispered.

Brooke's heart sank. David Price—who else could it be?

But it wasn't David. Instead, a tall, muscular stranger with high cheekbones and longish black hair rose from a chair to greet her. Brooke found his rugged outdoorsy vibe appealing, but there was something off in the way he kept his head tilted. As he shook her hand, she realized why. He was hiding a dark, purple bruise around his right eye.

"Seth Walker," he said. "Your uncle's been offering advice about a mess I ended up in last night."

Seth Walker. Jenna's old boyfriend. The heartthrob who'd unleashed a tsunami of murderous jealousy. What was he doing in Uncle Nelson's living room?

Brooke looked at her uncle for an explanation. In response, he picked up a newspaper from the coffee table and handed it to her. There on the front page was a photo of cops shoving a handcuffed Malcolm Mackenzie into a police suv.

"See," she said, a note of triumph in her voice. "I told you he killed Jenna."

Her uncle gave her a reproving glance. "I suggest you read the article before you jump to conclusions."

"With all due respect," Seth spoke up, "I'd be happy to provide a shorter version."

"Be my guest," Uncle Nelson said, and once they were seated, Seth began his story.

"I was at a bar last night watching a hockey game and eating a burger—my first contact with civilization since Jenna's murder. All of a sudden, someone came up from behind and dragged me off the barstool. I responded with a right hook to the jaw. Self-defense first—questions later. It turned out to be Malcolm who kept cursing and shouting and threatening to kill me because he thought I'd been messing around with Jenna. Other guys joined in and before long the place was swarming with cops. They hauled us to the station, charged us with disorderly contact and let us go, except Malcolm. They detained him overnight and charged him with public drunkenness, inciting a riot and resisting arrest.

Brooke looked at her uncle in amazement. "And how, exactly, do you factor into the equation?"

"I can answer that as well," Seth said. "As you know, your uncle sits on the board of the Tri-County Historical Conservancy. I'm a proud descendent of the Lenni-Lenape who once lived in this part of Pennsylvania, and I represent my people at Conservancy events. In addition, the Conservancy recommends my lectures, demonstrations and story-telling events to area libraries, schools and museums. But after last night, I'm worried that the damage done to my reputation will get me canceled."

"And you want my uncle to put in a good word for you."

"That's right."

"Of course I'll put in a good word," Uncle Nelson spoke up. "You were assaulted and you defended yourself. It's that simple. Under the circumstances, you have my full support."

"Thank you, sir. Forked Rivers Video Production Company is my bread and butter, but my speaking engagements and workshops are my passion." With that, Seth rose to his feet, shook their hands and went on his way.

"Well, that was a surprise," Brooke said once Seth was gone. "When you said you had company, I assumed it was David."

"I'm glad you mentioned David," Uncle Nelson said. "I meant to discuss this with you over the weekend, but Saturday's tragic events drove it from my mind. Now that the restoration's finished at David's house, he would like us to be his first dinner guests. I told him we'd enjoy that very much, but in the chaos following the murder, it completely slipped my mind. I know this is short notice, but he's expecting us at his house at 6:30 tomorrow evening."

Brooke glared at her uncle. There'd been too much of this sort of thing of late. She wasn't interested in David and she never would be. It was time to put a stop to this matchmaking and end it once and for all.

"I'm sure you understand why this is important to David," he said as though reading her expression. "And to me as well."

Brooke understood completely. A year-and-a-half ago, David had risked his life to help Uncle Nelson out of a dicey situation. But while Uncle Nelson might feel indebted, that didn't give him the right to hand her over as payment for that debt.

"Of course I understand. But you should have asked me first. As it is…" she hesitated. "I happen to have plans for tomorrow night."

The remark was greeted with a raised eyebrow. Uncle Nelson knew her evenings were spent working, watching a movie or reading. She needed a reason to wriggle out of David's invitation, but there was a hitch. She couldn't lie to her uncle. To do so would go against everything in their relationship. She needed an excuse—an honest one—but the only excuse she could come up with was the trip to Wellsboro. If she were miles away, she couldn't very well be wined and dined by David, could she?

"As it turns out," she said. "I'll be away for a couple of days. Starting tomorrow."

The announcement seemed to take her uncle by surprise. "That's not like you. You haven't been away since…" He didn't finish the sentence, but she knew what he was thinking. Her traveling days had ended when Karl died.

"My neighbor has some business in the northcentral part of the state. She asked me to go along for the ride, and after everything that's happened, I thought a change of scenery would do me good."

Uncle Nelson's face brightened. "I'm disappointed, but you're right. A few days away is exactly what you need. There'll be plenty of opportunities for David to have us to his house. I'll let him know right away."

Fifteen

David rose from his desk, his phone pressed to his ear. "Think nothing of it, sir. We'll have dinner some other time."

Hanging up, he crossed to the window and looked out over the grounds of the Tudor-Revival mansion that served as headquarters for the Tri-County Historical Conservancy. Gardeners would soon be planting seedlings in the knotted herb garden, buds would appear in the Elizabethan rose garden, and families with children would begin their explorations of the expansive and bewildering boxwood maze. But for now, March had painted the landscape a sullen gray—a perfect match for his mood.

He recalled that horrific night eighteen months ago and the way his heroic efforts had helped Nelson Roberts escape the flames. For that reason, he wanted the old gentleman and his niece to be the first guests to see his house now that it was restored to its late eighteenth century charm. He'd envisioned both a time of celebration and a time of closure—a chance to bring things full circle and start anew.

But now, at the last minute, Dr. Roberts was bailing out. To make matters worse, David had already ordered the meal from an upscale catering outfit and the deadline for cancelling the order had passed. He'd planned to pick it up on his way home tonight and stash it in the fridge in preparation for tomorrow's feast. But now he'd be feasting alone.

He thought of Dr. Roberts' excuse—something about Brooke going away for a few days. That was a joke. Brooke never went anywhere, and were it not for her uncle coaxing her out of her shell, she'd be stuck in her apartment day in and day out, cloistered like a nun among her books and editing projects. But Brooke wasn't a nun. She was a strong, beautiful, passionate woman as well as a talented artist, and he was tired of watching her act out a never-ending melodrama of tragedy and loss.

They'd met at a summer arts festival with white tents dotting the lawn beneath a vast blue sky. While meandering through the exhibits, he'd stopped to admire a series of paintings and after that, he'd lingered to admire the artist. It wasn't just her winning appearance in that floppy hat with flowers on the brim but also her quick repartee and melodic laughter that remained with him as he drove home that day. At the time he'd had no idea she was married to noted artist, Karl Ericson. And he'd certainly had no idea that while they'd spoken there at the festival, off in the woods somewhere, Ericson had fallen to his death. Since then, David often wondered if Brooke associated him with that tragedy, seeing him—David Jentzen Price—as the Grim Reaper who'd heralded her loss.

Would things be different, he wondered, if her uncle wasn't so keen on matchmaking? David had initially enjoyed the elderly gentleman's unspoken endorsement, but now that he knew Brooke better, he sensed that Nelson Roberts' repeated attempts at throwing them together had only increased her stubborn determination to keep him out of her life.

But if Nelson Roberts thought his niece was the only fish

in the sea, he was sadly mistaken. No, David had no trouble attracting female attention, and at the moment he was focusing his efforts on Julie Franklin, a stunning antiques appraiser he'd worked with on several occasions.

He scooped up his phone and placed a call. "Just a reminder," he said into Julie's voicemail, "I'll be picking you up at six on Saturday night for the Conservancy fundraiser. See you then."

He was about to leave the office when his phone buzzed. Julie, he wondered, returning his call?

But it wasn't Julie. It was Adele Smith, the harpy who chaired the Historical Conservancy's Board of Directors.

"The board has reached a decision," she announced. "Under the circumstances, we've removed Malcolm's name from our list of recommended contractors and workshop leaders."

David had anticipated this move and was ready with a response. "I thought a person was innocent until proven guilty."

There was silence for a moment. "There's nothing innocent about the way Malcolm assaulted Seth Walker in that bar last night. His behavior gives credence to the idea that he murdered Jenna Henley, and there's no way we'll allow a barroom brawler and murder suspect to represent our organization. As director, it's up to you to inform him of our decision."

The call ended on that note. This wasn't the sort of news David wanted to break by phone, text or email, and that meant making another trip to Malcolm's disaster area of a house with the reporters prowling like wolves around the door.

Feeling depressed, he left his office and headed down the stairs past an enormous stained-glass window of St. George slaying the dragon. In the foyer, he turned around for another look at St. George. The hero's sword was drawn as he stood before the dragon's fiery nostrils. It occurred to him that the dragon resembled Board Chairwoman, Adele Smith—not in looks but in personality.

Another thought occurred to him as he was about to leave the building. Rather than eating the caterer's overpriced meal by himself, he'd share it with Mac. And since there was nothing urgent on his schedule for tomorrow or Friday, he'd leave a message with the receptionist saying he was taking a couple of comp days—he'd accumulated tons of them already this year. He'd spend four days keeping Mac off the booze, and with the exception of Saturday night's fundraising event with Julie, he'd stay at Mac's side to offer solace and support.

It took only a minute to tell the receptionist, and once that was done, he left the building feeling good about his decision. He tended to hyperfocus on his work at the expense of relationships, but this was a chance to atone for past negligence and make a better man of himself.

After picking up the meal, he ran home to get Nessie and was greeted by a mess on the kitchen floor. "Bad dog," he scolded. "Bad, bad dog."

His anger faded when the puppy looked up at him with remorseful eyes. It was hard to stay mad at such a cute little thing. "I get it," he said softly. "You were alone all day, and you couldn't help yourself. After all, you're only a baby."

He hurriedly cleaned up the mess and before long he was elbowing his way through a crowd of reporters outside Mac's house while balancing Nessie in the crook of one arm and tonight's dinner in the other. The number of reporters had swelled since the barroom brawl, and they closed in on David with phones, cameras and microphones raised. As he squeezed through the door, he tried not to think of the photos and video clips that would soon be all over the internet.

Mac's appearance was as downcast as it had been the other night, but this time he had a gash on his upper lip and a nasty scrape on his razor-stubbled cheek. He turned away without speaking and led David through the cluttered hallway and into the living room. There were no embers on the grate to emit a warm glow; instead, a single, shadeless lamp cast a harsh glare on cracked plaster, rotting window frames and shards of glass still lying on the floor around the fireplace.

Concerned for Nessie's safety, David went to the hallway and found a broom and dustpan. As he swept up the glass, he thought of the sprawling Victorian house Mac had restored to perfection last year. By the time he'd finished with the place, every detail reflected the opulent optimism of the period. And not just the opulence of the period, but Mac's opulent optimism as well—a quality that was currently in short supply.

Once he'd disposed of the broken glass, David returned to the living room and broke the news about his conversation with the board chairwoman. Mac appeared to be listening, but his only response was a shrug of the shoulders. After that, he sank back against the sofa and closed his eyes.

"So, that's the bad news," David said, "but the good news is that I brought dinner. If you'll excuse me, I'll head out to the kitchen and heat things up."

He returned a few minutes later with an elegant pear-and-gorgonzola starter. Sadly, the subtle blend of flavors made no impression on Mac. Furthermore, he seemed indifferent to beef medallions in a wine reduction served with grilled asparagus and herbed baby potatoes. The final disappointment came when he refused a slice of Grand Marnier chocolate cake with ganache frosting.

By now, David was beginning to have second thoughts about the humanitarian mission he'd set for himself. He was accustomed to having his efforts appreciated—there were plaques all over his office testifying to his many achievements. But now, instead of feeling a warm glow of satisfaction, he was stumbling and faltering and wishing he'd scripted things out ahead of time.

Mac finally spoke up. "You probably think I'm a jerk for

starting that fight with Seth. But I kept picturing him with Jenna, and the thought made me crazy. I knew that beating the crap out of him wouldn't bring Jenna back, but I had to do it. You understand—don't you?"

David didn't know how to respond. He'd been devastated when his ex-wife cheated on him, but he'd never assaulted her lover, nor had he ever considered doing so. The divorce had been the struggle of a lifetime, but he'd accepted the breakup manfully and moved on.

"Instead of blaming me for Jenna's death," Mac said, "the police should be taking a look at Jenna's business partner, Nora Murphy."

The idea took David by surprise. He'd met Nora several times while helping the Tillmans launch the Stony Vale Historical Society. She seemed like an upbeat person who was happy to roll up her sleeves and complete any task she'd been assigned. He couldn't imagine her as a murderer.

When he said as much, Mac let out a laugh. "Nora's an insanely jealous control freak who believes every woman on the planet is trying to steal Seth away from her. I wouldn't put it past her to come up with a scheme to lure Jenna to the Tillmans' patio and have it out with her. Maybe she saw me and Jenna arguing and decided it would be easy to blame me for the murder."

"You've mentioned this to the detectives?" David asked.

"Mention it? I screamed it in their faces."

"And what did they say."

"Not much. The tall, thin guy wrote it down, that's all."

There didn't seem to be much to say after that. Sighing, David gathered up the dishes and carried them to the kitchen. There was a gaping hole where a dishwasher should be, so he washed the dishes by hand and took a few minutes to tidy things up. When he returned to the living room, there was a bottle of Scotch on the coffee table along with a half-filled glass.

"Haven't you had enough of that stuff?" he asked.

Mac looked at him and shrugged. "Until you've been through what I've been through, you've got no right to preach. So here's my advice: keep your mouth shut or get out of my house."

So much for humanitarian missions, David thought as he sat down on the sofa. His attempts at offering comfort had failed, and not only that, he'd lost the battle of the bottle. A long and torturous four-day weekend lay ahead of him, but there was a silver lining in this dark cloud. On Saturday night, he'd be seeing Julie Franklin.

Sixteen

Detective Radley's colleagues were gone for the day, and he liked being here in the briefing room with the phones quieted, the chatter silenced and the boss nowhere in sight. It gave him a chance to think and to probe the secrets guarded by each person whose face stared at him from the whiteboard.

A few hours ago, Burleigh's team had added Seth Walker, Jenna's old boyfriend and Nora Murphy's current love interest to the circle of faces surrounding Jenna. Opening his notebook, Radley reviewed the notes from the interview at Walker's video production studio earlier in the day.

Walker was a descendent of the Lenni-Lenape who'd once populated a broad swath of land extending from New Jersey, Delaware, Pennsylvania and New York. Five years ago, he'd moved to the area from Oklahoma and was currently living in a second-floor apartment above the video studio he owns. He'd been scheduled to lead a workshop on Native American genealogy on Saturday afternoon, and he'd arrived at the conference early to sign in and pick up the syllabus for the day. Rather than hanging around for the morning sessions, he went out for a run on the towpath along the Delaware Canal. He said he hated being cooped up, and after a week of miserable weather, he was happy to be outdoors enjoying the bright, spring sunshine.

He said that as far as he knew, no one had seen him leave the Center after signing in. He'd noticed plenty of folks hiking, biking and jogging on the towpath, but he didn't know any of them and they didn't know him. Afterward, he ran some errands and got back to the Center around 12:30 to set up for his workshop. Noticing a crowd outside the Tillmans' house, he went over to see what was going on. Nora Murphy spotted him as he approached and broke the news about Jenna. After that, everything was a blur.

Regarding his relationship with Jenna, he said she contacted him about three weeks ago and asked him to meet her for coffee. He said he'd never gotten over her, and he was disappointed when he realized she wasn't interested in rekindling their romance. Instead, she told him she needed a listening ear and he was a person she felt she could trust.

During their first meeting, she chatted about this and that without actually confiding anything that was on her mind. The second time they met, she talked about a commitment she made that she was trying to get out of. As she spoke, she kept gazing out the window as though afraid someone was watching from the parking lot.

Radley paused in his reading to mull that over. Was she worried about a commitment to Malcolm, he wondered. Maybe she'd agreed to marry him and changed her mind. Or was the commitment related to the financial deal that fell through— the one the vet at Family Friends Veterinary Clinic had mentioned. So far Burleigh's team hadn't found anything in Jenna's bank records that could shed light a financial deal. Had she opened an account somewhere and hidden the records?

Jenna's third and final meeting with Seth took place two

nights before the murder. As they talked, she kept fidgeting with her necklace—a silver cross on a chain. Walker noticed it, he said, because he'd never known her to be religious, and when he asked her about it, she said she'd been thinking about God a lot lately and wondering about decisions she'd made. Every now and then, she pulled a mirror out of her bag to check her lipstick, but Walker was pretty sure she wasn't worried about her lipstick—she was looking over her shoulder to see if someone was watching her. When her phone rang, she glanced at the screen, mumbled an apology and rushed outside to take the call. He watched through the window as she paced back and forth as she talked into the phone. When the call ended, she got in her car and drove off. He tried a dozen times to call her, but she wouldn't answer. Two days later, she was dead.

Radley tossed his notes aside. For his money, the key to this case lay in that phone call. Tracing it should have been easy, but the killer stomped on the phone and tossed the wreckage into the Tillmans' fishpond along with the rock that struck Jenna in the forehead. The police IT department was trying to retrieve the data from the phone, but so far—no luck. And now, instead of having arrest warrants signed, sealed and delivered, there was just a waterlogged piece of junk that refused to divulge its secrets.

Radley returned his gaze to Seth's photo. He claimed to be jogging at the time of Jenna's death, but without proof, he was a man without an alibi. He'd admitted to still carrying a torch for Jenna and being disappointed when he realized there was no hope for a relationship. Was unrequited love a motive for murder—if he couldn't have her, no one else would? But that didn't make sense. As long as she was alive, there was hope that she'd come back to him someday.

Radley shifted his gaze from Seth to Malcolm Mackenzie. Malcolm had a motive—jealousy—and judging from his altercation with Seth Walker, he had an aggressive streak that could be unleashed by a bellyful of booze. Like Walker he had no alibi for the time of Jenna's death.

The same was true of Nora Murphy—the detectives had asked around, but no one had seen her going home and returning to the conference an hour-and-a-half later. Her house was only a block from the Tillmans' house, and like Malcolm and Seth, she was in the vicinity of the murder at the time it occurred.

Might the three of them have been in this together, Radley wondered. Was there something strange about this love triangle—make that a love rectangle—that had yet to be discovered? He dismissed the idea as ridiculous and then circled back. No theory should be rejected until the evidence said to reject it.

And that brought him to Dr. Tillman. The guy had an alibi—he'd been at the genealogy conference listening to the keynote address at the time of the murder. Or was he? Perhaps he slipped out without anyone noticing. People would have seen him at one time or another during the morning and assumed he'd been there the whole time. And that's why, until the team figured out how Jenna ended up in his pond, the infamous Dr. Tillman held a place of honor on the whiteboard.

Radley moved on to a blank face—a ghostlike image that represented the person Maggie Jenkins had seen leaving Jenna's apartment the night before her death. The forensics team gathered tons of fingerprints from the place, but only a few were clear and none of them showed up in the police database. The building supervisor provided footage of a guy entering the building after midnight and leaving around two a.m., but he'd been looking at the ground and the hood obscured his face.

A second ghostlike image stood for the person or persons who'd offered Jenna the startup money that fell through. Had the money been withdrawn, he wondered, or did Jenna refuse it? What would make someone back out of a deal that promised to set her up financially? The answer was easy to come by. He'd heard plenty of stories about organized crime offering to fund a person's pet project without letting the person know the source of the money. Once the money changed hands, the thugs demanded repayment in terms of favors that put the debtor on the wrong side of the law. Is that what happened to Jenna?

Radley shifted his gaze back to her photo. *Talk to me beautiful,* he whispered. *Who called you that night at the coffee shop? And who was in your apartment the night before you died? And what was up with the money that sprouted wings and disappeared? And why were you so scared? Can you tell me what that was about?*

Of course, she couldn't. She was dead. But perhaps the answer to those questions lay, not in the faces on the white board, but in Wellsboro, four hours away.

Seventeen

Wellsboro's historic downtown was every bit as charming as the online travel sites claimed. There wasn't a chain store or restaurant in sight—just quaint shops and boutiques and a one-hundred-fifty-year-old brick hotel. Brooke and Maggie arrived later than planned thanks to a trip to Walmart for cat food and kitty litter followed by a stop at Bernie's to drop off the kitty supplies followed by numerous coffee breaks along the way. The trip had taken twice as long as it needed to, and it was pushing five o'clock by the time Maggie's van rolled into town.

The first item of business was dinner—something casual and not too expensive. They chose a landmark diner—a vintage 1930's place that looked like a train car. When they entered, a fifty-something woman with curly red hair introduced herself as Charlene. After seating them in a booth, she handed out menus featuring old-fashioned comfort food in keeping with the retro vibe of the place. Maggie ordered a burger and fries, and Brooke decided on fried haddock with onion rings.

A few minutes later, Charlene arrived at the table, a smile

on her face as she put the clunky diner plates in front of them.

"What's new in Wellsboro these days?" Maggie asked.

Charlene's cheerful expression faded. "I wish you'd asked me that question a week ago. I could have given you a rosier answer."

"Why? What's wrong?"

She shook her head sadly. "The whole town's in mourning. A dear, dear friend took a tumble down the basement stairs on Monday. By the time her son found her…" She sniffled and looked away. "A kinder, smarter, more generous person you could never have hoped to meet."

She pulled a tissue from her apron pocket and dabbed at her eyes. "Like I told my kids, if any good comes of this tragedy, it'll be to remind us that our time on earth is short. You never know when God might call you home, just like He did with our dear Kathryn Strauss."

Brooke sat up straighter. "Did you say Kathryn Strauss?"

Charlene nodded. "Do you know her?"

Brooke looked across the table at Maggie.

"We've heard of her," Maggie stammered.

"Of course, you have. Everyone has, and we all loved her. A more generous person you'll never meet in this lifetime. Where that woman found time to do all she did is beyond me. Took over her husband's business when the poor man passed away. Raised two wonderful sons. Taught early childhood development at the local university and trained generations of child psychologists and teachers. Gave endlessly of her time and money to worthwhile causes. The list goes on and on."

"I'm sorry to hear of your loss," Maggie murmured, her eyes filled with more than sympathy.

"Thank you, dear. But it's her sons who need our prayers. Both in their early twenties and recently married. I hear they're devastated."

At that moment, a party of four straggled into the diner

and with a nod of her head, Charlene tucked the tissue in her apron pocket and hurried off to seat them.

"So," Brooke said as Maggie looked back at her. "Kathryn Strauss's long-lost daughter suddenly materialized, and a few days later the daughter's murdered and two days after that, the mother's dead at the bottom of the basement stairs. Sounds pretty fishy to me."

"You're not kidding it sounds fishy," Maggie agreed. "And now, instead of giving Kathryn Strauss the photo album, we'll be going to her funeral."

"No we won't," Brooke countered. "We didn't know her and she didn't know us."

"True, but we knew Jenna."

"Maybe so, but no one in this town knew Jenna existed. And they certainly don't know us. We'd be intruding."

"Don't be an idiot," Maggie said with a roll of her eyes. "You heard what Charlene said. Kathryn Strauss was a college professor. She probably taught thousands of students over the years, and who's to say we weren't among them? We'll blend in with the crowd and no one will notice us."

Brooke eyed Maggie's spiky, neon-yellow hair and the purple shirt she'd paired with baggy aqua pants trimmed with red lace. "Don't be so sure about that."

"Listen, if you don't want to go to the funeral, you can stay at the motel, but I'm going and that's that. I feel like I owe it to Jenna."

At the register Charlene gave them the name of the funeral home and the time of the service—ten o'clock the following morning. "You ladies, take care. And remember what I said. You never know when the Lord will call you home."

By now, dusk was settling in, and in the west, a faint slash of coral broke through the clouds. On the way to the van, Brooke and Maggie passed the Penn Wells Hotel, it's bright lights shining out over the street.

"That place looks nice," Brooke remarked.

"Yeah, but I got us a better rate at a place not far from town. Look up the directions when we get in the van. It's called Maplewood Motor Lodge."

Soon they'd left Wellsboro behind and were making their way into a vast, dark wilderness with acres of trees as the only landmarks. Ten miles later, they turned left and then right and then left again. After a few more miles, a neon sign arose from the gloom to announce that they'd arrived at their destination.

Brooke's eyes swept the dark L-shaped structure. Not a single light shone from the various units, and other than Maggie's van and a beat-up pickup truck, the parking lot was deserted.

"It looks like the Bates Motel," Brooke said, "but without the scary house in the background."

"It looked a lot better on the internet," Maggie commented. "It's amazing what they can do with Photoshop." She looked over at Brooke. "This place is spooky, isn't it? Come inside with my while I check in."

Brooke stayed where she was. "I have a better idea. Let's forget about Maplewood Motor Lodge and go back to the hotel in Wellsboro."

Maggie shook her head. "It's late and I'm worn out. It won't kill you to come inside with me, will it?"

Sighing, Brooke followed her into a cramped space paneled in 1950's knotty pine. To the left, a large unlit room held a ping-pong table and a few lifeless arcade games, abandoned now for the season. At the counter, a heavy-set woman with cropped gray hair appeared to be playing a game on her phone. "I'll be right with you," she mumbled, her thumbs dancing over the screen. When the electronic music ground to a stop, she swore and looked up at them. "Which one of you is Maggie Jenkins?"

Maggie inched forward and handed over her credit card. The woman ran it through the machine and gave it back, along with a key card. "Your unit's the last one at the long end of the ell." As they left the office, the electronic music started up again.

"It's not the Ritz, but it'll have to do," Maggie said as they entered a room paneled, like the office, in knotty pine. The furnishings—two sagging double beds, a wobbly table, a pair of orange plastic chairs, and a laminated dresser—looked to be the same age as the pine-paneled walls.

Brooke had other thoughts on the matter. This place was depressing, and as she went about the business of getting ready for the night, she thought of the dinner she'd turned down. She pictured the warm, historic ambience of David's house and imagined a fire burning on the grate, candles on the table, wine sparkling in crystal glasses and soft music playing in the background. By rejecting David's invitation, she'd exchanged a memorable evening for two nights at the Bates Motel.

Maggie dozed off quickly, but Brooke lay awake thinking about Katherine Strauss's sudden death. Did she fall down the stairs as Charlene suggested, or did someone push her? If the latter, who had it in for both mother and daughter—and why?

Eighteen

"So," Maggie said the next morning. "Are you going with me to the funeral or staying here by yourself?"

Brooke gazed at her surroundings and then looked out the window. The beat-up pickup truck had vanished sometime during the night, and at the moment Maggie's van was the only vehicle in the parking lot. Once Maggie was gone, Brooke would be all alone in this dump.

"Okay, I'll go with you," she said.

Maggie gave her a triumphant smile. "I knew you'd come around. Now look up a place where we can get breakfast."

After a quick meal of omelets and home fries, they headed for the funeral home and stood in line to sign the guest registry. While waiting, it occurred to Brooke that by now the detectives back home had probably connected with the detectives out here and were sharing evidence back and forth. What would Burleigh think when he requested a copy of the guest registry and saw her name and Maggie's among the mourners?

"Good catch," Maggie said when Brooke mentioned it.

"We'll use fake names. No one out here knows us, so what does it matter?"

They scribbled their aliases in the guestbook and joined a line leading to a white coffin that seemed to be floating in a sea of roses, lilies and gladiolas. When it came her turn, Brooke searched Kathryn's Strauss's face for a trace of Jenna, but there wasn't much to go on. Even in death, Kathryn was guarding her secret.

Moving on, they expressed their condolences to Kathryn's young sons and their wives and followed an usher to overflow seating at the back of the room. A time of sharing followed the eulogy and it seemed that countless people got to their feet to honor Katherine. They praised her for keeping the family logging business afloat following her husband's death, for steering her sons, Derrick and Geoff safely into adulthood and for her work as a professor of early childhood development. The final speaker was a cousin who spoke of Kathryn's passion for genealogy and praised her for the meticulous research she'd done to deepen the family's appreciation of their ancestry.

This last remark was particularly touching. If allowed to live, Jenna and her birthmom would have explored their ancestry together, but they were gone without having had a chance to share that journey.

After the service, Brooke and Maggie joined the caravan headed to the cemetery. "*I am the resurrection and the life,*" the minster intoned from the graveside. "*He that believeth in me, though he were dead, yet shall he live.*"

When the reading ended, the Strauss brothers and their wives stepped forward to place roses on their mother's coffin. The minister concluded with a benediction, and then the mourners shuffled away in silence, unwilling to sully the occasion with words.

"Sad day, isn't it?" remarked a twenty-something woman whose car was parked next to Maggie's van.

"Real sad," Maggie agreed. "Were you a student of Dr. Strauss?"

She shook her head. "Derrick and I were friends in high school. He and his brother have made quite a name for themselves around here. In addition to running Strauss Lumber, they recently bought a ratty old motel they're planning to tear down and replace with an upscale resort and conference center. Their mom was in on the deal as well. Maplewood Motor Lodge the place is called."

Brooke and Maggie exchanged glances. Maplewood Motor Lodge was where they were staying.

"But that's not all," the woman continued. "Derrick and Geoff inherited their father's antique firearm collection, and they turned their dad's passion for collecting into a store and an online business."

Maggie eyed the woman curiously. "A store? Is it somewhere nearby?"

"About twenty-five miles that way," she said, pointing toward the west. "Strauss Antique Firearms. If you stay on the highway, you can't miss it." With that, she excused herself and got in her car.

"So," Maggie said as she unlocked the van. "What do you make of Kathryn Strauss's two wonderful sons?"

"They seemed like nice guys," Brooke said. "Smart too, from the sounds of it. And pretty successful for being so young."

"Oh, really? Those sad faces and teary eyes didn't fool me—not for one second."

Brooke looked at her, perplexed.

"Think about it," Maggie continued. "A lumber business wasn't enough for those guys. No—they had to turn their dad's gun collection into a business, and then they got their mom to go in with them on buying Maplewood Motor Lodge and turning it into a resort and conference center. You can bet they didn't want an illegitimate sister showing up to get her hands on the family cash."

Brooke stared at her, dumbfounded. "Are you suggesting Derrick and Geoff murdered Jenna?"

"It makes perfect sense, doesn't it?"

"Don't be absurd. They're not murderers—just two sad guys mourning their mother's death."

"Yeah—two sad guys who didn't want to divvy up the family fortune."

"Even if that were true," Brooke argued, "there's no reason to think they killed their mother."

"Think, Brooke, think. Derrick and Geoff knew that if their mom found out they killed Jenna, she'd do her civic duty and turn them in—she was that kind of person. They couldn't take the risk."

Brooke laughed at the suggestion. "Do you have any idea how crazy you sound? How in the world would Derrick and Geoff have known that Jenna would be at a genealogy conference in Stony Vale on Saturday? And even if they knew, how would they have known the location of the Tillmans' patio, and how would they have known the Tillmans wouldn't be home, and how would they have cooked up a scheme to lure Jenna to the patio so they could kill her? The idea's ridiculous."

"So, you say," Maggie said, her voice snippy. "But I intend to prove it."

"Oh really? How?"

"Buckle your seatbelt and I'll show you."

▼ ▼ ▼

A strip mall loomed in the distance against an outcropping of rugged hills. It wasn't much to look at. In addition to Strauss's Antique Firearms, there was a deli, a laundromat, and a bait-and-tackle shop.

Maggie pulled into a parking space directly in front of the

store. "While you were staring out the window," she said, "I concocted a plan."

Brooke reflected on Maggie's plans to date. Feeding Jenna's kittens ended with Burleigh ranting about fines and/or imprisonment for tampering with evidence. The Maplewood Motor Lodge turned out to be a dump, and Brooke could only imagine what would come of the plan that was about to unfold.

"So, here's what we'll do," Maggie said. "We'll go inside, and you'll stand by while I tell the clerk it's Bernie's birthday, and I'm looking for something special for his antique gun collection. Not true, but the clerk won't know that. While I'm discussing the guns, I'll casually steer the conversation around to Derrick and Geoff. You won't have to do a thing."

"And what, may I ask, do you know about antique guns?"

"Nothing. Why should that matter?"

"Because the clerk will expect you to have a vague idea of what you're shopping for."

"What's there to know? They're guns. You shoot them."

"Of course," Brooke said with a wave of her hand. "Why didn't I think of that?"

The Strauss brothers' store turned out to be surprisingly tasteful. Antique prints of soldiers, hunters and woodsmen created a museum vibe while on the ceiling, an array of security cameras kept a watchful eye.

A thin, gray-haired man in jeans, a tweed blazer and a striped shirt, appeared from an adjoining room. With his neatly trimmed beard, wire-rimmed glasses, and intense green eyes, he seemed more like a college professor than a gun dealer. After welcoming them to the store, he listened to Maggie's spiel about Bernie's birthday, and when she finished, he asked what period of firearms Bernie collected.

Maggie glanced at Brooke and then back at the clerk. "What periods of firearms do you have?"

The man suppressed a smile. "That's rather a broad question. We represent American military weapons from the early colonial era to more recent conflicts around the globe. In addition, we offer a wide variety of non-military weapons from the same periods as well as some excellent examples of historic European firearms. And over there…" he pointed to an adjacent room, "…we carry a selection of contemporary items."

Maggie looked back at Brooke. "Can you remember anything about the guns Bernie collects?"

Brooke pictured the muscle-bound, massively tattooed, former wrestler. "He strikes me as a *Don't Tread on Me* sort of guy. That would be the Revolutionary War."

"Really? I was thinking of the Civil War." Maggie smiled at the clerk. "Tell me everything you know about Civil War guns."

The man sniffed sharply. "With all due respect, ma'am, my knowledge of Civil War firearms is quite extensive, but perhaps you'd be interested in a recent acquisition." Reaching into the showcase, he brought out a small pistol and placed it on the counter. "This is the Philadelphia Derringer, the same model chosen by John Wilkes Booth to assassinate Abraham Lincoln."

"Really? John Wilkes Booth?" Maggie gazed at the small, single-barreled gun that featured a gracefully curved wooden body and metal work with carved acanthus leaves.

"Look, Brooke," she exclaimed. "Isn't it adorable?"

Brooke nodded. "It's a lot fancier than the double-barreled derringer Karl used to take with us when we went camping."

"I believe you're referring to the Snake Slayer," the clerk spoke up. "A popular model among hikers and outdoorsy types. But I believe we were discussing the Philadelphia Derringer?"

Maggie's interest faded when he mentioned a price in the thousands. "That's a little steep. I was thinking of something around fifty to a hundred."

He was silent for a moment. "You can't be serious."

"Okay, then. Two hundred."

He looked at her and said nothing.

"Make it three."

He shook his head. "I'm sorry, but we can't do anything at that price."

"All right—you win. How about a thousand?"

He paused to reflect. "That's somewhat limiting, but I could part with this 1853 Enfield rifle for that amount. Other than the 1861 Springfield, it was the most widely used weapon in the Civil War," he said as he removed it from the display case, and laid it on the counter.

Picking it up, Maggie looked through the sight. "Bang, bang," she said with a grin.

"Bang, bang isn't entirely accurate," the clerk said. "These were single-shot weapons that had to be reloaded after each firing."

"You're kidding. A person could get killed in the time it took to reload."

"I assure you, ma'am, many died in that manner."

Maggie took a moment to study the rifle as though she knew what she was looking at. "Your price seems a little high," she remarked. "Can you do any better?"

The ensuing silence was punctuated by the ticking of an antique clock behind the counter.

"I'd be willing to entertain an offer," the clerk mused. "Provided it's not too far off the mark."

Brooke sensed where this was headed. She'd seen Maggie at flea markets and knew her to be a tireless haggler. Once the negotiations began, she'd keep at it until she'd talked the guy down and committed herself to the purchase. After that, she'd walk away with hundreds of dollars on her credit card and an 1853 Enfield rifle nobody wanted.

She decided to intervene. "My friend needs time to think about her purchase," she spoke up.

Maggie seemed flustered by the interruption. "Time? Oh,

yes—of course. Time. And maybe I should find out if Bernie already has one like it." She smiled at the clerk. "Thank you for your help. I've learned a lot. And now, before we leave, I've got a quick question for you. A sad question, to be honest. I couldn't help but wonder if the people who own this store are related to the college professor who died a few days ago?"

The clerk nodded sadly. "Kathryn Strauss was their mother."

Maggie's eyes widened and she clapped a hand to her chest. "How terrible. Her sons must be devastated."

"Indeed, they are. Derrick was on his way home from a gun show on Monday when his brother called and broke the news. Can you imagine being in traffic on Route 80 and hearing something like that."

Maggie shook her head. "It's so very, very sad. "But where was this gun show, if you don't mind my asking?"

"Not at all. It's a major event held every year in Allentown."

Brooke had no trouble reading Maggie's thoughts. On Saturday morning, Derrick Strauss had been a mere 20 miles from Stony Vale. Did he leave the gun show, kill Jenna and return in time to haggle over the prices of antique firearms? Was it possible Maggie's outlandish theory was correct?

"I live just a few miles from Allentown," Maggie said, clearly shaken by what she'd just heard. "If I'd known about the gun show, it would have saved me a trip."

The clerk eyed her curiously, his forehead furrowed above his wireframe glasses. "It's funny that your boyfriend never mentioned the show. It's a huge event that brings out the finest dealers and collectors from around the country."

"Well, it hardly matters, does it? I found this store on the internet, and since my friend and I happened to be in the mood for a drive, we thought we'd check it out."

"Really? It's a long drive out here just to poke around in a random gun shop when you have no idea what you're looking for. What are we talking about? Four hours give or take? Why come all this distance when there are plenty of reputable dealers in the Lehigh Valley?"

"I like to drive," Maggie said. "And besides, you were highly recommended."

Sensing that the story was beginning to unravel, Brooke took Maggie's elbow and steered her toward the door. "Thanks for your help," she called out to the clerk. "You've given us a lot to think about."

Back outside, Maggie gripped Brooke by both arms. "Can you believe it? I told you Derrick was guilty. I said I'd prove it, and I did."

Over Maggie's shoulder, Brooke saw a black pickup truck ease into a parking space. "Don't look now, but Derrick Strauss just pulled in next to your van."

Maggie's triumphant expression faded. "Derrick? You're kidding!" She turned to look. "Oh no! We've got to hide before he sees us."

Grabbing Brooke's arm, she dragged her along the pavement and into the deli at the end of the strip. Keeping the door slightly ajar, she leaned forward so she could see what was going on.

"Can I take your order?" a young girl called from the counter.

Maggie waved a hand over her shoulder. "Quiet. I'm trying to concentrate."

The girl came over and stood behind her. "What is it?" she asked, standing on tiptoe so she could look over Maggie's shoulder. "Is something wrong?"

"I told you to be quiet," Maggie hissed. "Can't you understand English?"

The girl glanced at Brooke, confusion and fear in her eyes.

"Not to worry," Brooke said. "It's a personal matter."

"He's inside the store," Maggie shouted. "Let's get out of here—now!"

She dragged Brooke out of the deli, leaving the girl watching, wide-eyed, as they raced to the van. As they buckled their seatbelts, the door to the gun shop flew open.

"Wait a minute," Derrick shouted, "I need to talk to you."

Screaming, Maggie careened out of the parking lot and up an incline to their right. She slowed only slightly to round the curves on the winding stretch of narrow road, and as the pavement straightened out, Brooke glanced in the sideview mirror and saw Derrick's truck closing the space between them.

Nineteen

The van careened around a bend, coming dangerously close to a ditch that fell away to the right. Dirt and stones clattered against the chassis, and just when it seemed they might tip over, they lurched back onto the pavement. Brooke held her breath as the van swerved into the opposite lane, and she hung onto her seat as Maggie negotiated a series of hairpin turns. For a moment the center of gravity seemed to slip away, and then, as the road straightened out, Maggie jerked the steering wheel to the left and flew off the pavement, the tires clattering over loose, rocky soil. She slammed on the brakes just as they were about to fly over the edge of a steep embankment, and with a shudder, the van came to a halt, sheltered behind a wall of pine trees.

For a moment there was silence.

"How did you do that?" Brooke gasped in amazement.

Maggie placed a hand over her heart, her breath short and ragged. "I have no idea! All I knew was I had to shake him off before he caught up to us."

Brooke watched in the passenger-side mirror as Derrick's

truck flew by. "All clear," she said. "Let's get out of here before he realizes you fooled him."

Maggie backed onto the road and sped in the direction from which they'd come. Rounding a curve, she barely avoided a head-on collision with an suv ambling up the hill. The driver leaned on his horn, and the sound waves followed them as they passed the gun shop and turned east on Route 6.

"What are we going to do?" Maggie moaned. "The woman at the cemetery said Derrick and Geoff own the Maplewood Motor Lodge. They've probably got their friends and relatives from the funeral staying there. Once Derrick sees the footage from the store's security cameras, he'll have everyone he knows looking for us." She turned to Brooke, wide-eyed. "This is terrible. I'm scared to go back to the room."

"The sooner we leave, the better," Brooke said. "We'll get our stuff and head for home before anybody notices us."

Maggie ran a hand through her spiky yellow hair and glanced down at her purple outfit. "They might not notice you, but look at me. One glance, and they'll recognize me from the funeral. I can't take a risk like that. Think of something, will you?" She glanced in the rearview mirror and let out a shriek. "Derrick's back on our tail!"

Brooke turned around and studied the view through the rear windshield. Yeah—a vehicle was approaching, but at this distance, it could be Derrick or it could be anybody. She said as much, but that didn't keep Maggie from making an abrupt left and accelerating rapidly on a narrow road that, like all of them in this part of Pennsylvania, led through miles of state forests and game lands.

"I think we shook him," Maggie said fifteen minutes later. "And you'll be happy to know that while I was driving, I came up with a plan."

Brooke sighed. She'd about had it with Maggie's plans.

"We're near the Grand Canyon of Pennsylvania—and it's

popular tourist spot—right?" Maggie asked.

Brooke nodded.

"Okay," Maggie said. "Here's what we'll do. We'll find a souvenir shop—there's probably tons of them in the area. We'll buy a couple of oversized hoodies to cover our clothes and hide our hair. Once we put them on, we'll wait until dark to go back in the room and grab our stuff. If we're dressed like tourists, nobody will guess we were at the funeral today."

"Why wait until dark if we're in disguise?"

"Would you try thinking for once? People might get a good look at our faces in broad daylight. It only makes sense to wait until night."

Brooke resigned herself to Maggie's plan. The first souvenir shop they found was closed until later in the spring. The same turned out to be true of other gift shops, and it was late afternoon before they found one that was open. With minutes until closing time, they bought over-sized hoodies that said *I* ♥ *the Grand Canyon of Pennsylvania* and took them out to the van. After that, they grabbed a bite to eat at a redneck bar, and as night settled over the hills, they zipped up their sweatshirts, pulled up the hoods and returned to Maplewood Motor Lodge.

When they arrived, the parking lot was packed with vehicles that presumably belonged to Strauss friends and relatives. Lights gleamed in the room next to the office, and through the window Brooke saw people milling about while others played arcade games. A crowd of stragglers lingered outside, smoking cigarettes and drinking beer.

"See," Maggie said. "If we came back in broad daylight like you wanted to do, someone here could have recognized us. But now no one will know the difference. We'll grab our things and be back home by midnight."

They made it to their room without incident, and as Brooke was throwing things into her duffle bag, she heard a loud rumbling outside. Curious, she parted the curtains in time to see Derrick's truck roar into the parking lot. As he and his wife got out, people rushed forward to greet them.

"Your nemesis just arrived," she told Maggie. "He and his wife are talking to people outside the office. We'll leave as soon as they go inside."

Brooke went into the bathroom for her toothbrush and shower gel. As she was stuffing them in her bag, she heard a gasp. Returning to the room, she saw Maggie, her back toward Brooke as she peeked through a crack in the curtains.

"I don't believe it," she wailed. "Derrick's outside the window looking at my license plate. It's over, Brooke. We'll never get out of here alive."

"Don't be ridiculous. He won't kill us—not with so many people around."

"You're right. He'll wait for us to leave and then he'll follow us and force us off the road. No one will know what happened."

"He'll do nothing of the sort. In fact, I'll have a word with him and put this whole thing to rest."

"Are you crazy?" Maggie gasped. "You can't do that."

"Watch me."

Brooke tucked her hair beneath the hood and threw opened the door. "What do you think you're doing?" she asked.

Derrick looked up, startled. "Nothing," he said. I was just taking a walk."

"And taking a walk includes snooping around people's vehicles?"

Instead of answering, he took a step closer, his eyes narrowed as he tried to get a look at her face. "Were you at a funeral this morning?"

She lowered her gaze. "It's none of your business where I was. And this van is none of your business either."

He kept staring at her, twisting this way and that so he could see beneath the edge of her hoodie. "You look like someone who was at my mom's funeral today and later at my gun shop. You were with a woman about so tall." He held out his hand to indicate a height of about five-foot-eight. "She was skinny with a weird purple outfit and bright yellow hair. She asked the clerk a lot of nosy questions."

His description of Maggie was chillingly accurate, but Brooke couldn't let on. "I wasn't at a funeral today," she lied, "and I certainly wasn't at a gun shop. And if you don't get out of here, I'll call the cops and report a peeping Tom."

He took a few steps backward. "I'm not a peeping Tom—really. I had you mixed up with someone else. Sorry for bothering you."

She felt a sense of triumph as he retreated and went into the office. The encounter had gone better than she'd expected.

Back in the room, Maggie threw her arms around her and let out a sob. "I've never been so scared in my life. The whole time you were out there I was wondering if Derrick was the guy who sneaked out of Jenna's apartment the night before she died? What if he called her and said he was her half-brother, and since he'd be in the area, he'd love to meet her? What if he asked where she'd be the next day, and once she told him, he went to Stony Vale to check it out, and that's how he came up with a plan to kill her. It makes sense, doesn't it?"

"Sort of, but if it's true, it's all the more reason to get out of here."

"We can't do that. If he sees us leave, he and his brother will be after us with their vigilante buddies. Think of it—two women alone in a dark forest, and then—headlights in the rearview mirror. Not just one truck but a bunch of trucks and SUVs. No, Brooke. We'll have to stay here tonight and sneak out early in the morning."

"Not a good idea," Brooke argued. "You'll be awake all night, worrying about Derrick breaking down the door and killing us in our beds. I've got a better idea. Once things quiet down around here, we'll drop the key through the slot in the office door and head for home."

By two in the morning, every room was dark except for a few TV screen lights leaking through the curtains. Once they'd loaded the van, Maggie waited behind the wheel while Brooke dropped the key through the slot in the office door. As they hit the road, Brooke kept her eyes on the passenger-side mirror and breathed a sigh of relief as Maplewood Motor Lodge and its denizens disappeared from view.

Twenty

Detective Radley was lost in thought when he and the boss rolled into Stony Vale on Saturday afternoon. Yesterday, detectives from Wellsboro attended Kathryn Strauss's funeral, in part to pay their respects, but also to scope out the mourners—most notably those who stood to benefit from her death. Soon those people would get a knock on the door and the long, tedious cycle of interviews would begin.

Meanwhile, cops in both parts of the state were scrambling to find a link between Kathryn's death and Jenna's. But maybe there was no link. Maybe, in a moment of distraction, Kathryn tripped and fell. Such things were known to happen.

Either way, the business in Wellsboro had muddied the waters, and now there were two faces—Kathryn's and Jenna's— at the center of competing circles on the whiteboard back at headquarters. Would today's interview add another face to the orbiting suspects? If this continued, they'd need a bigger white- board.

They arrived at the Stevensons' house, showed their IDs and introduced themselves to Mrs. Stevenson. "I wondered when it would be my turn," she said. "And please—no formalities. I'd feel more comfortable if you call me Doris. And by the way, before we get started, I need to mention that we might be interrupted. My husband's resting upstairs, my grandkids are playing in the family room, and my son and his wife went out for a late lunch. I expect them back at any moment."

The first thing Radley noticed when he stepped into the foyer was a life-sized sculpture of a winged woman in a filmy gown. She was a pretty thing, but in his opinion, she was way too large for the space. She belonged in a park, or better yet in a cemetery where she could tower over the graves and warn people that life was short and they'd better get their act together.

Doris followed Radley's gaze. "Aurora, goddess of the dawn. The herald of a new age. She was a gift on the twenty-fifth anniversary of my husband's tenure at the Center for Spiritual Transformation. Hard to believe that was fifteen years ago."

That about wrapped up the art lesson, Radley thought. Or maybe not. A card table in the living room was weighted down with photos, paper cutouts, stickers and other artsy-craftsy stuff.

"Scrapbooking's a hobby of mine," Doris explained. "And, if you don't mind, I'd like to continue working while we talk. These days I rarely get the opportunity to indulge my passion."

"No problem," the boss said. "We appreciate your willingness to talk. Let's begin with a description of your activities between eight and ten-thirty Saturday morning?"

Doris took a moment to move a photo here and there on a page. Was that a stalling tactic, Radley wondered. A chance to get her ducks in a row before she opened her mouth?

"I arrived early to help Eleanor and Prescott set things up," she said. "At nine, I introduced our keynote speaker and sat in the front row during his talk. Afterward, I went back to the podium to announce that we were serving refreshments in the break room. During the break, I mingled with the crowd, and after that I led a session on family history scrapbooks. Things were running smoothly until lunchtime when we heard the sirens.

"As far the rest of the family is concerned," she continued, "my husband's an Alzheimer's patient, and he was in the house the whole time as were my three grandchildren—we had a friend watching them. My son Ryan was at the Center helping out where he could, and my daughter-in-law, Heather, left before dawn for a conference at Penn State." She looked up and smiled. "As you can see, we're all accounted for."

"Did you hear anything that morning that might have a bearing on the case?" Burleigh asked. "Or since then, for that matter?"

Doris picked up some paper cutouts and fiddled with their placement on the page. "That doesn't work," she murmured before looking up at Burleigh. "To answer your question, Monday evening we had a few guests here for dinner. Eleanor Tillman arrived by herself and said that Prescott had gone off to search for an ancestor's grave. I found the news surprising because it was pouring rain—hardly a day for wandering in old cemeteries. He arrived late and boasted about finding the gravestone, but when we asked to see pictures, he said he'd gone off without his camera and had forgotten to charge his phone. It struck us as odd because a seasoned genealogist documents every discovery, and knowing Prescott as we do, the omission was striking.

"Anyway," she said, "it seemed as though we'd caught him in a lie. The situation was awkward, and to tell you the truth, my heart went out to Eleanor. Why would her husband run out on her just two days after a body was found in their pond? And why would he lie about it?"

She paused to adjust a photo, and leaned back to study the results. "Shame on me," she said. "Here I am, casting doubt on a dear friend. But it's hard not to entertain suspicions. Prescott's quite a gad-about—always running here and there. Eleanor normally doesn't mind—she's a prolific author, and she cherishes time to herself. And yet, I'm sure she wonders if her husband might be…"

She caught herself before completing the thought. "Forgive me. I shouldn't be gossiping. It's just that people talk—how can they help it? But please, strike those words from the record."

Radley had no intention of striking the words from the record. Instead, he underlined them. Nora Murphy had mentioned seeing Tillman and Jenna together last winter at the casino in Bethlehem. So far, there'd been no other witnesses to verify the claim, but the show wasn't over yet.

Doris fished a photo out of the pile and smiled wistfully. "My husband's first Sunday as leader of the Center. He'd been involved with its founding, and it was quite an honor when he was asked to be in charge. And it was lovely for both of us that this house was part of the package. And so sweet of my son and his wife to make it possible for us to continue living here." Sighing, she handed the picture to Burleigh who glanced at it and passed it to Radley.

No doubt about it—Ralph Stevenson was a handsome guy way back when—robust with wavy, blond hair and a smile that hinted at a keen sense of humor. He'd been tall and sturdy as well, with the looks of an outdoorsman rather than a leader of a metaphysical society. Radley hadn't known many leaders of metaphysical societies, but he pictured a spaced-out, pale sort of guy with a turban and a prayer shawl. Ralph Stevenson didn't fit the bill.

The same could be said of the younger Stevenson whom the detectives had met briefly the day of the murder. Like his dad, Ryan Stevenson seemed too hale and hearty to be a shaman or a spiritual guru. But if Radley'd learned one thing over the years, it was that looks could be deceiving.

Taking the picture back, Doris gazed at it lovingly and placed it on the page. "Alzheimer's is such a dreadful curse," she said. "Ralph used to love camping, hiking, horseback riding—all kinds of outdoor activities. He used to say that the fishing weekends he spent with Ryan were some of the most meaningful of his life."

She turned her face away, struggling to control her feelings. Her obvious distress tugged at Radley's heart. He had an uncle with Alzheimer's and he knew how tough it could be.

"Forgive me," she said. "Our family's had a difficult time of it lately. Just a few weeks ago we learned that Ryan carries the genetic marker for early onset Alzheimer's. The doctor says it doesn't mean that he'll be stricken like his father—just that the odds are higher. Ryan tries to be brave, but I can tell he's upset. I tried to talk to him about it a few days ago, but he flew into a rage and said that he and Heather gave up their dreams of homesteading in Wyoming to help me deal with his dad. And now he doesn't know how many good years he has left, and he doesn't know if he'll be able to give his wife and children the life they'd hoped for."

She looked away down at the floor. "I shouldn't be telling you my problems. That's not why you're here."

"Don't give it a thought," Burleigh said. "But I'm curious. Why Wyoming?"

"His wife, Heather, grew up there, and that's where they were married—there on her uncle's ranch. Ryan fell in love with the wide open-country, and from the start, they dreamed of living there one day. It breaks my heart to know that Ralph and I are the reason for their unhappiness. It was different before the DNA results when they thought they had all the time in the world, but now..."

The front door opened and a voice called out from the foyer. "Hey kids, we're home." At the sound, a little tyke darted into the living room from an adjacent hallway and ran to greet his parents as they came into the room. Smiling, Ryan gathered him in a bear hug, but the look of paternal warmth turned icy when he spotted the detectives.

The boss rose to his feet and showed his ID. "Detective Burleigh," he said. "We spoke briefly on Saturday when by team was searching the building."

"I remember."

"Well then, my partner and I have been chatting with your mother, and we'd like a word with you as well."

Ryan looked at his mom as if wondering what she'd told them. "Of course," he said as he handed his son to his wife. "We can speak in my study."

He led the detectives through the foyer and into a small room directly across from the goddess Aurora. The room was lined with bookshelves, and behind the desk, a stained-glass window glimmered in the sunlight shining through it.

The conversation began with the usual question—where were you at the time of Jenna's death?

"I was going to attend the keynote address," Ryan said, "but I decided instead to sneak down to the basement office to review my notes for a workshop about ancestor worship I'd be leading in the afternoon. I was there from about 9:15 to 10:30."

"Is there anyone who can confirm the fact?"

"Not that I'm aware of."

"Correct me if I'm wrong," Burleigh said, "but I seem to remember that the basement office is directly across from a door leading in and out of the prayer garden."

"That's right."

"Did you happen to notice Malcolm and Jenna in the garden?"

He shook his head. "The office door was closed. All I noticed was the material I was working on."

"Were you acquainted with Jenna Henley?"

He didn't answer at first. "No," he finally said. "We never

met, but I noticed her once or twice when my wife and I visited the Artisans' Emporium. With looks like that, it was hard not to notice her."

"And your wife—were she and Jenna acquainted?"

"It's possible. You'll have to ask her yourself."

"I'd like to do that. Would you send her in?"

Nodding, Ryan excused himself, and a few moments later, Heather Stevenson entered the study, her eyes bright and her cheeks flushed. She seemed in good spirits—like a kid coming down the stairs on Christmas morning. She took the seat her husband vacated and didn't wait for introductions. "Can you keep a secret?" she asked.

"We're in the business of keeping secrets," Burleigh said.

"Well, my secret has nothing to do with the investigation. It's just that I'm dying to tell someone. I can't mention it to Ryan's mom until he's had a chance to speak to her. Promise you won't tell?"

"You have our word of honor."

Heather leaned across the desk, her green eyes glistening. "Drum roll, please. Ryan and I are headed for Wyoming—sooner rather than later. To live there, not to visit."

"Well, this is sudden," Burleigh remarked.

"It happened pretty fast," she agreed. "Two weeks ago, my uncle called to tell me about a ranch that went on the market. I haven't been able to stop thinking about it, and today over lunch, Ryan and I made up our minds. We'll buy the ranch and take his parents to Wyoming with us."

"That's a big decision," the boss said. "I'm sure there's a lot to work out between now and then."

She nodded. "It'll be a tough adjustment for his dad. And his mom will hate leaving her friends and her work at the Center. But Ryan decided it's time to put the health and well-being of our children first. We've got a few financial details to iron out, but he expects things to come together nicely."

"Congratulations." Radley spoke up. "It sounds like you have a lot to look forward to."

Heather rewarded him with a smile. "We owe it all to the Sustainable Agriculture Conference I went to last weekend. The speakers were phenomenal, and all I could think about was getting home and telling Ryan about it. He said the things I learned at the conference helped him make up his mind."

She sat back and crossed her arms. "But enough about me. Ryan said you needed to ask me something, and here I am wasting your time."

"Just a quick question," the boss said. "Your husband mentioned that he recognized Jenna Henley from visits to the Artisans' Emporium. On your visits to the store, did you and she ever speak?"

"Never, but I'm not surprised she took Ryan's eye—he never misses a pretty face."

"I see. And one final question: what time did you leave Stony Vale on the morning of the murder?"

"A little after five in the morning."

"And there are people who can testify to that?"

"My family. And friends at the Community Supported Agriculture Conference at Penn State who saw me there all weekend."

She rattled off three names, and once Radley'd written them down, the conversation ended.

Back in the car, Radley and the boss discussed the interviews. Prescott Tillman had gone somewhere last Monday, and a roomful of people thought he lied about it. The matter seemed unrelated to Jenna's death—unless, of course, it established a habit of philandering, in which case, it might shed light on Nora Murphy's claim of seeing Jenna and Dr. Tillman leaving the casino together last December. But in one sense, it didn't matter because Tillman had an alibi for the time of the Jenna's murder.

Ryan Stevenson, on the other hand, was a man without an alibi. He'd supposedly been alone in the basement office at the time of Jenna's murder, but there was no one who could verify the claim. And now, just one week after the murder, he'd made a snap decision to pack up the family and move to Wyoming. Was he hoping for a chance to live out his dreams before time ran out, or was he determined to get out of Dodge before suspicion shifted in his direction? There was no way to answer that—not yet. But Radley suspected that by the end of the day, Ryan's face would join the others on the whiteboard back at headquarters.

Twenty-one

The evening shadows stretched out across Main Street in Stony Vale, and all along the block, tiny pink and white buds dotted the trees. *Spring*, Ted thought to himself. *The time of year when a young man's fancy lightly turns to thoughts of love.* Not that he was all that young. He was pushing forty, but who was he to argue if Cupid chose to take aim and fire.

He turned up a steep driveway that led to a large, seventeenth-century fieldstone house. This relic of the past had undergone a few upgrades over the decades, notably a two-story addition, a two-tiered deck, an attached three-car garage and a glassed-in conservatory that reflected back the colors of the setting sun. Amazingly, these disconnects from early-American architecture blended in naturally, as though they'd been here all along.

As he got out of the Jeep, Ashley emerged from the house to greet him. For tonight's reunion, she'd opted for beauty over brains—contacts instead of dark-rimmed, high-IQ glasses. Her hair was piled on her head in a heap of gold with wispy tendrils escaping to frame her face. Her outfit—cream-colored leggings and a pink sweater—was a simple look that on her was stunning.

"Hey," she said, turning her face to him for a kiss.

"Hey, yourself." he said, He delivered the kiss on cue and held her close. This was it, he thought as the sweet fragrance of her perfume teased his nostrils. This was the week that would determine if he and Ashley had a future together.

They separated and he glanced at his surroundings. "Nice place your folks have here."

"It's not bad."

"Not bad at all. A bit small, don't you think?"

The remark was facetious, and it earned him a smile. "My folks need space to entertain. Believe it or not, several couples have held their weddings here."

"I can believe it. The view from your deck must be incredible."

He wondered then if Ashley was imagining her own wedding here in this country-club setting. Was she picturing him in the wedding photos, duded up in a tux while she stood next to him like a goddess in white?

"My parents are dying to meet you," she said as she led him up the walkway to the door.

Ted didn't say anything, mostly because he wasn't exactly looking forward to meeting them. No matter a man's age, the first encounter with the individuals who—for better or for worse—might one day become his in-laws was always a daunting experience.

Opening the door, Ashely welcomed him into a well-lit foyer with a cathedral ceiling that reached up beyond the second story. He wasn't a historian of colonial architecture, but he knew enough to realize that houses of this vintage rarely came with cathedral ceilings. But it hardly mattered because the effect was incredible.

The living room they entered was a huge space with massive windows overlooking the river valley. The furnishings were tasteful—a chocolate-brown leather sofa with matching chairs, a Persian rug, a huge stone fireplace and a grand piano.

"Steinway," he observed. "I'm impressed. Do you play?"

"Years of lessons," she said, "but not much to show for them."

"Your parents?"

"None of us play. Not my brothers. Not my parents. And certainly not me. It's here for parties. My mom likes to book a piano player for special occasions—live music creates a wonderful ambience."

"I couldn't agree more. All my friends have Steinways for that exact reason. I've got two—one in the living room and one in the second-floor hallway. The surround-sound is amazing."

Before Ashley could say, "very funny," two people materialized in front of them. The first was a meek-looking guy of average height with thick glasses and thinning dark hair slicked into a shiny combover. When Ashley introduced him as her dad, he insisted on being called George. Ted felt comfortable greeting him that way, but Ashley's mom didn't offer to put things on a first-name basis. Instead, she nodded a greeting, her dark eyes appraising him from beneath a helmet of gray hair. He couldn't quite read her expression. It might have been a smile, but it was hard to tell. He dutifully addressed her as Mrs. Stoddard, and although he was tempted to add *Your Royal Highness*, he refrained from doing so.

He and Ashley took seats on the leather sofa, being careful not to sit too close together. Her dad picked up a remote-control device, and with the touch of a button, ignited a fire in the stone fireplace—a trick his historic forebears would have found remarkable. He asked Ted what he'd like to drink, and while Ted was known to knock off a beer now and then, his drinking days were behind him. He opted for seltzer and lime while the others chose something stronger—gin and tonic for Mrs. Stoddard, white wine for Ashley, scotch and soda for her dad. From there they turned their attention to a tray of crab-stuffed mushrooms, shrimp and something meaty on chunks of toasted bread. There was more than enough for a full meal, but even though Ted was ravenous, he restrained himself from devouring everything in sight.

Before long, the conversation drifted to the subject on everyone's mind—the Jenna Henley murder investigation.

"A friend of mine used to date Malcolm Mackenzie," Ashley remarked, a crab-stuffed mushroom in one hand. "She said he's a narcissist, and she had to get out of the relationship to save her sanity."

"Malcolm's not a narcissist," her father spoke up. "He's confident, and why shouldn't he be? Look at how successful he is. His company was recently chosen to restore an important historic building in Philadelphia. Quite a feather in his cap, wouldn't you agree?"

"I'm not talking about his work," Ashley argued. "I'm talking about narcissistic personality disorder. My friend said he's manipulative and controlling and incapable of understanding how his behavior makes other people feel. She said that whenever he hurt her feelings, he had a way of twisting things to make it seem like his bad behavior was her fault. He could never admit he was wrong, and he was always hinting that she needed to improve herself to be worthy of him. She said that when she tried to get out of the relationship, he made her life miserable. With what I know about him, it's easy to believe that Jenna Henley tried to dump him, and he killed her rather than releasing control.

She took a bite of the stuffed mushroom and chewed thoughtfully. "I think I should tell the detectives what I know about him."

"I totally agree," her mother said. "It makes me shudder

when I think of the number of times we had him here working on the house. My word, if you'd gotten mixed up with him, you might have been the one floating in the Tillmans' pond."

"So, if he's as terrible as you two seem to think," George said, "why haven't the police arrested him?"

Ashley shrugged. "They must have other suspects in mind. Like Prescott Tillman, for instance. After all, Jenna's body was found in his pond,"

"That doesn't mean a thing," her father said. "Prescott's right as rain—I'd put money on it. But I'll let you in on a little secret. The man needs to polish up his golf game. I'd be embarrassed to show my face at the country club if that was the best I could do."

He shifted his gaze to Ted. "What about you? How's your game?"

Ted shrugged. "I'm not a golfer."

"Not a golfer, eh? We'll have to get to work on that, won't we? I'm sure Ashley can give you some pointers."

"Now, Daddy, if Ted doesn't want to play golf, he doesn't have to."

"Nonsense. A man has to play golf if he expects to get anywhere in this world."

Frowning, Mrs. Stoddard rose to her feet and announced that it was time for dinner. They followed her to a dining room that offered a spectacular view of the river valley, but other than that, the space was too stuffy and formal for Ted's taste. He felt like he was in a museum display with valuable period furniture arranged just so and every detail chosen to create the impression of a long-vanished era. Adding to his discomfort were portraits of grim-faced ancestors who scowled at him from the walls. Noticing a butler's pantry off to one side, he considered lightening the mood by asking if the butler and footman had been given the night off, but a look at Mrs. Stoddard's granite face made him reject the idea.

After George said grace, Ashely darted off to the kitchen and returned with bowls of mushroom soup—a rich, creamy concoction with a hint of some exotic spice that Ted couldn't identify. The soup was followed by an arugula salad with strawberries, followed in turn by grilled salmon with rice pilaf and asparagus. The dessert, a lemon ricotta pie, was the perfect ending to a springtime dinner. Ashley made her forays to the kitchen and back again with the grace of a ballerina, and when Ted complimented her on the meal, she confessed that everything came from a catering establishment with which her family did business.

Following dessert, they adjourned to the living room to sip coffee and wrack their brains for topics to discuss. Mrs. Stoddard kicked things off by describing the process she'd followed in tracing her genealogy for the Daughters of the American Revolution. "It took some doing," she said, "but I was affectionately welcomed into the fold the moment I established my pedigree back to the late 17th century in Barnstable, Massachusetts."

Pedigree—the term was hilarious. Ted pictured Augusta Stoddard as a poodle being trotted around the circuit at the Westminster Kennel Club by an aging DAR matron in sensible shoes. The image was entertaining, at least until Mrs. Stoddard shifted gears and asked about Ted's lineage.

He froze at the question. An aunt had done copious research into his family's history, but Ted had never bothered to take a look. Should he make something up? Something funny about being descended from pirates on his father's side and Chicago mobsters on his mother's? Ashley's dad might laugh, but Ted was pretty sure her mom wouldn't, so he opted for the truth—namely, that he'd paid little attention to his ancestry.

The conversation faltered after that, and feeling uncomfortable, he thanked the Stoddards for a lovely evening and excused himself. Ashley walked him to his Jeep, and they shared a kiss beside the driver's side door beneath the harsh glow of the motion detector light above the garage.

"Don't worry about my mom," Ashley said, her blue eyes reflecting back the floodlight's glare. "She's a stickler for family history and she expects everyone else to be as well. And as far as my dad's concerned, work and golf are all he thinks about. But I promise that in time they'll learn to love you."

Ted seriously doubted it, but the ordeal was over with, and he and Ashley had the rest of the week to spend together—without her parents. As he drove away, he imagined a piano player at the Steinway in the living room while on the deck, servers offered hors d'oeuvres and flutes of champagne to well-dressed, well-coifed guests. He pictured Ashley in a white gown decked with lace and pearls while all around her roses bloomed and the scent of lilacs filled the air. He imagined her eyes, bright and radiant as she accepted congratulations from her mother's DAR pals, and he pictured her face beaming as she welcomed kisses on the cheek from her father's country club buddies and law firm partners. But oddly, when Ted tried to imagine himself—tall, handsome and debonair in a bowtie and tux—the picture refused to stay in focus.

Twenty-two

The Conservancy fund raiser on Saturday night had been a huge financial success. David was thrilled with the praise his efforts received, but he was even more thrilled that his evening with Julie was just as successful. He recalled the way her eyes sparkled when he'd been called to the podium to thunderous applause as Conservancy members shared their commendations of his work. Later, Julie had eagerly accepted his invitation to attend a concert next week at Lehigh University's Zoellner Arts Center. He thought back to the kiss they'd shared on her doorstep. It had taken a lot of willpower to limit himself to just one, but this was a budding relationship, and he didn't want to mess it up by being too assertive.

A knock on Mac's door brought David back to reality. All at once, he was no longer on Julie's doorstep seeing himself reflected in her eyes. Instead, he was in a decaying wreck of a house, trying to cheer up a hungover, unappreciative, self-absorbed person-of-interest who seemed completely oblivious to the things David was doing on his behalf.

"Reporters," Mac growled from the sofa. "Ignore them, and they'll go away."

When the pounding continued, David went to the window to take a look. "Bad news," he said, his eyes fixed on a vehicle at the curb. "It's the cops."

Wincing, Mac placed a hand to his head and tried to sit up. When the effort failed, he sank back against the cushions with a groan. "They're here to arrest me for Jenna's murder You'll tell them I didn't do it—won't you?"

David didn't answer. A week ago, that's exactly what he would have done—but now?

He left Mac to his hangover and went to the door, his mind reeling at the thought of what was about to happen. He pictured officers cuffing Mac and leading him to their car. Off to one side, reporters would snap photos and shoot videos, not just of Mac but of David watching from the door.

Taking a deep breath, he threw back his shoulders and opened the door. Two cops, a woman and a man, flashed their IDs at him. "We'd like a word with Malcolm Mackenzie," the female officer said.

David beckoned for them to follow, and when they entered the living room, Mac struggled to his feet, a look of hopeless resignation on his face.

"I assume you were aware," the female cop began, "that Jenna Henley was pregnant at the time of her death?"

The announcement wasn't what David had expected and apparently Mac hadn't expected it either. He looked at David in bewilderment, and then back at the cops. "Pregnant? Jenna? She never mentioned…" His voice wavered and fell silent.

"We'll need a DNA sample to determine paternity," said the male cop. "It's no big deal—just a swab inside the mouth."

"Okay. So, give me a swab and get it over with."

"Sorry," said the male cop. "It has to be done in a lab to establish chain of custody and guarantee the sample's integrity.

The lab's open today until three."

There didn't seem to be much to say after that. David showed the officers to the door but stopped them as they were about to leave. "For the record, how far along was Jenna at the time of her death."

"From what I understand," the male cop said, "she was about three mon…"

The female officer cut him off, her eyes flashing at her partner. "We aren't privy to that information," she said.

Nodding, David closed the door and went back to the living room. Since Mac was in no shape for driving, he offered to give him a ride. Even so, it took nearly an hour for Mac to pull himself together enough to make his way through the reporters and crawl into David's Miata. The drive was a short one, and it wasn't long before the car came to a stop in front of a squat brick building.

"I didn't even know she was pregnant," Mac said for the hundredth time. "How am I supposed to deal with the fact that I lost Jenna and my child as well?" He clenched his fist and sank back in the seat, his eyes closed. "What if I find out it wasn't my kid? If it turns out to be Seth's, I'll kill him. I mean it this time."

Sighing, he glanced over at David. "Thanks for sticking by me, pal. I couldn't have faced this alone."

The comment lifted David's spirits. He'd struggled all weekend to offer support, and it was good to know that in spite of the challenges, his efforts were appreciated.

He watched Mac get out of the car and head for the building, shoulders slumped and eyes downcast. Once Mac shuffled through the door, David replayed the cops' visit in his mind. Today was Sunday, and Jenna had died a week ago yesterday. It wouldn't have taken much time for the forensics people to discover the pregnancy, so why did they wait so long to request a DNA sample? Did it always work this way?

His phone jangled in his pocket. Julie, he assumed, calling to thank him for a lovely time last night. But a look at call waiting told him it wasn't Julie. It was Adele Smith, Chairperson of the Board of Directors.

"Enjoying your long weekend?" she began in way of reminding him that he hadn't given the required 48 hours' notice prior to taking two comp days. "And by the way," she added in the same snarky voice, "I wanted to talk to you at last evening's fundraiser, but you seemed to disappear whenever I approached."

He tried not to laugh. He and Julie had made a game out of avoiding Adele's company.

"What I intended to tell you," she said, "is that due to the negative publicity surrounding Seth Walker's fight with Malcolm Mackenzie, the board is cancelling Seth's speaking engagements and withholding our referrals—at least until the Jenna Henley case is resolved. As director, it's up to you to break the news, just as you did with Malcolm."

David felt sick at the thought. Seth's Native American genealogy workshops, his lectures on Lenni Lenape culture and his story-telling sessions were among the Conservancy's most popular events. But more importantly, Seth was a good guy who'd defended himself from an unexpected assault. He deserved better than this.

Thankfully, David had anticipated this move and was ready to counter it. "Will I be making a similar call to Prescott Tillman?" he asked. "The media hasn't been shy about asking how Jenna ended up in his fishpond. Don't you think that if we're canceling Seth, we should cancel Tillman's genealogy lectures as well?"

A lengthy hesitation told David he'd touched a nerve.

"Dr. Tillman is a generous donor," Adele said, her voice frosty. "And in case you've forgotten, we rely on generous donors to keep the Conservancy afloat. As of now, we have no intention of severing our relationship with him."

David knew better than to argue. While the idealist in him was furious at the board's double standard, the realist in him knew how things worked. Without the largesse of the moneyed class, there'd be no Tudor Revival mansion to serve as Conservancy headquarters. No funds to pay salaries. No money to maintain the lawns and gardens. And no means of preserving regional farmland, forests and historic properties, and certainly no resources for seminars, workshops and consultations to schools, museums and community organizations. No—there was nothing to be gained from alienating Prescott Tillman. In the world of nonprofits, money didn't just talk—it sang.

The call ended, and a few minutes later Mac emerged from the lab. He seemed even more dejected than before when he climbed back into the Miata, and his mood darkened further when they got back home and faced the reporters who, judging from their questions, had gotten wind of Jenna's pregnancy.

Inside the house Mack leaned against the door, and sank to a sitting position with his knees drawn to his chest. "Why can't they leave me alone? I didn't murder her. I swear I didn't. I'm grieving. Can't those idiots see that?"

He smiled—sort of—when Nessie waddled into the foyer and sat in front of him. Sighing, Mac reached for the Scottie and held him close, like Nessie was the baby he and Jenna might have had together. But as he stroked the thick, black fur, a confused expression stole over his face. "The cops didn't tell me how far along Jenna was."

"I asked them as they were leaving," David told him. "One cop said she was three months, and the other cut him off and said they weren't privy to the information."

"But the first one said three months—you're sure of that?"

When David nodded, Mac drew in his breath and closed his eyes. "That settles it then. The baby wasn't mine."

"What? How can you be sure?"

"I can be sure because three months ago I was in Scotland visiting my family for Christmas. I stayed on to visit friends around the UK and got back in the middle of January. That means that while I was away, Jenna hooked up with somebody. When things didn't work out, she decided to make me think the baby was mine."

"But why would she bother?" David asked. "Most women in her position would have aborted the fetus and been done with it."

"Don't ask me why she did what she did. All I know is that it wasn't my kid, and it isn't my problem."

Shooing Nessie off his lap, he struggled to his feet and headed for the stairs without further comment. Moments later David heard water running, and when Mac returned, he'd showered and shaved and put on clean jeans and a pin-striped Oxford shirt.

"It's time to put this behind me," he said. "Stiff upper lip, as the Brits say."

Nessie looked up at him with eager eyes, but Mac ignored him and went into the living room. Picking up his phone, he spent the next half hour making calls and pacing back and forth as he gave orders to his work crew and asked for updates on their progress.

The transformation was remarkable, and as David watched, he found it hard to hard to believe that Mac had mourned Jenna's passing at all. But did he murder her? The question nagged at him, and David was still thinking about it when he said goodbye to Nessie and left the puppy sitting alone in the cluttered foyer.

He got in the Miata, but as anxious as he was to get away, he couldn't bring himself to start the engine. Nessie was Mac's birthday gift from Jenna. Would Mac conflate the dog with Jenna and treat it accordingly? Or would he reject the little creature and take it to a shelter where it would spend its days in a cage waiting to be adopted? Unable to bear the thought, David got out of his car and returned ten minutes later with Nessie in his arms.

Twenty-three

*J*ust *friends,* Ted told himself as steam rose from his coffee cup and drifted toward the light above his head. *Brooke and I are just friends.*

Eighteen months ago, he'd gotten a call from a complete stranger saying someone gave her his name because they thought he might have information to explain her husband's out-of-the-blue religious conversion a few months before his death. Would Ted meet with her?

He'd been intrigued from the start, first by the story she'd told on the phone and later by her as well. More than intrigued. But it didn't take long to realize the hopelessness of his infatuation. Brooke wasn't interested in him beyond the fact that he happened to hold the keys to a mess her late husband had landed in.

He'd tried to keep things in perspective, but in spite of his efforts, the infatuation had lingered for well over a year. And then he met Ashley. Last night's dinner with her parents had been a little rocky, but the time he'd spent with her today— church in the morning, brunch at noon and later a tour of Bethlehem's historic sites—had smoothed things out considerably. She had plans tonight with friends from high school, and so he'd phoned Brooke to suggest coffee. It was time, he'd decided, to put his pointless infatuation to rest and rebuild his relationship with Brooke on a foundation that had nothing to do with a hope of romance. From now on, they'd be friends—period.

"Hey," a voice said from over his shoulder. "A penny for your thoughts."

He looked up and there she was, gazing down at him. "A penny for my thoughts? My thoughts are worth way more than that. Sit down and I'll prove it."

"Coffee first."

He watched Brooke glide over to the counter and return with something hot and steamy in a ceramic mug. He remembered that about her—she preferred ceramic mugs to disposable cups because she didn't like the feel of hot cardboard on her lips—an odd quirk that he found amusing.

She slid into the seat across from him, and as their eyes met, he felt that something he always felt when he looked at her. He couldn't help himself—the mottled blues and greens of her eyes sent his pulse racing.

I'm seeing Ashley, he reminded himself. *Ashley and I have things in common. Things that define us as a couple. Brooke is just a friend.*

He watched Brooke blow a puff of air over her coffee, her lips the subtle shade of coral he remembered so well. Taking a cautious sip, she frowned and set the mug down. Too hot to handle, apparently.

"So," she said. "Tell me these thoughts of yours that are worth more than a penny."

Before long, he was dazzling her with descriptions of his upcoming video series on the subject of transhumanism. For once, she didn't make fun of what he said. In fact, she added to the conversation with observations from and sci-fi films and novels, and soon they were talking about cyborgs, replicants, brain-computer interfaces, terminators, clones, androids, robots and more. From there the conversation segued naturally to alien abduction stories with their claims of forced medical experiments related to human reproduction.

"Nobody talks much about that anymore," Brooke remarked. "Makes you wonder though, doesn't it? What were the 'aliens' (air quotes) doing with the sperm, eggs, embryos and DNA they harvested in all those abductions?"

She leaned closer across the table. "Here's a question for you—were those 'alien' experiments part of the Human Genome Project in the 1990s? And how about this? Are the same 'alien' experiments somehow related to the modern transhumanist movement?" She glanced around at the customers sipping coffee and studying their phones. "They look like us, but how many are actually alien-human hybrids?"

Ted could tell she wasn't serious, and it was nice to see her lighten up for a change. Most of their shared experiences had been rooted in some urgent and dangerous crisis. This easygoing banter was a welcome change of pace.

The chatty mood continued with a discussion of recent feats of genetic engineering. They talked about the rebirth of the dire wolf after millennia of extinction and the mice embryos implanted with wooly mammoth DNA—a step toward bringing the long-extinct creatures back to life. Further experiments were in the works to reanimate Tasmanian tigers and dodo birds.

"I think they should bring back T-Rex," Brooke said with a smile. "What could possibly go wrong?"

From there, the conversation shifted to transhumanist guru, Dr. Prescott Tillman. Last week, Brooke had attended a dinner at the Stevenson's house in Stony Vale. Tillman arrived late after spending the day searching for and finding an ancestor's grave. The other guests thought it strange that he'd failed to take photos of the gravestone—a significant oversight for a dedicated genealogist.

"Anyway," Brooke continued. "I happened to overhear an argument later between Tillman and his wife. She seemed to think he was lying about where he'd been all day. It struck me as suspicious, coming just two days after Jenna's body showed up in his pond."

"Suspicious," Ted agreed, "but maybe not in the way you mean. Tillman's a rock star to a whole generation of science geeks. Is it hard to imagine a transhumanist groupie indulging in a fling with her hero? That would be a reason to lie to the missus—wouldn't it?"

"I'm sure everyone at the table was thinking the same thing—especially this grumpy lady named Augusta Stoddard. She wasn't about to let Tillman off the hook."

Ted nearly choked on his coffee. "Did you say Augusta Stoddard?"

"That's right? Do you know her?"

"You might say that. I'm seeing her daughter."

The comment drew a look of surprise.

"I'm happy for you," Brooke said after an awkward hesitation. "That you're seeing someone, I mean."

He struggled to find a response. Brooke had just handed him the perfect segue to the topic he'd hoped to discuss with her, so why couldn't he find the words? He wanted to tell her that while he hoped he and she would remain friends, he was seeing Ashley, and their relationship was gaining steam. Most of all, he wanted to emphasize that Ashley shared his faith and believed in the work he was doing.

But the words never made it from his brain to his lips. Instead, he returned to the topic at hand.

"I have a suggestion for Tillman's wife," he said. "She needs to buy a digital tracking device and plant it in the wheel well of her husband's car. Next time he wanders off, she can track his location on her phone. I have one of those gizmos myself, but so far, I've never used it."

Brooke's expression shifted from upbeat to anxious, a look Ted had seen plenty of times before. "A tracker?" she said. "I never thought about…" Suddenly flustered, she got her phone out of her bag. "Excuse me. I'll just be a sec."

She averted her face and lowered her voice as though trying to keep him from hearing what she said. Leaning closer, Ted picked up something about a motel and a guy named Derrick and a van. Silence followed and then she told the person she'd called to calm down—she'd take care of it.

That settled, Brooke grabbed her bag and rose to her feet. "Sorry, Ted. I have to run."

"What is it? Can I help? Is someone in trouble?"

She shrugged and mumbled something about a friend being trapped in a house with two Rottweilers and two kittens named Donnie and Marie. The friend's significant other was out running errands and the friend's van was back at the Beacon Arms.

Reaching out, she squeezed Ted's hand—an unexpected gesture, given that she'd never reached out to touch him before. "I'll explain later," she said.

And then she was gone.

Twenty-four

All was quiet when Brooke got back to the Beacon Arms. While she hadn't bought into Maggie's theory about Derrick Strauss murdering Jenna, she couldn't shake the suggestion that Derrick was the guy who'd been in Jenna's apartment the night before her murder. If that were true, did he recognize Maggie that day at the funeral, and did he plant a tracker to confirm that she was the same person who'd seen him race for the elevator?

She slipped a hand beneath the driver's side wheel well and probed the rough metal surface. Finding nothing, she moved on to the other three wheel wells. Nothing. A second more thorough inspection confirmed her first impression. She phoned Maggie with the good news, and as they ended the call, Brooke heard a car door slam in the distance. Brooke glanced in that direction and saw Anita, the crazy psychic from the first floor, getting out of a Mini Cooper.

Hoping to avoid another visit to crazy land, Brooke ducked behind the van. But it was too late.

"Brooke!" Anita shouted, her long black skirt swirling

around her ankles as she hurried toward the van. "I have something important to tell you."

As far as Brooke was concerned, so-called psychics were self-deluded manipulators who'd learned to read body language, facial expressions and verbal cues in order to prey on people's fears. She wasn't about to let Anita play those games with her.

"I dreamed of you last night," Anita announced.

"That's nice. Now if you'll excuse me…"

She grabbed hold of Brooke's arm. "I saw you in a dark forest, unable to find your way out. When you approached a stream, Melusine leapt out and tried to drag you beneath the water. It's a warning—I'm sure of it."

Brooke was determined not to play along. "For the record, Melusine is a shape-shifting mermaid depicted in medieval European legends. As far as I know, there are zero accounts of her leaping out of streams to drag women to their death. And now if you'll excuse me, I've got work to do."

Anita tightened her grip on Brooke's arm, her eyes dark as coal. "It's a warning from the spirits. You see that, don't you?"

A chill crept up Brooke's spine. Not because she believed this nonsense, but because she was in no mood for spooky talk—not after being freaked out by thoughts of Derrick sneaking out of Jenna's apartment just hours before she died.

Letting go of Brooke's arm, Anita got out her phone and scrolled around. "I have an opening tomorrow," she said. "If you'll come to my apartment at one, I'll cast a spell to guarantee your safety."

"Oh really? Your spells didn't do much for Jenna, did they?"

Anita recoiled, her eyes dark and angry. "You'll be sorry," she hissed. With that, she went to the building and disappeared from sight.

Back in her apartment, Brooke made a cup of mint tea and tried to put the unpleasant encounter behind her. She put no stock in psychics, and yet she'd found the conversation disturbing, given all the uncertainty surrounding Jenna's death.

Her thoughts drifted to a book her mother used to read to her—the one about mermaids. She recalled Irish merrows with long, green hair. Scottish selkies shedding their skin to become human women. Greek Nereids protecting sailors from the terrors of the deep. Undines frolicking in waterfalls. The Rhine Maidens of Wagnerian fame. And of course, the French water spirit, Melusine.

The phone rang and the memories faded.

"Sorry to bother you," Doris Stevenson said. "I got a text early this afternoon from the publicity person for the Stony Vale Summer Fest. She's been called away on a family emergency and we need someone to fill in. Your uncle said you might be willing to lend a hand. We're meeting tomorrow at ten at my house. There's only a few of us—me, Eleanor Tillman and Augusta Stoddard—you would be the fourth. Sadly, we can't afford to pay anything—it would be strictly volunteer."

Brooke accepted, not just because Uncle Nelson would be pleased, but because doing so would allow her to smooth things out between herself and Eleanor Tillman. They'd ended on a sour note that night in Ryan's study, and Brooke welcomed the opportunity to improve her relationship with a noted author who'd expressed interest in her editing abilities.

Later, she lay awake thinking about Ted. Eighteen months ago, it had been evident that he was interested in more than friendship. But being the nice guy he was, he'd kept his distance out of respect for her grief following Karl's death. And now that he'd fallen for Augusta Stoddard's daughter, Brooke was troubled by conflicting emotions.

It was for the best, she decided. Instead of being worried about Ted's intentions, from now on she'd be free to kick back and enjoy his company. The idea was liberating, and she looked forward to this new chapter in their relationship. No more ignoring the way Ted looked at her. No more self-censoring to make sure she wasn't giving him the wrong impression. And no more keeping her distance for fear of what might develop between them.

And yet something about this new arrangement troubled her. She'd taken for granted that Ted would always be there. Like her laptop and her phone and her TV, he was a fixture in her life—always there when she needed him. The idea was silly, she realized. More than silly, it was self-centered and childish, and she hadn't been aware of it until this very moment. She had to let go and accept that he was moving on with his life while she was idling in neutral, unable to shift gears.

▾ ▾ ▾

Huge, wet snowflakes fell from the sky as Brooke entered Stony Vale the next morning. She hurried up the walkway to the Stevensons' house and when she rang the bell, Doris welcomed her inside and showed her to the living room.

"A mug of coffee to warm you?" her hostess asked.

"That would be lovely."

As Doris filled the mug and handed it to her, the phone—a landline—rang noisily.

"Pay no attention," Doris said. "It rings in three places—Ryan's study, the living room and the office at the Center. Heather's working there this morning, and she'll answer it. We've had some awkward moments when Ralph answers. He thinks he's still in charge, and his remarks have led to quite a few mix-ups." She sighed. "It would be amusing if it weren't so sad."

The doorbell sounded from the foyer, and Doris scurried off to answer it. She returned a moment later with Eleanor Tillman and Augusta Stoddard, and as they got seated, Brooke studied Augusta from across the coffee table. Was Ashley as prim and proper as her mom? Maybe not, but they say that with the passing of time, women turn into their mothers. If that were true, Ted was in for a rough ride.

The meeting kicked off with a list of Brooke's responsibilities—press releases, flyers, promotional items and so forth. After that, the discussion moved to related matters, and when it concluded, Doris went to the kitchen and returned with a chocolate-chip poundcake.

"I assume by now you've heard the latest," Augusta remarked as Doris passed slices of cake around. "I refer, of course, to the fact that Jenna Henley was pregnant at the time of her death. One can assume that Malcolm's the father, but from what I hear, the police are taking DNA from every man in Jenna's circle."

Eleanor changed the subject by commenting on Doris's cake and asking if she could have the recipe. After that, the conversation seemed strained, and it wasn't long before Augusta set her empty plate aside. "I hate to break up the party, but I have errands to run."

"Before you leave," Doris said. "I have an announcement to make."

Augusta glanced at her watch. "Make it quick. I have a hair appointment in half-an-hour."

"I'll be as brief as possible. I want you and Eleanor to be the first to know Ralph and I are moving with Ryan's family to Wyoming."

"Wyoming?" Augusta exclaimed. "Out in the middle of nowhere? Whatever prompted a notion like that?"

Tears welled in Doris's eyes, and she struggled to speak. "As you know, Ryan inherited the genetic marker for early onset Alzheimer's. He's always dreamed of homesteading in Wyoming, and with that timebomb ticking inside him, he can't afford to procrastinate any longer. Heather's uncle in Wyoming notified her of a 500-acre ranch that's come on the market, and we're moving ahead with the purchase."

"How wonderful," Eleanor said.

Doris cast her a grateful smile. "I'm afraid there's a hitch. Ryan and Heather are strapped for the cash to make a down-payment and get the ranch up and running. Ralph and I have made a few investments over the years, and given Ryan's situation, I've decided it makes sense to cash in now."

"How lovely that you're in a position to help out," Eleanor said. "I'm sure things will work out beautifully."

With that Doris broke down in tears. "How can they? I can't bear the thought of leaving my friends and the work I've devoted my life to. How will I manage when I'm far away from Stony Vale and everything I love?"

"Don't fret," Augusta chimed in. "Before long you'll be making scrapbooks about life in the great state of Wyoming. And now, if you'll excuse me, I really must be going."

Doris pulled herself together enough to show Augusta to the door. In their absence, Eleanor reached for a folder on the sofa next to her and paged through it. "That's funny," she said with a frown. "Everything's here except the list of milestones in Stony Vale's 300-year history. I must have forgotten to print it." She let out a sigh. "I suppose I could email it to you, but I'd prefer to send you off with a complete packet. Would you mind coming over to the house? It shouldn't take long."

After agreeing to the plan, Brooke waited by the door while Eleanor hugged Doris.

"If you need anything at all just ask," Eleanor told her. "Packing, watching your grandkids, running errands—whatever you need, I'll be there."

Doris dabbed at her eyes with her sleeve. "I'm afraid I'll never find friends like the ones I've got right here."

"Oh, yes you will. In no time at all, you'll be settled in a community with wonderful people like yourself."

The lovefest wrapped up and Brooke followed Eleanor out

the door. By now, the morning's snow had given way to icy drizzle, and they had to watch their step as they hurried along Main
Street.

"March is certainly going out like a lion," Eleanor remarked. "Funny, but I don't remember it coming in like a lamb."

As they entered the house, the Corgis galloped out to greet
them, and Tillman appeared from a room halfway down the
hall.

"Nice to see you, Brooke," he said. "Did you ladies have a
productive meeting?"

"It was a rather emotional one," his wife said. "But we'll
talk about that later." Nodding toward the living room, she told
Brooke to have a seat while she went to her office to print the
missing information.

"I've got a fire going in the study," Tillman told Brooke.
"You're welcome to join me if you don't mind the clutter."

"A fire sounds lovely," Brooke remarked.

The study was every bit as cluttered as Tillman had suggested. Books, papers and files lay strewn across a huge mahogany desk, and Brooke had to wend her way through stacks of
scientific journals that created an obstacle course on the floor.
She took a seat in a leather wing chair, while to her right, eight
generations of Tillman patriarchs kept watch from above the
fireplace.

"I'm halfway through what may very well be my swan
song," Tillman said as he sat down behind his massive desk. "As
you can see, the project's reached the spiraling-out-of-control
stage. They tell me you're an editor. Maybe you could help me
get organized."

She laughed at the suggestion. "I'm afraid your subject
matter calls for a level of expertise I don't possess."

"Not in this case. I've had it with writing for stuffy, know-
it-all academics. Instead, I'm reaching out to average folks to
let them in on the amazing developments that are about to

completely transform life on this planet." He handed her an image of a family tree, its branches soaring into the air while its roots burrowed deep into the earth.

"The cover design for my book," he announced. "A reverse family tree with the roots representing our ancestors and the branches representing generations yet to be born. I'm calling it *A Genealogy of the Future*. A provocative title, don't you agree?

"Nice," Brooke said, "but I'm a little confused. Isn't genealogy concerned with the past?"

"Of course it is, and that's what makes my title so intriguing. I'm challenging folks to look *forward* to their descendants, not *backward* to their ancestors. I'm asking my readers to consider the biological inheritance they're leaving to those who come after them. Will their offspring inherit disease, disability and death, or will their legacy be the keys to health, vigor and longevity?"

He leaned back in his chair, his fingers laced over his chest. "Consider, if you will, the fears that keep expectant parents up at night. Consider also, the concerns a woman faces while carrying a child. What if those concerns could be eliminated? Imagine what it would mean if women were no longer taxed with the inconvenience, pain and health risks of pregnancy and childbirth? If fetuses could gestate safely in artificial wombs, these threats to a woman's health and career would vanish."

Brooke laughed at the thought. "It sounds like science fiction to me."

"Ah, but it's closer than you imagine, and that's only a small taste of the good news my book conveys."

He looked at her intently, his glasses reflecting back the orange glow of the fire. "Naysayers will say nay—they always do. Ethicists will sermonize, and novelists and filmmakers will conjure up dystopian hellscapes like they've done for decades. But here's what I say to all of them. Yes—mistakes will be made.

Experiments will fail. Expectations will be dashed. That, my friend, has always been the way of progress. But that's no reason to wring our hands and cry foul. Not when a glorious future awaits us."

The door opened. "I just got a text from my sister," Eleanor said. "Her colonoscopy's scheduled for Wednesday morning, and the ride she was counting on fell through. Do you think we could take her?"

Tillman scowled at the question. "I can't help you with that one, my dear. I'll be out all day on Wednesday."

Eleanor's eyes narrowed. "More grave digging?"

"My book, Eleanor."

She glared at him from the doorway, but instead of commenting, she turned to Brooke and held out the pages she'd printed. "File these with the other documents and call me if you have any questions."

With that settled, Brooke hastened back to her suv with the icy wind at her back. As she started the engine, she thought of something she'd forgotten to do. She'd hadn't called Ted to apologize for walking out on him last night. She needed to take care of that before it slipped her mind.

Twenty-five

The boutique was crammed to the rafters with overpriced merchandise, most of which no one actually needed. As Ashley poked through the glitz and glitter, Ted's thoughts drifted to Brooke. Why did she run out on him last night? Was she okay? He'd intended to explain that he wanted to be just friends, but they'd been interrupted before he could venture down that path. Would she misinterpret his motives if he called to make sure she was alright?

"What about these?" Ashley asked.

The question jolted him back to the present. Ashley expected him to have an opinion about the dishes she was examining, but he hadn't been paying attention. A quick glance revealed that the plates were flat with raised edges to prevent food from falling on the floor. The bowls looked deep enough to keep cereal and soup from sloshing over the sides, and the mugs, while a bit flimsy, could probably hold a dozen or more gulps of coffee.

"Nice," was the best he could do, but apparently that wasn't good enough because she kept after him for more.

"The pattern I mean. Do you like it?"

"Roses? Sure. What's not to like about roses?"

"They're not too fussy?"

They were, but he'd already committed to liking them. "I'm a fan of roses, aren't you?"

She put the item back on the shelf. "I prefer something more contemporary. Like these." She picked up a pale gray plate with a band of darker gray around the rim. "What do you think?"

What he thought was that this whole business reminded him of twelve years ago when his ex-wife dragged him from store to store to pick out stuff for her bridal registry. His feelings on the subject hadn't changed much in the intervening years. He didn't care what dishes looked like as long as they got food from the stove to the table to his stomach. And besides, he already had dishes—nothing special—just functional items he'd picked up at Walmart. He assumed Ashley had dishes as well, and it seemed like a waste of time to be fussing over the twenty-or-so options in this store when they already had enough between them to serve sixteen at a pop. But he suspected there were more significant issues at stake. This was a prenuptial exercise—a multiple choice exam to make sure their tastes were in sync.

Ted's phone buzzed in his pocket. Fishing it out, he saw that the caller was Brooke, probably phoning to apologize for her abrupt departure last night. Excusing himself, he left Ashley to the dishes and went outside to take the call.

It was exactly as he'd expected. After a hasty apology Brooke explained that her fears had come to nothing. Then she mentioned that she'd just found out that Prescott Tillman would be heading out on Wednesday morning for one of his magical, mystery tours.

Ted thought of the tracking device—the one he'd never used. Too bad he'd promised to take Ashley to the University of Pennsylvania Museum on Wednesday. He thoroughly enjoyed looking at relics of the past, but tracking Tillman's whereabouts would make the day even more interesting. But there was a problem. Ashley was certain to notice if he kept checking his phone for updates and she'd probably demand an explanation for why he was distracted.

"Too bad I've got plans on Wednesday," he told Brooke. "Otherwise, I'd make use of the tracker I told you about. I've followed Tillman online for years, and it'd be a kick to follow him in person for a change."

They wound up the call, and he returned to the store, his mind buzzing with thoughts of the things they'd discussed. The tracking device would allow him to know the location of Tillman's vehicle, but once Tillman got out, there'd be no way to know who he was with or what he was doing. A better plan would be to plant the tracker and follow Tillman at a safe distance while the device mapped out the route. Once he arrived at his destination, Ted could follow on foot to figure out what he was doing. But none of that would be happening, because he'd be wandering through the Penn Museum, looking at ancient artifacts—most notably Queen Puabi's funerary ensemble that Ashley'd been raving about.

Back in the boutique, he found Ashley in the scented-candle aisle, her phone pressed to her ear. As he approached, she covered the phone with her hand and made a shushing sound.

"My mom," she whispered. "She wants me to go to a Daughters of the American Revolution tea party on Wednesday. I told her I can't because we're going to the museum."

Ted felt his hopes rise. If Ashley went to this shindig with her mom, he'd be free to spend the day following Tillman around. Should he do it? Of course he should.

He leaned closer and whispered in Ashley's ear. "Your mom must be dying to show off her smart, gorgeous daughter to her DAR pals. Tell her you'll go. We can hit the museum on

Thursday."

Ashley leaned over and kissed his check. "It's sweet of you to put my mom's feelings ahead of your own. I'll make sure she knows it was your idea."

Twenty-six

Brooke was about to dig into the contents of Eleanor's folder, when her phone pinged. *Change of plans for Wednesday,* Ted texted. *Looks like I'll be free to track Tillman after all—not from afar, but from just out of eyeshot. If he stops, I'll follow on foot to see what he's up to. You're welcome to ride shotgun, but either way, the hunt is on. Tally ho!*

Brooke sat back in her chair to consider her answer. Thanks to Ashely, her relationship with Ted was on safer footing, so yeah—it might be fun to tag along. She texted him back, and they agreed to head for Stony Vale before dawn on Wednesday. They'd plant the tracking device and once Tillman hit the road, they'd trail him from a distance of about a mile.

That settled, she turned her attention to the documents in the folder. Among them was a receipt for a deposit paid to Forked River Studio, the video company owned by Seth Walker. Try as she might, she couldn't find a description of the work he'd been hired to do. She sent him an email, and he responded quickly, saying he was creating two 30-second ads and a fifteen-minute endless-loop video about Stony Vale's history to be shown in the Center the weekend of Summer Fest. He hadn't heard back from the committee, but he was free later that day and would be happy to meet with her to review his work to-date. They agreed to meet at six in a sports bar within walking distance of Brooke's apartment.

She arrived at the bar at a little before six and spotted Seth chatting with the bartender. He greeted her with a smile, his rugged features illuminated by a large screen TV where a hockey game was underway. As they exchanged greetings, he picked up a leather portfolio and ushered her to a booth.

"I met with the publicity committee a few weeks ago," he began. "Since then, I've worked up a few scripts and story-boards. I'm ready to start shooting as soon as I get the okay. And a second check, of course."

Brooke glanced over the material and made some sugges-tions based on what she'd learned at today's meeting. After that, Seth showed her a montage of old photos and postcards depicting Stony Vale in the early 1900s. These images would be prominently featured in the fifteen-minute endless-loop video.

As they talked, a loud cheer erupted from the people at the bar—the Flyers scored a goal!

"It's getting noisy in here," Seth shouted over the din. "What do you say we take a walk and keep the conversation going?"

Brooke glanced toward the door. "You're sure you want to venture out in the cold?"

"Cold is a good thing. It clears the head and sharpens the instincts."

She wasn't sure about that, but Seth was right—the noise was deafening. Minutes later, they were out on the street, jackets zipped up to their necks as they walked east onto the pedestrian walkway of the Northampton Street Bridge. Stop-ping in the middle, they watched the Delaware River journey southward to join the Lehigh, less than a mile away.

"My people called this place, *Lechanwitauk*," Seth said softly. "Translated, it means the place of the forks."

"Like the name of your business," Brooke said. "Forked River Studio."

He nodded. "According to our legends, the Lenni-Lenape were the original people—the tribe from which all others sprang. Further legends explain that we originated at the spot where the Delaware and Lehigh meet. As a child in Oklahoma, I used to lie awake thinking of my ancestral home. I knew there were roads, trains, houses, industry and so forth, but I liked to picture the rivers as my people saw them. Two mighty powers uniting in peace."

Brooke glanced at the buildings crowding the banks on either side, their lights gleaming as twilight descended. "You must have been disappointed when you got here and found all this."

"It's a far cry from a child's view of paradise," he acknowledged." But I'm grateful beyond measure to be in the land of my ancestors. At night I open the windows, and if I listen hard enough, I can almost hear them whispering in the darkness." He turned to look at her. "I suppose that sounds crazy."

Brooke recalled the eerie sense of Karl's presence long after his death. "No," she said softly. "It doesn't sound crazy at all."

"Nostalgia is a weakness of mine," Seth continued. "At times, an uncontrollable grief steals over me when I think of what my people have lost."

Brooke understood his feelings. Grief was a current running through her life—sometimes a trickle—sometimes an unstoppable force that uprooted everything in its path. Either way, it was always there.

"Your ancestors," she said. "Have you discovered records of family members in the region?"

He shook his head. "Geneticists tell us the Eastern tribes are too admixed for meaningful study, but that doesn't keep me from trying. I might never know the names of those whose DNA shaped my own, but I honor them by keeping their stories and customs alive."

He fell silent, his eyes fixed on the river as cars rumbled behind them. "Jenna loved to hear the legends of my people. We had that in common—we'd both grown up as keepers of our ancestor's stories. That's why she searched so diligently for her birthmother. She wasn't just seeking her biological mother—she was seeking her tribe and the stories they told."

He glanced over at Brooke. "You and Jenna were friends?"

"Acquaintances," she clarified. "We'd barely gotten to know each other when she died."

He was silent for a moment. "I'd give anything to know what was troubling her in the days and weeks before the murder. I thought she might confide in me, but all I could find out was that she was worried about a commitment she'd made and wanted out of.

"What sort of commitment?"

"I never found out."

Brooke gazed at the water flowing southward beneath the bridge. "Is there anyone else she might have told?"

Seth paused to think. "She mentioned a couple of Mormon missionaries she'd spoken to a few times. And there was a psychic lady who lived in your building. Beyond that, I can't think of anyone.

"Whether you believe in psychics or not," Seth continued, "you have to admire their skill at weaseling information out of their clients and making it seem like they—the psychics—are receiving news flashes from beyond."

Seth's thoughts mirrored Brooke's exactly and seemed to confirm an idea forming in her mind. "I'm not on the best of terms with Anita," she said, "but I've got a sense of how she works. Maybe I could use some of the same tactics she uses on clients to get her to open up and reveal the things Jenna discussed with her."

"You'd be willing to do that?"

"I could give it a try," she said.

"Would you mind recording the conversation?"

"Good idea. I'll send you the results later tonight."

Smiling, Seth reached for his wallet and pulled out some bills. "Here's fifty dollars. Let me know if it runs to more."

Twenty-seven

No one was around when Brooke entered the Beacon Arms. She walked down the deserted hallway and activated the recording app on her phone before knocking on Anita's door. It opened a moment later, and a weathered face looked back at her. "Brooke," Anita said, an odd smile wrinkling her lips. "I've been expecting you. Won't you come in."

Brooke tried not to laugh. *I've been expecting you* is exactly the sort of thing a fake psychic would say when someone dropped by unannounced. But what Anita didn't realize was that Brooke was a fake client intent on learning Jenna's secrets.

Anita's apartment was a gloomy, claustrophobic space illuminated by flickering candles and a tiny light bulb shining from within an eight-inch amber glass pyramid. The scent of incense and patchouli oil assaulted Brooke's nose, and as she made her way through the semi-darkness, something dark and furry rubbed against her ankle and scurried back into the shadows. Hah! What would the building supervisor think if he found out Anita was harboring a cat in her apartment? But maybe Jake already knew. Maybe Anita offered free readings in exchange for his silence.

"Have a seat, my dear," she said. "Make yourself comfortable."

Comfort wasn't an option, Brooke realized as she sat down on a sagging futon covered in Indian print fabric. Once she was settled, Anita arranged herself on a kilim pillow separated from the futon by a brass coffee table cluttered with assorted crystals, a stick of burning incense, tarot cards and other tools of the psychic trade.

"I hope Merlin didn't startle you," Anita began.

"Merlin?" Brooke had to stop and think. "Oh, you mean the cat."

"That's right. As intuitive creatures, cats bring their unique energy to psychic readings. No doubt, we'll hear from Merlin before we're done."

Brooke fought back her cynicism and instead concentrated on fidgeting with an earring. Success depended on appearing anxious and vulnerable—a ploy to disarm Anita and make her think she had the upper hand.

"If I seem ill-at-ease," she said, "it isn't because of Merlin. It's because I can't stop thinking of what you said about Melusine."

Anita studied her through narrowed eyes. "Last night you mocked the timeless wisdom I offered. And now you've come to me for assurance. What changed?"

Brooke chose her words carefully. "I keep thinking of the legends about Melusine hiding the secret of her dual nature from her husband. When he finally found out that one day a week she turned into a water spirit—half woman and half fish— she left him, never to be seen again. Scholars say that Melusine represents the secrets women keep hidden—even from their closest friends. And now I can't help but wonder what secrets Jenna took with her to her grave, and I keep wondering why Melusine is threatening me with a similar fate."

Anita sat in silence, her coal-black eyes studying Brooke's face. "Before I respond," she said slowly, "you must answer a question. Have you come here to mock or to listen?"

Brooke felt herself squirming beneath Anita's gaze. Did Anita see through her act? Was she being obvious? Somehow, she had to persuade Anita that she was sincere.

"I came here to learn what was on Jenna's mind at the time of her death. I need to protect myself from similar danger. To do so, I need to understand Jenna's secrets. Can you help me with that?"

"Of course. Assuming that your request is sincere." Dropping her gaze, Anita reached for the deck of tarot cards on the coffee table and made an elaborate show of shuffling them. After that, she turned over the top card—a woman with a crown of stars on her head.

"Ah, the Empress," Anita said. "In the normal position, she represents the blessings of motherhood and abundance, but in this case, the card is upside down. She's telling us that Jenna experienced deep anxiety about her unborn child and about her ability to support it."

No kidding, Brooke thought to herself. Anyone in Jenna's situation—pregnant, unmarried and with her long-term relationship on the rocks—would be anxious. There was nothing psychic about that revelation.

The same seemed to be true of the next four cards. The things they represented could apply to Jenna's circumstances, but they could apply to hundreds of other circumstances as well. It was up to the person reading the cards to artfully match the interpretation to the client's situation, making the reading more like a Rorschach test than an otherworldly revelation.

"It's uncanny that the cards can tell us so much," Brooke said, her fingers crossed behind her back. "But they haven't addressed my questions. Is there another avenue we could explore?"

As if answering the question, Merlin leapt from the

shadows and landed on the coffee table. With a swish of his black tail, he knocked the incense over and sent it toppling onto the Empress card. His mission accomplished, he jumped gracefully to the floor and disappeared.

Startled, Anita snatched up the card. "I don't believe it!" she exclaimed. "The burn mark beneath the crown matches the wound on Jenna's forehead."

She looked around, her eyes wild. "Jenna, are you here with us? You must be. I can think of no other explanation."

The coincidence was amazing, but even more amazing was the fact that for once, Brooke was pretty sure Anita wasn't faking it. She leapt to her feet, the incense smoke surrounding her like the mist encircling the Oracle of Delphi. She closed her eyes and raised both hands in the air. "I'm listening, Jenna. Speak to me."

There was no response. No tapping on tables. No rushing wind. No sighs or whispers from the shadows.

This was the moment Brooke had been waiting for. Snared by her own delusions, Anita was vulnerable in a way she hadn't been earlier.

"I came here to learn Jenna's secrets," Brooke said. "And she came here to make sure you tell them to me."

"Jenna," Anita moaned into the shadows. "Come forth and speak to us."

A long silence ensued before the so-called psychic spoke again. "The child," she murmured, her eyes still closed. "Jenna's grieving her lost child." With her arms still raised, Anita swayed back and forth like an antenna searching for a signal. "Wait!" she cried suddenly. "She's telling me something. Yes, I remember now. She's telling me about the baby and saying it was…"

A sharp knock on the door brought Anita out of her trance. Opening her eyes, she glanced around as though uncertain where she was. "Jenna," she murmured. "Where have you gone? Are you still with us or have you fled?"

"Please, Anita," Brooke begged. "What was she about to tell you?"

When the knock repeated itself, Anita struggled to her feet and held out her hand. "She's gone now. That will be one-hundred dollars."

"For twenty minutes?"

"Drop-in sessions always cost more and so do tarot readings."

Brooke added fifty dollars to the money Seth gave her. At the door she said a brief hello to Anita's next client, a handsome, well-dressed guy in an expensive-looking suit who didn't seem the type to be consulting a phony psychic like Anita. Brooke was about to warn him about a cat lurking in the shadows, but thought better of it. If he'd been here before, chances are, he and Merlin had already met.

She was halfway to the elevator when Anita's voice rang out from behind her.

"Wait," she called as she ran toward Brooke, her long skirt threatening to trip her. She drew close and seized Brooke's arm in a claw-like grip. "As you left, Jenna appeared and spoke a single word."

She fell silent as thought recalling the moment.

Brooke didn't believe for one minute that Jenna had actually appeared to Anita, but rather that Anita remembered something Jenna said in one of their sessions. "The word, Anita," she urged. "What is it? Jenna wants me to know what she told you."

"Unholy," Anita said, her voice barely a whisper. "She was telling me the baby was unholy."

Brooke's heart sank. "That's it?"

Anita nodded. "I don't expect to hear from her again."

Back in her apartment, Brooke entered *unholy* into an on-line thesaurus and stared at the responses.

Depraved.
Diabolical.
Godless.
Iniquitous.
Unsanctified.
Irredeemable.
Why had Jenna described her unborn child that way? Was it because it had been conceived out of wedlock, or was there a darker reason for Jenna's choice of words?

Twenty-eight

Tuesday began with someone knocking on the door. "It's me, Maggie," a voice called out. "I've got a favor to ask."

Brooke braced herself for a confrontation. She'd had it with Maggie barging into her apartment and asking for favors. This time, she told herself, she'd stand her ground and say no.

"This'll only take a minute," Maggie said when Brooke opened the door. "Long story short, Bernie found a home for Donnie and Marie."

"Wow—good news for a change. How did that happen?"

"That's what I need to tell you. Once you've heard the story, you'll understand the favor I'm asking."

Steeling her resolve, Brooke waited for Maggie to continue.

"Okay, so the other day two Mormon missionaries approached Bernie on the street. To his surprise, they turned out to be the same missionaries who were friends with Jenna. When they found out that Donnie and Marie were living in Bernie's basement, they offered to find them a home. Bernie didn't expect anything to come of it, but they texted him yesterday to say they knew a family who'd love a pair of kittens. After they'd been so nice, Bernie figured the least he could do was listen to their spiel. Long story short, he loved it and he wants me to hear it as well. And here's the problem—I'm scared they'll pressure me into joining something I don't want to join. I'm not good at debating, but you are, and that's why I need you to go with me. They're meeting at Bernie's place this afternoon at three."

Brooke was about to say a firm no when a thought streaked through her brain. According to Seth Walker, the missionaries had acted as Jenna's spiritual advisors. Did she tell them her secrets? Anita didn't have much to offer. Would things be different with the missionaries?

"Sure," she said. "I'll meet you at Bernie's at a little before three."

Maggie seemed surprised. "Really? You mean I don't have to beg and plead and twist your arm?"

"Not this time. It's a worthy cause and I'm glad to help."

At two-forty-five, Brooke met Maggie outside the bungalow-style dwelling that doubled as Bernie's tattoo parlor. Since Bernie's clients entered through the front door, they went around to the back where a door led into a mudroom off the kitchen.

When they stepped inside, a pair of Rottweilers galloped out to greet them. "Back off," Maggie shouted. "Behave yourselves!" The dogs paid no attention. Instead, they cavorted and played, their sturdy bodies bumping into Brooke like battering rams as she worked her way into the kitchen.

In the distance she heard a baby crying.

"Trevor," Maggie said. "I forgot to mention that Bernie's watching his six-month-old nephew while his sister travels for business."

A muscle-bound, tattooed giant wearing flannel pajama

bottoms appeared in the kitchen with a baby on his hip. "What took you so long?" he snarled at Maggie. "Take this creature, would you. He kept me up all night."

"Stop whining," Maggie shouted as the Rotts added their howls to the din. She took the shrieking baby and held him at arm's length. "When's the last time you changed him?"

"I can't remember."

"So, change him already."

"I was waiting for you to do it."

"Me? He's not my nephew."

"Don't you think I know he's not your nephew? Help me out with this—would you?"

Frowning, Maggie glanced around the kitchen. "Look at this place. Dishes in the sink. Sticky stuff all over the table. Trash on the floor. And you're not even dressed. You've got company coming any minute. Why didn't you straighten up?"

"How am I supposed to straighten up when this spawn of Satan won't stop bellowing. He carried on all night, and if that wasn't bad enough, the dogs kept howling, and the cats kept screeching, and long story short, it was a helluva night. A helluva night, and I've had it."

A sound from beyond the mudroom put an end to the conversation. "Anybody home?" a voice shouted.

Bernie glanced at his watch. "Figures they'd be early. Put on some coffee, would'ja?"

"They're Mormons," Maggie reminded him. "They don't drink coffee."

"Okay, tea."

"They don't drink that either."

"Fine," Bernie snapped. "Get them some milk—they drink that, don't they? And don't stand there gawking," he shouted at Brooke. "Let them in—we can't keep them out on the stoop all day."

Maggie headed out of the kitchen with Trevor on her hip

while Bernie went off to get dressed. Left to play hostess, Brooke opened the door and greeted a pair of young, bright-eyed, clean-cut kids in dark suits and ties. The older of the two boasted classic good looks—chiseled features, a firm chin, deep-set brown eyes and wavy dark hair. His shorter companion was more of a geek with curly reddish hair, freckles and blue eyes surrounded by thick glasses.

The freckle-faced guy reached out to pet one of the Rottweilers. "Nice doggy. Nice big old doggy." When it let out a throaty snarl, he drew back his hand and stepped away.

Mr. Classic Good Looks introduced himself as Elder Bolton and his younger partner as Elder Douglas. When Brooke offered them milk and a handful of Oreos, they wolfed them down like they hadn't eaten in weeks. As they were finishing, Bernie showed up in jeans and a muscle shirt and invited them into the living room.

Maggie appeared a few minutes later and handed a much happier Trevor back to Bernie. She shook the younger elder's hand, but as she turned to greet Elder Bolton, her eyes widened and her mouth dropped open. She cast Brooke a quick glance and then returned her startled gaze to Elder Bolton. "I think I left something in the kitchen," she managed to say. "Excuse me for a sec and excuse my friend as well."

Grabbing Brooke's arm, she steered her out of the living room. "That's him," she whispered.

"Who?"

"The guy I told you about. The one who was in Jenna's apartment the night before she died."

"You said that was Derrick Strauss."

"I made a mistake," Maggie said. "I only got a glimpse of the guy's face for the split second before he looked down at the floor and took off for the elevator. But it all came back to me just now. It's him—I'm sure of it."

"Well then, the problem's solved. He was there on a

missionary visit."

"At two in the morning? And wearing jeans and a hoodie instead of his missionary outfit? And sneaking out the door and making a mad dash for the elevator the moment he noticed me?"

"Hey, you two," Bernie shouted from the living room. "Get your butts out here. These bad boys don't have all day."

"What should I do?" Maggie whimpered.

"Pretend you don't recognize him. Act like you've never seen him before and try to steer the conversation away from the presentation and onto Jenna."

Maggie glanced nervously over her shoulder. "Okay, but I'll need your help."

"That's why I'm here."

Back in the living room, Bernie handed Trevor to Maggie and turned his attention to the missionaries.

"I've got to hand it to you guys," he said. "Finding a home for those cats was nothing short of a miracle. And then you pulled off an even bigger miracle by talking me into becoming a Mormon. Me, of all people. Who would have thought?"

He glanced at Maggie. "You're gonna love their story—especially the part about an angel telling some guy where to find a bunch of gold tablets. Solid gold—can you imagine what they'd be worth in today's market? What's an ounce going for these days? We're pushing three grand or more—right?"

He grinned at the two young men. "You're good at this missionary stuff. Really good."

"We're not all that good," the younger elder said. "Until you came along, Jenna was the only person who took us seriously. And she didn't actually convert. She said she liked talking to us because as a kid, she used to be a Mormon."

"Well, that's a good place to start," Bernie said. "But speaking of Jenna, Brooke's the gal who found her body."

Both elders turned to stare at her.

"How terrible," Elder Bolton, the older elder, gasped.

"Yeah, and the story keeps getting more terrible every day," Maggie said. "According to the news, Jenna was pregnant when she died, but so far, no one knows who the father was."

The missionaries looked at each other and said nothing.

"I'm sure you guys must have been a help to her," Brooke remarked. "It's great to have someone to confide in when you're in a tough situation."

"It sounds like she was planning to keep the baby," Maggie remarked. "Lots of women in her situation would have had an abortion."

"She was going to," Elder Bolton blurted out. "It was scheduled, but she started thinking about it and decided to…"

The younger elder bolted out of his chair and stared, red-faced, at his partner. "You are off script, Elder Bolton—way off script. We're here to do a presentation. Do I need to remind you of the rules?"

"I could recite the rules in my sleep," Elder Bolton shot back. "But this isn't just any missionary visit. These people are Jenna's friends. They cared about her and…" His voice wavered and he slumped forward, his head in his hands. "Go ahead—do the presentation without me."

Elder Douglas sniffed and straightened his tie. "All right then, I will." With that, he got a flip chart out of his carryall bag, set it on the coffee table and paused to adjust the glasses that had slid down his nose. Soon he was deep into a story about an angel who'd appeared to a man named Joseph Smith in 1823 to tell him about golden tablets buried in…

Brooke tried to concentrate, but her mind kept wandering. Jenna. An unborn child. A cancelled abortion. Would Elder Bolton have said more if his friend hadn't interrupted? How could she find out?

Twenty-nine

Eleanor rapped on the door to Prescott's study. "I'm leaving now. Dinner's in the fridge."

"Give me a sec. I'm just finishing up in here."

Soon he emerged and walked her to a Prius parked next to his Mercedes. "Drive carefully," he said as she slipped behind the wheel. "And have a nice time."

"A nice time? My sister's colonoscopy's at eight tomorrow morning. She'll be doing her prep tonight. It's not like we'll be having a million laughs."

"Even so, you and Olivia always enjoy being together."

It was true. Eleanor's petite younger sister was a source of joy in good times and a rock of support in tough times. There'd never been a tough time like the one Eleanor was currently facing, and she looked forward to unburdening herself to the person who knew more about her than anyone on earth.

Tonight, she'd chosen the scenic route to Philadelphia, through Chestnut Hill and along the Wissahickon Drive. She arrived around seven at her sister's Rittenhouse Square apartment and found dinner—kung pao shrimp from a Chinese take-out restaurant waiting for her. At the table, Olivia picked at a bowl of lime Jello and looked enviously at Eleanor's meal.

"It's been a nightmare," Eleanor said, a pair of chopsticks poised in her hand. "When I'm not lying awake imagining noises and worrying about a killer, I'm plagued by reporters asking if Prescott and Jenna were lovers, and was he the baby's father, and did he have to provide a DNA sample. I guess it's to be expected. If a pregnant woman shows up in someone's fishpond, people want to know how and why she got there."

"Do you trust Prescott?" Olivia asked.

The question was jolting, and when Eleanor didn't respond, her sister leaned across the table and squeezed her hand. "I know what you're thinking. You're worried the baby was his, and he killed her to keep it quiet."

Eleanor nodded. "I want more than anything in the world to trust him, and yet…"

Suddenly she was crying. "I've tried to stay focused on my work, but with all this on my mind, the words swim on the page."

"Forget your book for now," Olivia said. "Go shopping. Visit a museum. Take a walk along the canal. A change of pace will help settle your mind."

"That won't work. When I'm walking the canal path, I can't shake the feeling that someone's watching me. And when I run an errand—the bank, the grocery store, the Emporium—complete strangers come up to me and ask questions. When I tell them I threw Jenna in our pond, they give me this odd look. It's easy to guess what they're thinking: *The wife is always the last to know.*"

She wiped her eyes on her sleeve, but the tears wouldn't stop. "At times I've wondered about the book I'm writing. In it, I expose some pretty dark individuals—corporate sociopaths you might say. Was it possible Jenna was killed by mistake when

I was actually the target? Or was I being told to stop writing the book or this is what would happen to me?"

She looked across the table at her younger sister. "Do you think I should give up on the book? Should I yield to my fears or…" Unable to speak, she buried her face in her hands.

Olivia was out of her seat in a flash and kneeling beside her older sister. "Cry, my dear. Cry long and hard, and you'll feel better once it's out of your system. And don't worry so much. As far as your book is concerned, keep at it. You're doing a great service by exposing forces that control us without our realizing it. And as to Prescott—he's a brilliant man. If Jenna were pregnant with his child, he would have known better than to bring attention to the fact by killing her and tossing her in his pond. Only a moron would do something so stupid."

"Unless it was a crime of passion," Eleanor said through her tears. "What if he demanded that she get an abortion and then flew into a rage when she refused? What if he lost control and it was over before he realized what he'd done?"

"You're forgetting his alibi," Olivia said. "He was at the genealogy conference at the time of her death—right?"

That question only made things worse. Prescott hadn't been at the conference. He'd been in his study, and just this morning Eleanor asked if he'd informed the detectives as to his whereabouts at the time of Jenna's death. "Why stir up trouble?" had been his hasty response. After that, he retreated to his study and closed the door. So, no—to answer Olivia's question, he didn't have an alibi. But for all Eleanor's trust in her sister, she couldn't bring herself to say as much.

"Of course he had an alibi" she said instead. "I'm a fool for letting my imagination run away with me."

"You're not a fool. You're dealing with something most of us can't even imagine."

Later they sat in the living room reminiscing about the cruise they'd taken last fall around the Grecian islands. Soon their phones were out as they compared pictures of the Monastery in Corfu, the whitewashed buildings and blue-dome churches of Santorini, the Valley of the Butterflies in Rhodes and other spots that had made the cruise a memorable experience.

The pleasant moments ended when Olivia announced that she had to excuse herself—it was time to start her prep for tomorrow's procedure.

In the guestroom, Eleanor lay awake thinking about the sundrenched beauty of the islands dotting the Aegean and Ionian Seas. When she'd returned to Stony Vale in mid-October, she learned that there'd been a misadventure while she was away. One of the Corgis had a medical emergency, and finding the usual vet closed for the day, Prescott located a 24-hour clinic that offered emergency services. He had a good laugh when he realized the catastrophe that had the dog howling was simply a bee sting.

He'd never mentioned the name of the clinic and Eleanor had never asked. And now, in the quiet of her sister's guest room, she couldn't help but wonder if it was the Family Friends Veterinary Clinic where Jenna worked parttime. If so, had she been working that evening? Eleanor pictured the pretty blond removing the stinger from the dog's paw and chatting with Prescott as she applied salve to the site. Did they discuss the book she was writing—the one about genetic problems affecting inbred dogs? Had she asked him for professional advice on the project or perhaps an endorsement once the book was ready to publish? Had they met later to discuss it over coffee, and had one thing led to another?

How could Eleanor find out? She rejected the idea of calling the clinic to ask if Prescott brought the Corgi there on a night when Jenna was working. Doing so would raise red flags and get the gossip wheels turning and spilling over to the media. There had to be another way to find out, but Eleanor couldn't imagine what it might be.

But as the hours ticked by, a plan began taking shape. Prescott was in the habit of saving store receipts in a desk drawer so he could reconcile them with his check book and bank statements. He typically let months go by before he got around to the task, and by then there was usually a thick wad of register tape to sort through. Could there possibly be a receipt from Family Friends Veterinary Clinic all these months later?

He kept his desk locked, but that was no obstacle because he'd hidden a backup key in the heating duct in case the original got misplaced or in case something happened to him and Eleanor needed to access his papers. He'd be out until five or six, but by the time she drove Olivia to her colonoscopy and stayed for lunch afterward, she wouldn't be back to Stony Vale until two or later. Would that give her time to snoop through the desk before he returned?

She felt a sense of unease at the thought. Prescott's study was his sanctuary, just as her office on the second floor was hers. In thirty years of marriage, she'd never violated his space, and she assumed he'd been equally respectful of her. Tomorrow that was about to change, and the thought of it filled her with dread—not because she'd be violating his trust, but rather that she was afraid of what she'd find.

Thirty

Brooke was awake and dressed when her phone pinged at five Wednesday morning. In minutes she was out the door and climbing into Ted's Jeep.

"Mmm, bacon," she said as the warm aroma hit her nose.

"Bacon, egg and cheese on toasted Kaiser rolls, to be specific." Ted pointed to an insulated coffee mug in the cup holder. "I know you don't like cardboard, so I brought this one from home."

She was touched by his thoughtfulness. "You didn't have to go to the trouble."

"No trouble. It helps to start the day out right. We'll hold breakfast until we've planted the tracking device on Tillman's car. After that, we'll relax and enjoy."

The village of Stony Vale was dark when they arrived—lights out everywhere, including the Tillmans' house. Brooke stood guard while Ted planted the tracking device, and once that was done, they returned to the Jeep and headed south a couple of miles. Ted found a spot to pull over so they could eat breakfast and watch daylight break above the river. Around eight, his phone emitted a shrill beep.

"Tillman's headed our way," he announced. "Unless he breaks the speed limit, he'll pass us in about three minutes. We'll give him a head start, and pick up the chase."

The Mercedes cruised by right on schedule and after another minute, Ted set off in pursuit while Brooke kept an eye on the app on Ted's phone. The route led south on scenic River Road along the Delaware. At New Hope, they crossed the bridge to New Jersey and veered left just south of Lambertville. They continued to follow Tillman east to Hopewell and from there, in the direction of Princeton. As they approached the historic university town, Ted narrowed the distance until Tillman's car was visible on the road in front of them. That was Brooke's cue to slouch down in the seat—the last thing they wanted was Tillman glancing at his rearview mirror and recognizing her. She kept watch on the app as their quarry drove through town, entered the campus and came to a stop minutes later at the entrance to a parking lot.

Ted pounded his fist against the steering wheel. "Parking by permit only," he said. "By the time we find a spot on campus, we'll have lost him."

"Not necessarily," Brooke spoke up. "Assuming you trust me to drive this thing, you can hop out and follow Tillman while I drive around and find a parking spot. We'll stay in touch as planned, and once he heads back to his car, you'll text me, I'll pick you up, and we'll be back in the game."

Ted grinned at her. "Good thinking. I knew there was a reason I wanted you along on this trip."

Once Ted was gone, Brooke slithered over the console and into the driver's seat. Unable to find a visitor's space on campus, she cruised up and down the streets in town and finally located a spot just a block off of Nassau Street. She texted her location to Ted, and he texted back to say he'd watched Tillman enter a classroom building, but by the time he'd followed him inside, Tillman was nowhere in sight. Ted was presently walking up and down the halls, but he had no idea which room Tillman entered.

"Wait near the main door," Brooke suggested. *"That way you can follow him when he leaves the building."*

With that settled, Brooke rolled down the window and looked out at the pedestrians hurrying by. It was warm for late March, and she felt bored and restless trapped in the Jeep. When a word game on her phone failed to entertain her, she got out to take a walk—just a short one to pass the time until she heard from Ted. Her steps took her to Palmer Square on Nassau Street, and as she window shopped, her thoughts drifted to the event that had precipitated today's outing—Tillman's late arrival at the Stevenson's house and his wife's refusal to believe that he'd actually gone "grave digging" that day.

A thought crossed Brooke's mind as she studied a display of spring fashions in a boutique window. Tillman had been late for dinner on the same day Kathryn Strauss fell to her death. Was there a connection? Probably not, but it might be fun to play with the idea and see where it led.

By now it was common knowledge that Kathyrn Strauss was Jenna's birthmother, but in spite of all the reporting on that subject, there hadn't been a word of speculation regarding her biological father. An amusing thought sprang into Brooke's mind. What if Tillman was Jenna's father? A big if, to be sure, but given that Kathryn Strauss had a PhD in early childhood development, a field in which genetics played a huge role, it was possible their paths may have crossed. Had she been a grad student in one of Tillman's classes, and did a crush on a charismatic professor lead to a love affair and an unwanted pregnancy?

It wasn't likely, but Brooke was enjoying the narrative, so she let it unfold in her mind—at least until she hit a stumbling block. Assuming Jenna was Tillman's long-lost daughter, why would he kill her and then rush off two days later to kill Ka-thryn? A scandal raised by a thirty-year-old love affair would have died down in no time, and while Tillman's wife, kids and grandkids would have been upset and embarrassed, the rest of the world would have yawned and turned the page.

And that meant, in order to keep the story going, Brooke had to come up with something to explain why a person would risk everything to avoid a scandal hardly anyone would care about. Maybe the whole thing revolved around Jenna's unborn child. What if Tillman, not realizing that Jenna was his biolog-ical daughter, had an affair with her? And what if Jenna, not realizing that he was her biological father, told him she was pregnant and then announced that she'd found her birth-mother? Once Tillman heard Katherine's name, he would have been mortified to realize that Jenna was his daughter while at the same time, being pregnant with his child. That would have made him the baby's father as well as its grandfather while Jenna would have been the baby's mother and sister. A scandal like that would shake up the branches on the Tillman family tree, and the genetic implications of such inbreeding would be catastrophic.

Brooke imagined Tillman insisting that Jenna have an abortion and flying into a murderous rage when she refused. Once that happened, he couldn't risk Katherine learning that Jenna—the child they'd had together—had died in his pond. It would have taken no time at all for the police to put those puzzle pieces together. For that reason, he had to silence Ka-thryn to keep her from revealing his secret.

And that's why he was late to dinner at the Stevensons' house.

Brooke didn't actually believe the scenario she'd just created. How could she when it was every bit as crazy as the theories Maggie kept coming up with? And yet the pieces seemed to fit as long as the what-ifs were true.

She continued window shopping and was deep in thought when a text came through from Ted. *"Tillman left the building a few minutes ago. I'm on his tail. Sit tight and stay tuned for updates."*

Okay, so she needed to get back to the Jeep, ASAP. Heading in that direction, she stopped at the sight of a shock of unruly white hair just a few yards in front of her. Panicked, she ducked into a doorway and peered around the edge. Yes—it was Tillman. He was outside a restaurant reading something, probably a menu, in the window. Had he seen her? She ducked back into the doorway, and when she looked again, he was gone. Did he enter the restaurant, she wondered, or did he keep walking? Would he notice her if she kept walking? If he did, would it matter? It was a nice day for shopping and sightseeing, and Princeton was a perfect spot for both. A coincidence, she'd tell him if their paths crossed.

But their paths didn't cross, and as she climbed into the Jeep, a second text arrived.

"He went into a restaurant. I'm going in to scope things out. Drive there and wait for me outside. BTW, was that you I saw ducking into a doorway?"

Ted ended the text with the address of the restaurant— the same place where she'd spotted Tillman. She was there in a few minutes, and finding no parking space on the crowded street, she double-parked with the engine running. Minutes later, Ted was out the door and diving into the passenger seat. Grinning, he held his phone beneath her nose.

"Look at this," he crowed. "I think we found out why he lied to his wife."

Brooke scrolled through the photos. The first showed Tillman in a booth across from a pale, late twentyish woman with mousy brown hair. She was slender with a pleasant face, but not glamorous, at least not in a trophy-girlfriend kind of way.

In the second picture the woman seemed to be arguing

with Tillman, and in a third, she'd scooted over to the edge of the booth as though intending to leave. In the fourth, his hand rested on hers—possibly persuading her to stay.

"See," Ted said with a grin. "It's just as I thought. He's hitting on a grad student."

"Possibly," Brooke said. "But while you were following him around, I came up with a theory. It's kind of crazy, but let's grab lunch and talk about it."

Thirty-one

Only two reporters were waiting when Eleanor got home. Since the news broke about Jenna's pregnancy, she'd become accustomed to more. Perhaps the threat of bad weather was holding them at bay.

Ignoring their questions, she darted up the walkway and into the house. As she closed the door, the Corgis scampered into the foyer, their nails scratching at the hardwood floor. "Would you guys settle down?" she said as they clambered around her. "I know you're hungry, so stop nagging already."

In the kitchen she stopped at the sight of daylight pouring into the sunroom. Prescott had opened the blinds and failed to close them before he left this morning. He knew she didn't want them opened until the investigation was over, and this was just another sign of his lack of concern for her feelings. As she gazed through the windows, an irrational fear swept over her. Something terrible awaited her out there—something monstrous and evil waiting to destroy her life.

"Get a grip," she told herself. "Nobody's going to attack you. Not with reporters standing guard outside."

Back in the kitchen the Corgis kept after her, anxious for their meal. "I said I'd feed you," she scolded and then felt guilty for her tone of voice. There was no reason to be upset with the dogs—quite the opposite. One of these rascals was the reason for the trip to a 24-hour emergency veterinary clinic, and that visit might turn out to be the evidence Eleanor needed to prove that Prescott and Jenna had met before. What then, she wondered. Would she confront him? Would she share her suspicions with the police? She knew that wives didn't have to testify against their husbands, but did a similar provision exist about reporting evidence to the authorities? Would failing to do so make her an accessory to a crime? She had no idea, but whatever the case, she had to know the truth.

After filling three bowls with dogfood, she went to the utility closet for a screwdriver and stepstool. She was nearly at the door to the study when she heard a car door slam. Was it Prescott? Had he come back early? She raced to a window in time to see Doris Stevenson's car heading up the street. Prescott's Mercedes was nowhere in sight.

Feeling relieved, she carried the screwdriver and stepstool into the study, and in the silence, her gaze drifted to the enormous mahogany desk that was nearly as old as the house. She tried to picture the scenario Prescott had described to her just two days after the murder. She imagined him sitting at the desk, headphones on as he transcribed a lecture, completely oblivious to the fact that out on the patio someone was slamming a rock into Jenna's head and pushing her into the pond.

An icy chill crept up Eleanor's spine, and it seemed to her that a vast evil spirit had entered the room with her. *Nerves*, she told herself as she hurriedly climbed the stepladder, removed the screws and pulled the grate off the air duct. A moment later the key was in her hand and she was at the desk, sliding the key into the lock and turning it. She held her breath and then a sharp click announced that all seven drawers were unlocked and ready to be accessed.

The wide top drawer was filled with office clutter: paper clips, pens, pencils, loose change, assorted business cards and notes scribbled on bits of paper—but no receipts. A second drawer contained material related to Prescott's current book while other drawers held insurance papers, investment documents, appliance warranties and so forth. The bottom right-hand drawer seemed to be a catch-all for odds and ends, and as Eleanor rooted through the contents, she found what she was looking for—thick wads of receipts from grocery stores, gas stations, drug stores, big box stores, doctors' offices and more. But nothing from a veterinary clinic. She went through them a second time, this time checking for dates. The incident had occurred early in October, but these receipts went back no further than the first of January of this present year.

She sank back in Prescott's chair. All this excitement and she'd found nothing. Sighing, she put the receipts back in the drawer and was about to lock the desk when she recalled the business cards carelessly strewn about in the shallow top drawer. Opening it, she sorted through them one by one. There were dozens—not just from businesses in the Lehigh Valley but from Prescott's colleagues and individuals he'd met at conferences around the world.

She picked one up and as she read it, her breath caught in her throat. *Family Friends Veterinary Clinic: 24-Hour Emergency Service,* the card said. But did it prove anything? Did Prescott pick it up at the clinic, or did a friend give it to him, or did he get it from a bulletin board in a store or office? There was nothing to prove that he'd taken the dog there, and there was certainly nothing to prove that he'd spoken to Jenna Henley. Eleanor turned the card over and in the stillness, a gasp escaped her lips. There on the back, written in Prescott's familiar scrawl was Jenna's name, phone number and email address.

Hands shaking, she put the cards—all except this one—

back in the drawer and tried to recreate the disarray she'd found there. A thought occurred to her as she mixed the cards up with paper clips, pencils and pens. Prescott had a nearly photographic memory. Would he open the drawer and realize the contents had been rearranged?

She would deal with that later. For now, she had to put the room back in order. Tucking the card in her pocket, she climbed the stepstool and when she reached inside to return the key, her fingers made contact with a hard, narrow object. When it slid further back in the duct, she stood on tiptoe and stretched to get hold of it. Just a few centimeters more, she told herself. She strained to reach it, and just when she had it in her grasp, the stool teetered beneath her. She tried to keep her balance, but gravity won out, and as the stool careened and tipped over, the object flew across the room and she fell with a crash on the hardwood floor.

Thirty-two

"I like your Tillman theory," Ted remarked as he and Brooke ate takeouts in the Jeep. "It's got drama. Intrigue. Pathos. And the idea of Tillman being both the father and the grandfather of Jenna's child scores points in the scandal department. Too bad there's nothing to back it up. He could have been anywhere last Monday."

"Like I said, I was having fun creating a narrative," she said. But it strikes me as odd that no one seems to be wondering about the identity of Jenna's biological father."

"Good point. After all, it takes two to tango."

Brooke fell silent, recalling that night at the Stevensons' house. "And don't you think it's a coincidence that Tillman was out all day on the exact same day Kathryn Strauss died? And why was his wife accusing him of lying about where he'd been? I'm convinced there's a lot more to Tillman's story than meets the eye."

"And that's why we're on this reconnaissance mission," he reminded her.

She let out a sigh. "All we've learned so far is that he had lunch with a nondescript woman who's probably his editor."

"I'm not so sure about that. If she's his editor, why did she get upset and try to slither out of the booth? And why did he convince her to stay?"

"They were probably arguing about his manuscript. Authors can be pretty stubborn about the words they put on the page."

"Well, you should know about that," Ted acknowledged. "But we seem to be forgetting about other suspects. Take Malcolm Mackenzie. As far as we know, he hasn't been written out of the script."

"Same with Nora Murphy," Brooke said. "There was some news coverage on her early on, but lately, nothing."

A ping from Ted's phone put an end to the discussion. "Our man's back on the road," he announced. "Time for you to ride shotgun."

Brooke kept her eyes on the screen as Tillman headed south along Route 206. Near Trenton, he cut over to Route 1 and turned east a bit later.

"Some reconnaissance mission," Brooke said with a laugh. "Our man of mystery just entered a Walmart parking lot."

"And we shall do likewise," Ted told her. "Slouch down so he won't see you."

Brooke hunkered down, her eyes still on the phone. "He seems to be looking for a parking spot. Hold on a sec—he just pulled into a space about a dozen cars back from the entrance."

"I've got him in my sights," Ted responded. "We'll stay close enough to keep an eye on him and far enough away so he won't notice when I nonchalantly get out and follow him into the store."

"All this trouble," Brooke laughed, "so you can get a glimpse of the world-renowned Dr. Prescott Tillman buying socks and underwear at Walmart."

"And if the world-renowned Dr. Prescott Tillman buys

socks and underwear at Walmart, you and I will be the first to know about it. But in the meanwhile…"

There was a pause. "He got out of his car, but he's not going toward the store. He's talking on his phone and walking deeper into the parking lot." There was a pause. "Hand me my phone. I need to video this."

"Why? What's happening?"

A few seconds passed before Ted answered. "An Asian guy got out of a Lexus. He and Tillman are shaking hands. Well, isn't that interesting?'

"What's interesting? Tell me already."

"The Asian guy just handed Tillman something small—probably a flash drive. Tillman gave him one as well, and now the guy's walking back to the Lexus and Tillman's returning to the Mercedes. He just opened the door and got in."

"No socks and underwear for our man of mystery today," Brooke remarked. "This was obviously a pre-arranged meeting to swap thumb drives. And you know what that means—they want to keep the information private and off the internet."

"Agreed," Ted remarked. "I don't know about you, but I'd give anything to know what's on those drives."

Once Tillman was on his way, Brooke sat up straighter and kept her eye on Ted's phone. Staying just out of sight, they followed him west into Trenton and north on Route 29 along the Delaware River. Twenty-five minutes later, they crossed the bridge into Pennsylvania.

"Bor-ing," Brooke said. "This entire day has been a waste of time."

"Patience, my friend. Profiling a target involves days and weeks of the sort of stuff we've just done. But look on the bright side. You and I possess the only video in the entire world of not one, but two international men of mystery swapping thumb drives in a Walmart parking lot. Pretty exciting business, if you ask me."

She smiled over at him. He was adorable in a goofy sort of way. And not bad looking either, something she'd barely been conscious of before. She liked his uncombed vibe and the way his eyes sparkled when he laughed. And she liked how he could slip from goofy to serious in a nanosecond and then back to goofy again. After eighteen months of fending him off, it felt good to chill.

After that, the trek continued without incident, and then, just south of the village of Upper Black Eddy, Tillman made an unexpected left. A minute later, Ted made the same turn and followed the Mercedes along a winding road that inclined sharply above the river. A right turn took them down a narrow dirt lane through acres of gloomy woods. In spite of their relative proximity to civilization, only deer and squirrels were on hand to notice the Jeep as it passed.

A few more miles and Tillman made a left onto what appeared to be a long driveway. Bringing up an aerial view, Brooke showed Ted an image of a hedge surrounding a large building and a couple of outbuildings.

"No point in venturing up the drive," Ted remarked. "We'd only be announcing our arrival. What do you say we park on the side of the road and cut through the woods on foot?"

"And then what?" Brooke asked. "You'll accost Tillman and wrestle the thumb drive from his hand?"

Ignoring the question, Ted pulled off the road, cut the engine and fished a compass and binoculars out of the glove compartment. "Not much to see," he said as he got out of the Jeep and surveyed the surroundings. "Just trees and thick undergrowth. Oh—and a bunch of no-trespassing signs."

Brooke didn't need binoculars to see the signs. They were everywhere. And she didn't need binoculars to see the clouds thickening overhead. A quick glance at a weather app announced a pending downpour. "They're calling for rain in the next few hours," she said. "Maybe we should call it a day."

Ted threw his hands in the air. "Twenty minutes ago, you were chewing my ear about being bored. Don't tell me you're wimping out just as things are getting interesting."

"Fine, but we can't exactly pretend we don't see the signs."

"Okay," he said. "What do you suggest?"

She paused to consider the matter. "If suppose we could pretend to be birdwatchers. That would explain the binoculars."

"Not bad," Ted said with an approving grin. "Keep it up, and you might become an investigative reporter."

"I don't want to be an investigative reporter."

"Too bad. You're a natural. But at any rate, we need to figure out what sort of bird would lure people into a forest filled with 'no trespassing' signs." He hesitated, thinking. "How about a goldfinch?"

"Too common. Same with the red-winged blackbird." She thought for a moment. "I've got it. The pileated woodpecker."

"The pileated woodpecker? Never heard of it."

"Sure, you have. A large black-and-white bird with a pointy, red head. Shape-wise, it looks like a miniature pterodactyl."

"I'm a fan of pterodactyls. That settles it. The pileated woodpecker it is!"

Leaving the Jeep behind, they ventured into the woods. There was no discernible trail, only occasional deer paths that vanished into networks of briars and scrubby undergrowth. Ted relied on his compass for direction, and Brooke followed along, burrs clinging to her jeans and roots threatening to trip her.

A few minutes later, they came to the hedge surrounding the property. A close inspection revealed a chain-link fence running through the middle of it.

"No chance of sneaking through this thing," Ted remarked. "Not without wire cutters. Let's find a spot where the hedge thins out so we can get a look at what goes on around here."

Brooke glanced up at the treetops. "What'd do you wanna

bet they've got security cameras all over the place."

"So, what if they do? We're not snooping. We're following the pileated woodpecker—remember?"

He started forward, but Brooke lagged behind. "Are you comfortable telling lies? Being a Christian and all?"

He stopped to consider the question. "Back in my investigative reporter days, I did whatever it took to get a story. The pileated woodpecker would have been a tactic—a means of getting the truth out of unscrupulous characters who'd rather not divulge the truth. But I'm touched that you've taken this sudden interest in my spiritual well-being."

"I'm not one bit interested in your spiritual well-being," she said. "I'm trying to talk you out of this."

"Not possible. We're in it too far. Go back to the Jeep if you want, but I intend to stick it out."

Brooke paused to consider her options. Did she really want to sit in the Jeep and be bored for as long as it took Ted to get tired of snooping around?

"All right," she said with a sigh. "You win."

Near the front of the property, a section of hedge thinned out enough to allow a view of a sprawling, three-story house made of white stone and stucco. A driveway circled from a gate in the hedge to a portico at the front of the house and branched off toward a garage made of the same white stone and stucco as the house.

Ted raised his binoculars. "No pileated woodpeckers that I can see," he remarked as he studied the place. "The blinds are closed on the first floor, and I can't seem to get a good angle on the second-floor. As far as the garage is concerned, Tillman's Mercedes is parked outside next to a Porsche, and…" He hesitated. "Holy cow—is that a Ferrari?"

As Ted studied the distant Ferrari, the gate in the hedge slid open and a white stretch limo glided around the circular drive and came to a stop at the portico. A uniformed driver got out and opened the backdoor for three women who appeared to be in their late twenties or early thirties. They weren't dressed like women who rode in limos and partied with the owners of Porsches and Ferraris. Instead, they wore jeans and hoodies, and they didn't seem to be in a partying mood as they huddled together on the pavement, their eyes fixed apprehensively on the house.

The front door of the house flew open, and a dark-haired woman in a tight-fitting white jacket and matching skirt exited the building. Smiling broadly, she extended an armload of bracelets and shook the newcomers' hands. After some chit-chat, she escorted them toward the house, and then turned around, her expression stern when one of the three women lagged behind.

Ted focused the binoculars on the laggard's face. "Unbelievable," he whispered. "That's the same woman who had lunch with Tillman back in Princeton."

Leaving the binoculars dangling around his neck, he grabbed his phone and started shooting video. Peering through the hedge, Brooke watched Tillman's friend join the others as the woman in white ushered them into the house. Once the door closed behind them, the driver returned to the limo and drove to the parking area outside the garage.

"So, what's this all about?" Ted asked as watched the video he'd shot.

"Beats me. But this place is giving me the creeps. What do you say we get out of here?"

"In due time, my friend."

Crows cawed overhead, their cries splitting the silence. Crows were known to be intelligent creatures who warned one another of approaching danger. Did they see Brooke and Ted as a danger, or was a darker threat close at hand?

"I think we should go," she said.

Ted remained silent, his eyes glued to his binoculars which

were in turn, glued to the house.

She glanced up at the sky. "It's going to rain. I can feel it in the air." She sensed something else in the air as well. Forest sounds. Squirrels scampering in the underbrush and setting the leaves rustling. Perhaps a rabbit or a fox, curious as to who was invading its turf.

The crows cawed a warning, their voices signaling an alarm. At the same time, a twig snapped close by.

A deer—what else would it be?

But it wasn't a deer. It was a towering, muscle-bound guy with a shaved scalp, a bushy red mustache and a gun in the waistband of his jogging suit. And there was something else as well—a Doberman gazing at Brooke with murder in its eyes.

Thirty-three

"Ted," Brooke called over her shoulder. "I think you'd better…"

"Chill," Ted said, his binoculars still aimed at the house.
"Really, you need to turn around."
"Stop worrying. You're starting to sound like my mother."
"No, I mean it. There's…"
The Doberman uttered a low throaty growl.
Lowering his binoculars, Ted turned around and looked first at the dog and then at the hulking creature controlling it. The Doberman snarled again, and just as it was about to lunge, the guy with the mustache tugged on the leash. "Easy, Mitzi," he said.
"We're birdwatchers," Ted stammered. "We saw a pileated woodpecker and figured it must have a nest nearby. Just think—before long you'll have a bunch of baby birds that look like tiny pterodactyls. Lucky you—right?"
The man's eyes were dark pools in which evil creatures swam. "I have no idea what the f--- you're talking about."

"The pileated woodpecker," Ted explained. "Black and white with a red pointy head. It led us here."

The man's gaze shifted from Ted to Brooke and back to Ted. "Funny you two didn't notice the *No Trespassing* signs."

Brooke forced a laugh, hoping to ease the tension. "It's obvious you're not a birdwatcher. Do you seriously expect birds to change their flight patterns because of a few signs?"

His eyes raked over Brooke like she was a bag of dogfood he'd be happy to rip open. "Lucky for you I've got Mitzi on a leash. I hate to think what would happen if I let her go."

Brooke pretended to be offended when in fact, she was terrified. "If that's the way you're going to be…" She nodded toward Ted. "I guess we'd better be going."

When she turned to leave, the guy extended a beefy hand to stop her. "You're headed the wrong way."

"No, we're not," Ted spoke up. "We're retracing our steps. We tracked the woodpecker through the woods, right along the hedge until…"

The man grabbed Ted's collar and yanked him close, so close that his bushy, red mustache nearly touched Ted's nose. "You'll go the way I tell you, understand?" Scowling, he released Ted with a shove that sent him sprawling onto the ground. "As it so happens," he said, "Mitzi's got brothers and sisters who enjoy a romp in the woods about this time every day. If you know what's good for you, you'll be out of my sight by the count of ten.

"One." He tugged on the leash. "Two." The Doberman lurched forward, struggling to break free. "Three."

At the count of four, Brooke and Ted took off at a run. By now the air was damp with the loamy scent of impending rain. Would it hold off until they reached the Jeep? If it didn't, would they find their way when the rain began?

There was no trail to guide them as they forced their way through the underbrush. Once they were safely out of view,

Ted paused to check his compass.

"That way," he said. "We'll steer a straight line and come out on the dirt lane. The Jeep will be somewhere to our left."

A gust of wind howled through the trees, setting the branches clawing at the sky. A drop of rain touched Brooke's cheek and then another and another until, with a roar, the sky split open. The deluge was blinding, and without a path to follow, she and Ted stumbled forward, nearly falling as they dodged rainswept saplings and the spindly branches that reached out to tear at their faces.

A sudden drop in temperature left Brooke shivering in her wet clothes, and the mud pooling at her feet made the going slow and treacherous. As she pressed on, a vine snagged at her ankle and brought her crashing down in the mud. Winded, she rose on one elbow to wipe the dirt from her face, but when Ted reached out to help her, she was already on her feet.

They forged their way through the forest, brambles ripping at their skin and rocks and vines threatening to trip them as they struggled against sheets of driving rain. Up ahead the sky seemed to brighten. Was it merely a break in the trees, she wondered, or were they nearing the road?

Ted came to a sudden halt, his arm extended to stop Brooke in her tracks. Ahead of them a shallow ravine extended to their right and left. It looked to be only four or five feet deep, but a muddy stream raged through the middle of it. At this distance, it was impossible to gauge the water's depth.

"That way," he said pointing to their left. "We'll follow along the edge and hope the ground levels out at some point."

A few steps later, the water-soaked earth gave way beneath his feet, unleashing an avalanche of rocks and mud that carried him and Brooke down the embankment and into the stream. The water was only a few inches deep, and once they'd caught their breath, they slipped and slid out of the water and up the slippery slope on the other side.

"Almost there," Ted shouted. Near the top, he grabbed a vine to steady himself and let out a yell as it came loose in his hand, sending him careening backward and taking Brooke with him. They landed in the stream, face-to-face in the muddy water with their noses nearly touching.

The situation struck Brooke as funny—like a scene from a romantic comedy where the male and female leads find themselves suddenly thrown into each other's arms. She imagined the music swelling above the shrieking winds as the couple gazed into each other's eyes. Their lips would meet, tentatively at first and then with growing passion while in the distance, the howl of approaching Dobermans soared like a descant above the storm.

Wait a minute, she told herself. That wasn't her imagination. The howling was real.

"The dogs!" she screamed. "The lunatic set them free."

She and Ted wasted no time scrambling up the embankment. This time the earth held, and once they were free, they raced toward the road with the dogs baying and howling in the distance.

"Run," Ted shouted over his shoulder as she lagged behind, water-logged and nearly tripping on rocks and vines.

She didn't answer. At this point, breath was a precious commodity she couldn't afford to waste. In spite of the obstacles underfoot, she kept up her pace, and just when it seemed that her lungs would burst, the trees thinned out up ahead. Another hundred yards, and they were back on the dirt road that by now had turned into a sea of mud. But this wasn't the time to stop. Not with the dogs drawing closer.

Her breath clenched in her lungs as she splashed through the muddy puddles, and just when she thought she couldn't take another step, a shape loomed in the distance. The sight of the Jeep propelled her forward, and in spite of her breathless state, she almost laughed for joy. They were outrunning the lunatic and his crazed dogs, and before long she and Ted would be miles away and this awful ordeal would be behind them.

Ted must have pushed the unlock button on his key fob because suddenly the Jeep lit up like a lighthouse. A mere fifty yards from their destination, he let out a yell and teetered wildly in an attempt to catch his balance. His arms waved like windmill blades, but it was no use. He came down with a splash, and at the same time, a dense shadowy mass appeared among the trees. The dogs—a pack of them—moving as a single unit.

Brooke ran to help him, but he pushed her away. "I've got this," he shouted. "Get in the Jeep."

Reaching her destination, she dove into the passengers' seat and leaned over to open the driver's side door. At the same moment, the dogs burst out of the woods and came at Ted like heat-seeking missiles. By now he was on his feet, and he barely managed to make it to safety before the dogs converged on the vehicle in a whirlwind of gnashing teeth, slavering snouts and thrashing paws.

Without thinking, Brooke threw her arms around him. "I thought the dogs would kill you."

"I thought that too," he gasped, his arms wrapped around her, his hands pressing against her back, and water dripping from his hair and down her neck. "Believe me," he said, his breath warm against her ear, "that's not how I want to die."

They stayed that way until it occurred to Brooke that she was in Ted's arms while outside, the dogs were intent on assaulting the Jeep. "The Dobermans," she said as she tried to extricate herself from his embrace. "They're wrecking your paint job."

"Mother Nature wrecked it long ago," he said, still clinging to her as though his life depended on it. She allowed him another moment, and then gently eased herself away.

Pushing his muddy hair back from his face, he started the engine and the Jeep inched forward. The dogs kept after them, howling leaping and snapping at the rear bumper. But they couldn't keep pace and before long, the only sound was the sloosh of tires through the mud and the swish of wiper blades against the windshield.

Thirty-four

Eleanor's fall had left her with a goose egg at the back of her head and with something else as well—a flash drive hidden in the duct. She glanced at the time. Four o'clock and she'd about had it with skimming through page after page of scientific documents packed with mathematical and chemical formulas, unfamiliar medical terms and names of people she didn't recognize. Add to that the endless descriptions of meetings at universities, biolabs and research facilities around the world, and it was no wonder she needed a break. So far, she'd found nothing on this flash drive that was out of the ordinary, and it was beginning to seem that her search had been a complete waste of time.

Three more documents, she promised herself and then she'd treat herself to a square of dark chocolate and a cup of coffee.

The first two docs were similar to the others—formulas, lists of prominent researchers and journal articles that only an insider could understand. She opened the third and last one, expecting more of the same, but something unexpected took her eye, and she wondered if she'd understood the first few paragraphs correctly. A second reading confirmed her fears. The document detailed her husband's leadership in designing gene-specific bioweapons in laboratories around the world—weapons designed to infect certain ethnicities while bypassing others. And then came the shocker—in several instances the bioweapons had been tested on unsuspecting human subjects.

Reading further, she learned about laboratories hidden in deep underground installations where secret experiments were conducted on undocumented immigrants trafficked to this country for precisely that purpose. No one seemed to care if these individuals died as a result of the experiments. After all, the only ones who knew they existed were their traffickers and the scientists and technicians who performed the experiments.

She sat back, sickened by what she'd read. This was MKUltra and the Tuskegee Syphilis Study all over again—but on a much grander scale. MKUltra, a secret CIA program involving medical and mind-control experiments, had theoretically been shut down in the late 1970s when Senate hearings exposed the program to public scrutiny. But here it was again, reborn as something even more monstrous—and her husband was playing a leading role.

A noise at the front of the house set the Corgis barking. Startled, Eleanor glanced at the time and saw to her dismay that it was nearly five. She'd been so engrossed in her search, that she hadn't notice the minutes slipping by. She expected Prescott to get back at six. Why, of all days, had he decided to come home early?

A gust of wind rattled the shutters and drove the rain against the roof. The storm must have put an end to his plans, and now he was back before she'd had a chance to put things right in his study.

Panicked, she ejected the drive and stuck it in her pocket. There was no way she could put the study back together in a fraction of a minute. Instead, she'd greet him at the door and send him upstairs for something. But what would that be? *Think*—she told herself. But she couldn't think—not when she was paralyzed with fear at the thought of him entering the study and finding the stepstool beneath the vent and the cover removed.

Taking a deep breath, she hurried to the foyer to look out the window. As she did, relief washed over her. It wasn't Prescott, it was the mailman walking away from the house, his black poncho glistening with rain. Opening the door, she reached into the mailbox and brought out today's offering of bills and advertising circulars. She thumbed through them and stopped when she came to a padded envelope. The tracking device she'd ordered four days ago was finally here. She'd considered hiring a private detective to see what Prescott was up to when he went out for hours on end, but this little gadget would save time, trouble and expense. The police weren't permitted to use these things without a warrant—to do so would constitute an unreasonable search and seizure. But there were no such restraints on a wife.

She hurried back to the study, climbed the stepladder, returned the thumb drive to its hiding place and screwed the cover back on the air duct. After that, she put the stepladder and screwdriver back in the utility closet and took a few deep, cleansing breaths. She was safe, she told herself. She'd make a nice meal, open a bottle of wine and put on her best smile to keep Prescott from guessing what she'd been up to all afternoon.

At six-fifteen, the Corgis perked up at the sound of the Mercedes pulling into the driveway. They wriggled off to greet their lord and master while in the kitchen, Eleanor freshened her lipstick and ran a comb through her thick, silvery hair. Tonight, there'd be no nagging questions about where he'd been all day. Just pleasant conversation to camouflage the battle raging inside her.

But as it turned out, Prescott wasn't in the mood for conversation. He seemed agitated, and once he'd gobbled down his dinner and put away two glasses of wine, he disappeared into his study, leaving Eleanor to load the dishwasher and tidy up.

Afterward, she slipped on her raincoat, went outside and knelt beside the Mercedes, her fingers probing beneath the driver's side wheel well. She encountered something unexpected, but when she tried to get it loose, it remained right where it was. It took a bit of fumbling, but eventually she pried it free. There in her hand was a tracker, much like the one she'd just purchased.

Rain rolled down her coat and soaked her jeans, but she stayed rooted in place, her eyes fixed on the device. Where did it come from? Did a reporter plant it? Or worse—were federal agents following Prescott? She thought of the biolabs scattered around the globe. Perhaps he'd made a misstep and was on the radar of dangerous foreign operatives. She glanced back at the house. Did his enemies know where they lived? Was she safe with him in Stony Vale?

Fingers trembling, she put the newly discovered tracker in her pocket and placed the one she'd purchased in the wheel well. When she returned to the house she found Prescott—not in the study where he belonged—but in the kitchen, frowning as he poured a cup of coffee. She thought of his top desk drawer and the jumble of business cards. Had he noticed something amiss?

"An odd night for a walk," he remarked.

She fingered the tracker in her pocket. *Think fast,* she told herself. *Don't give yourself away.* "I misplaced my lipstick," she said. "I thought it might have fallen out of my bag in the car, but I guess I left in it my sister's apartment. I'll pick up another at the drugstore."

"What's wrong with the stuff you're wearing?"

She shrugged, rain running off her coat and puddling on the floor. "Nothing's wrong with it. It's just that I prefer the other."

The conversation died there. Taking his coffee mug with him, Prescott retreated to his study and closed the door.

Thirty-five

Ted lay awake, replaying the events of the day. Funny, but Brooke had never looked more beautiful than when she'd splashed down next to him in the ravine, mud streaming down her face and the storm shrieking overhead. For a brief moment, the rain and the mud had seemed to vanish until all he saw was her blue-green eyes. Her gaze seemed more welcoming than he remembered—warmer somehow—and if they hadn't been interrupted by those stupid dogs howling in the distance…

He recalled her sitting next to him in the Jeep, mud-soaked and sopping wet as she speculated about what was going on in that house. Most women would have been ticked at him for dragging them into a mess like this one. But Brooke had responded, not with anger, but curiosity.

And that brought him to the house in the woods. What was happening in there that merited the protection of an armed bodyguard and a pack of savage dogs? On the way home, he and Brooke had speculated about the house being a research lab where Tillman and his cohorts conducted creepy genetic experiments on women they'd recruited as subjects. That lead to a discussion of a book they'd both read as kids— H.G. Wells' *The Island of Dr. Moreau*, a sci-fi novel about a mad scientist who was turning animals into human-like creatures known as the Beast Folk. Moreau's island was crawling with animal-human hybrids, but what if that sort of thing were being done in reverse with humans being re-engineered to possess specialized capabilities of the animal kingdom. What would it be like to have the eyes of an eagle or the strength of a lion or the lifespan of a Galapagos giant tortoise? If such upgrades were possible, would the wealthy pay hefty sums to enjoy the benefits—benefits, they'd pass on to their offspring? If so, what would happen to ordinary humans who remained unenhanced? Would they become a slave class doomed to serve the needs of an elite race of superhuman overlords?

Ted pictured the Dog Man, the Sloth Creature, the Pigmen, the partially transformed Puma-woman and the other hybrids that inhabited the Island of Dr. Moreau. Had this novel, like so many other sci-fi narratives, been predictive programming—a look into a crystal ball to prepare the public for what loomed on the horizon? He drifted off to sleep with that and similar questions on his mind and woke at four to the alarm shrieking in his ear—the second morning in a row he'd been jolted awake before dawn. He pushed the snooze button and in no time at all the shrieking started up again. After a shower and coffee, he got in his Jeep and headed to Stony Vale to reclaim his tracking device.

The streets were deserted as he parked the Jeep and made his way to the Tillman's house. It took only a few seconds to retrieve the small rectangular object and when he got back home, he stood in the kitchen, staring at it in the light above the sink. Was it his imagination or did it seem bigger than he remembered? Turning it over, he glanced at the serial number. Well, this was interesting. The number ended with the digits 3-

7-0, but the device he'd planted ended in 0-1-2. Startled, he got out his phone, and checked the monitor. Astonishingly, the tracker he'd planted in Tillman's wheel well was currently inside Tillman's house.

The realization left him stunned. Tillman had obviously found the thing—how else would it have made it through his front door and into the house? But why was there a second device, and what would its owner think when Ted's house popped up on his or her phone?

He glanced out the window. Was someone out there at this precise moment? He imagined a hitman eyeing the house from a parked car, and while it appeared that the coast was clear he needed to get rid of the tracker before someone broke down his door.

Twenty minutes later he pulled into the parking lot at Lehigh Valley International Airport. Entering the terminal, he hurried to the men's room and placed the magnetic device on the wall of a metal stall, just above the toilet paper dispenser. He chuckled to himself as he pictured some shady character thinking he was closing in on Tillman, only to discover that he'd been conned. The scenario would be hilarious if it weren't so bewildering.

He arrived home just as the sun was peeking over the horizon. He spent an hour cleaning the mud from inside the Jeep and then hurried to a drive-through car wash. From there, he drove to Ashley's parents' house to pick her up for their big day at the Penn Museum. They chatted pleasantly on the way to breakfast at her favorite diner, and soon were in a booth, sipping coffee and gazing at the breakfast items on the enormous, eight-page laminated menu.

"You seem distracted," Ashley commented as she set her cup down in the saucer.

"Guilty as charged. I didn't sleep well the last couple of nights." He didn't bother explaining the reason for his lack of sleep—namely that he'd been running around in the early morning hours planting and retrieving tracking devices.

"Anything on your mind?" she asked.

Anything on his mind? She had no idea what she was asking.

He had no intention of describing the guy with the mustache or his pack of four-legged killers. Instead, he mumbled something about an issue with a video he was working on, and by the time the omelets and home fries were delivered, Ashley was chatting happily about the tea party she'd attended with her mom. The ladies from the Daughters of the American Revolution were charming, she told him. And the food was yummy—scones, clotted cream, cute little sandwiches, petit-fours and...

Ted's thoughts wandered to the house in the woods. Who were those women in the limo? Why were they there, and why did they get the red-carpet treatment when they weren't exactly dressed in red-carpet clothes? The situation made no sense.

"While we were sipping and eating," Ashley continued, "the guest speaker told us about the history of tea-consumption in the colonies. To make it seem more authentic, she and the hostess wore period costumes and..."

Ted thought about the security cameras that must have been watching as he and Brooke prowled along the hedge. Once Tillman got a look, he'd have instantly recognized Brooke. Would he press charges for trespassing? Not likely—not if he wanted to keep his shady business out of the spotlight. A more chilling thought sprang to mind. Would he send hired thugs to keep an eye on Brooke? Or worse—would she meet a fate like Jenna's? The thought made his pulse race. Had he dragged Brooke into something more dangerous than the dogs?

And what about himself? His videos were all over the internet and face-recognition software would have identified him in seconds. He pictured returning home today and finding an SUV idling in front of his house while a hit man watched through tinted windows. He pictured the next day's headlines: *Podcaster Mowed Down in Cold Blood. So Far, No Suspect and No Motive.*

He thought again about Brooke. Instead of being available to help if danger came calling, he'd be in West Philly, wandering around a museum and looking at…

"Did you hear me?" Ashley asked. "Are you even listening?"

"What? Oh—sorry. Can you say that again?"

Her expression darkened. "I said we should do something to bring you up to speed on your genealogy. I think we should talk to your aunt—the one who traced your family history."

"My aunt?" He had to think for a minute. "Oh, you mean Aunt Claire. Sad to say, she died years ago."

Ashley rolled her eyes at the news. "Well, someone in your family must have the genealogy records." She glared at Ted through her smart-lady glasses. "I insist that you find them."

He stared back at her, speechless. *I'm about to be gunned down by snipers and you're insisting that I dig up my ancestors?* He studied her face to figure out if she was serious or just clowning around. Okay—she was serious. He wasn't thrilled with her tone and he wasn't exactly happy with the insisting business.

"Who's actually doing the insisting," he asked. "You or your mom?"

Ashley appeared to take umbrage at the question. Chin raised. Nose in the air. A frown on her pretty, pink lips. "Just what are you implying?" she asked.

"I'm not implying anything. I merely want to know if dragging my family skeletons out of the closet was your idea or your mom's. It's a simple question and all it needs is a simple answer."

Ashley tossed her perky blond ponytail like she was batting off horseflies. "For your information, the DAR tea reminded me of the importance of staying connected to our roots. My heritage and tradition are important aspects of who I am."

"I've got no problem with heritage and tradition," Ted said. "And since these lofty concepts are so important to you, how would you feel about roughing it like your ancestors did? I'm picturing a cabin with an open fireplace, a vegetable garden just off the kitchen, a few chickens and a cellar full of produce you grew and canned yourself."

She turned her nose even higher at the idea. "I picture myself in a townhouse in Society Hill, attending balls and formal teas with our country's founders and their wives. So, to answer your question, cabins, woodstoves and chickens hold no appeal."

"What about camping?" he asked. "Ever do much of that?"

"I prefer clean sheets and hot showers. With a few luxuries thrown in."

"A few luxuries, eh? Like complimentary champagne, a chocolate truffle on the pillow and a hotel spa with terrycloth robes?"

"Exactly."

"Then let me ask you this," he continued. "How would you feel about falling into a muddy ravine and nearly being killed by a pack of savage Dobermans?"

She looked like at him like he was crazy. "Sometimes you say the oddest things."

Ted didn't respond. Instead, he stuffed a chunk of rye toast in his mouth and chased it with a swig of coffee. He was tired and cranky, and while he didn't want to be tough on Princess Ashley, it was beginning to appear that there were more than a few things they didn't have in common.

Thirty-six

Brooke stared at the article she was attempting to edit—a piece about PPE (personal protective equipment) used on construction sites. In it, the author reviewed the latest in hard hats, safety glasses, lanyards, air-purifying respirators—the list went on and on. She could have used some PPE yesterday, designed specifically to ward off savage dogs and to cushion an individual against injuries sustained when plummeting down embankments into muddy streams. At this point, every muscle in her body ached, and even the act of thinking was painful. But there was work to do and with deadlines looming, she needed to get moving.

Except that she couldn't concentrate. What about Malcolm Mackenzie, she wondered. He seemed to have vanished from the news cycle. Was he off the hook for Jenna's murder, or were the detectives digging up new evidence and keeping it under wraps? The same with Nora Murphy. There'd been a lot of gossip initially and now nothing. She wondered too about Derick and Geoff Strauss. Was there anything to Maggie's theory, or was it as ridiculous as it seemed?

Brooke had no sooner put these questions out of her mind when someone pounded on her door. By now Maggie was at work, so who was it?

Detective Burleigh, that's who, followed by Detective Radley. And judging from their frowns, this wasn't a friendly visit.

"Good morning," she managed to say. "To what do I owe the pleasure?"

"Pleasure?" Burleigh barked. "That's not what I'd call it. But that's beside the point. May we come in?"

Since there didn't seem to be an option, Brooke showed them to the sofa and took a seat next to the window.

"I'll make this brief," Burleigh began. "Did you and Maggie Jenkins make a visit to Wellsboro last week?"

The question took her by surprise. After yesterday's adventure, the trip to Wellsboro was a distant memory.

"A visit to Wellsboro?" she echoed. "Why do you ask?"

"Why do you think I asked? I asked because I want an answer. Were you in the vicinity of Wellsboro, Pennsylvania, last Thursday and Friday?"

When she didn't respond, he kept going. "We don't have time for games, Ms. Roberts. Sources tell us that two women bearing a striking resemblance to you and your tall, skinny neighbor were seen at a diner in Wellsboro on Thursday evening. The next day you appeared at the funeral of Jenna Henley's birthmother and later at an antique gun shop owned by the sons of the deceased. Later, someone who fits your description was involved in a less-that-friendly chat with the deceased's older son outside the motel where Ms. Jenkins was registered. Would you care to comment on that?"

There was no room for denial, not after such an accurate summary. Instead, Brooke offered an explanation—she'd agreed to keep Maggie company on a trip to Wellsboro to deliver Jenna's photo album to her birthmother. Until they'd stopped at the diner for dinner, they had no idea Kathryn Strauss was dead.

Burleigh wasn't impressed by the explanation. "So you're telling me that Ms. Jenkins had a photo album that belonged to Jenna Henley? Why didn't she tell me about it when I interviewed her?"

"I guess she didn't think it was relevant."

He threw his hands in the air. "It's my job to decide what's relevant—not hers and not yours. But let's see if I've got this straight. You and Ms. Jenkins drove halfway across the state to give a photo album to Jenna's birthmother. How did you end up at the funeral?"

"The waitress at the diner told us about Kathryn's death and she mentioned the location of the funeral. Maggie thought we should pay our respects."

Burleigh fell silent, his forehead knotted as though he were having trouble matching Brooke's answers with whatever narrative he and his sidekick had already constructed. "Okay," he finally said. "Saying I accept the story that you and your friend were all innocence and light as you traipsed out to Wellsboro on a mission of mercy. How, then, do you explain your visit to the gun shop?"

"That's where things get complicated." Brooke summarized Maggie's theory about the Strauss brothers murdering Jenna and then their mother. When she finished, Burleigh shook his head.

"For your information," he said, "both Derrick and Geoff Strauss have alibis for the time of both deaths. They're grief stricken at losing their mother, stunned by the knowledge that they had a half-sister they never knew and heart-broken by her untimely death. By your actions that day, you and Ms. Jenkins heaped unnecessary distress upon two grieving young men and increased their suffering in a situation that was already unimaginably painful."

"We never meant…" Brooke stammered. "I mean, when Derrick Strauss came after us in his truck, we naturally assumed…"

"Derrick Strauss came after you because he wanted to know why you and your goofy friend showed up at his store spouting a harebrained story about buying a birthday gift and then pestering the clerk with nosy questions about Kathryn Strauss's death. If you thought his actions were suspicious, what do you think he thought of yours?"

"I see that," Brooke acknowledged. "But to be honest, the only reason I went on that trip was to avoid my uncle's attempts at matchmaking. I'm sorry things turned out badly."

"I should hope so," Burleigh huffed. "Not only did you put yourselves in harm's way, but you and your friend jeopardized the safety, privacy, and emotional well-being of everyone who has a stake in the Jenna Henley/Kathryn Strauss investigation. From now on, I'll expect you to keep your nose out of police business. Do you understand?"

Brooke nodded but said nothing. She wanted to tell him about Prescott Tillman and the house in the woods, but it didn't seem right to drag Ted into the conversation without his okay. Maybe she should talk to him first, and then the two of them could meet with the detectives and share the highlights of their experience.

The detectives finally left, but by now Brooke had lost all interest in personal protective equipment. Instead, she decided on a walk to clear her head and loosen up the knots in her aching limbs. She headed out into the bright sunshine, but the bright, gleaming day was unable to chase away the dark sense of someone watching her. The feeling lingered as she made her way along Northampton Street and headed for the pedestrian lane on the bridge crossing the Delaware. *It was nothing,* she told herself—*just the memory of the terrors she'd lived through the day before.* Even so, she glanced over her shoulder, half expecting to see the bald-headed guy with the Doberman closing in on her. Instead, a petite woman in jeans and spiked heels studied her phone as she walked a tiny Yorkie along the street.

Get a grip, Brooke told herself, but the message sent by her brain never made it to her central nervous system. Had Tillman seen video footage of her and Ted snooping around the house in the woods, and did he dispatch thugs to keep an eye on her? Was someone lurking nearby, a phone to his ear as he reported her exact location and waited for instructions?

The feeling of being watched intensified when she paused to look at a display in an art gallery window. She tried to focus on a grouping of three landscapes but her thoughts were elsewhere.

She'd just decided to head back home and lock herself in her apartment when a male voice shouted her name and sent her heart pounding. Afraid to turn around she shifted her gaze from the landscapes to the reflection in the plate glass window. She watched cars heading to and from the bridge, and she saw people strolling, jackets unbuttoned in the spring sunshine. But as far as she could tell, there were no thugs on cell phones and no lunatics walking Dobermans. So, who called her name? Was it a friend or a foe?

The question was answered when the reflection revealed two smiling faces. The Mormon missionaries—Elder Bolton and Elder Douglas.

"I didn't think you heard us," Elder Bolton said as she turned around. She wanted to embrace both of them, but not knowing if missionary protocol permitted such shows of affection, she refrained.

"We've got good news," Elder Bolton's freckle-faced partner spoke up. "The people got Donnie and Marie from Bernie's place this morning, and they're safe and sound in their new home."

"Wonderful," Brooke said. "I'm so glad the story has a happy ending."

The missionaries filled her in on the details of the family who'd adopted the kittens—two parents, three kids, two dogs, five chickens, an aging tabby and now Donnie and Marie.

The topic ran its course, and as Brooke was about to excuse herself and head for home, a plan arose unexpectedly in her brain. At Bernie's two days ago, Maggie insisted that she'd seen Elder Bolton leaving Jenna's apartment the night before the murder. At Bernie's on Tuesday, Elder Bolton had seemed eager to say something significant about Jenna, but his partner cut him off before he could finish his thought. This might be Brooke's only opportunity to find out what Jenna confided to him in the hours before her death.

"The news about the Donnie and Marie calls for a celebration," she told them. "How about if I treat you to lunch?"

They heartily accepted the offer and with that settled, the three of them walked to a deli in the center of Easton. As they entered, Brooke recalled Burleigh's warning about poking her nose into police business. But this wasn't police business. It was just three people tying up the details of a conversation they'd left hanging two days ago.

Thirty-seven

Eleanor stared at the app on her phone. Somehow the tracker she'd planted on Prescott's car had traveled from Stony Vale to Allentown and from there to Lehigh Valley International Airport. Stranger still was the fact that it ended up, not in the airport parking lot where cars belonged, but somewhere inside the terminal.

She glanced out the window at Prescott's Mercedes gleaming in the sun. Something had gone dreadfully wrong.

"I'm taking the dogs for a walk," she called through the door to his study. "We won't be long."

Outside, the Corgis scrambled at her feet, their impatience evident as she knelt beside the Mercedes and felt inside the wheel well. An eerie feeling stole over her as she realized the device was gone. While she'd been tossing and turning all night, someone had crept through the darkness and removed it. But who? And why? Who were they and what did they want?

The dogs tugged at their leashes, eager for the walk she'd promised. Acquiescing, she let them steer her down the path from the house and into the woods along the canal. All around her trees were in bud, birds sang and frogs chirped, but she barely noticed these harbingers of spring. Instead, she recalled the day she and Prescott retired to Stony Vale. She'd been happy to settle into in this pleasant, hopeful place where people trusted their neighbors and worked together toward a brighter future. But now she knew better. In the last two weeks the illusion of peace, security and brighter futures had vanished.

Her thoughts flew to the biolabs she'd learned about yesterday. Maybe, just maybe, she'd drawn the wrong conclusions. Maybe Prescott wasn't complicit in those foreign shenanigans. Maybe he was an investigator tracking down rogue scientists and reporting his findings to the federal government. The thought raised other fears. Did an enemy find out that he was a mole? Did they dispatch hitmen to silence him before the truth got out? And Jenna—did they kill her and toss her in the pond as a way of warning him to watch his step?

But what if Prescott were actually involved in illegal experiments at biolabs around the world? If so, was Jenna Henley involved as well? Is that why he'd lied about knowing her—because the story went deeper than anyone would dare to imagine? And is that why he—or someone associated with him—killed her?

If so, Eleanor needed to catch him in his lies. But what signals should she look for? What facial expressions? What instances of questions dodged or inadequately answered?

The Corgis waddled in front of her, their legs too short and stubby for their bulky bodies. She tried to picture the dogs before breeders intervened to shorten their legs and make it easier for them to nip at the hooves of the cattle they herded? Their disproportionate body parts were an example of human-directed evolution. Would transhumanist efforts to direct human evolution lead to equally freakish results? Prescott made it sound so wonderful with his lofty descriptions of increased longevity, improved health and enhanced mental capability. But what if something went wrong? What if Humans 2.0 turned out like these Corgis—mutated in unspeakable ways?

Trust the science, people liked to say. But what if science didn't merit the trust people placed in it?

Arriving at the towpath, she watched the Corgis wriggle and run, completely happy in their springtime romp. Happy, little mutants, Prescott always called them. And why not be happy? Ignorance is bliss.

Back at the house, she found Prescott rooting around in the fridge. "I'm ravenous," he announced with a smile. "It's a beautiful day, so what do you say we open the blinds and have lunch in the sunroom? I'll make sandwiches while you slice some fruit."

Eleanor glanced at the windows that once filled the room with light. She couldn't open the blinds. Not until Jenna's killer was behind bars. She couldn't bear to gaze at the sunlight sparkling in the pond where that beautiful young woman met her death.

"I'd rather we ate in the kitchen," she said softly.

Prescott looked up from the counter where he was slathering mayo on slices of multi-grain bread. "You always said the sunroom was your favorite spot in the house."

"I'm sure I'll enjoy it once again as soon the case is settled."

"What if it's never settled? What if it goes cold?"

Is that what you want? she felt like shouting. But she didn't. Instead, she swallowed the words before they could escape her lips. The same thing had happened last night at dinner. She'd drowned her questions with sips of wine before accusations could start flying.

"We can eat in the sunroom," she said, "but we'll keep the blinds closed."

He sighed at the remark. "Never mind. We'll eat in the kitchen if you prefer."

Hands shaking, she cut up chunks of cantaloupe and

placed them in a bowl. Is this how she'd spend the rest of her life—walking on eggshells and stifling questions that begged for answers? She wondered if Prescott could sense the shift in the energy between them. Could he tell that her doubts about him had turned to profound fear and distrust?

"By the way," he said. "I have an errand to run after lunch. I'll only be gone a few hours."

"Take me with you," she said, the words spilling out. "Please. I want to go with you."

He raised an eyebrow. "Still not trusting me?"

When she didn't answer, he crossed the kitchen and drew her close. "This has been an awful ordeal," he said, his breath warm against her neck. "Instead of offering support, I've left you on your own to sort things out. So, here's an idea. Let's do something special tonight. Pick a place for dinner, and I'll make a reservation."

She pulled away and went back to cutting cantaloupe. "I'd rather not."

"Of course you would. We'll enjoy a meal with a first-class bottle of wine and wrap it up with something decadent for dessert."

She put down the knife. "Think about it, Prescott. For almost two weeks, your face has been all over the news. The moment we enter a restaurant—any restaurant—people will start whispering. That doesn't sound like much of a night out to me."

He shrugged his shoulders. "Point well taken. So how about this? We'll have dinner delivered, and I'll set the stage. Candlelight. Soft music. And wine. *In vino veritas*—in wine there's truth."

Truth. The word struck Eleanor as absurd. How would she ever learn the truth when there'd been so many lies?

Thirty-eight

A glob of Russian dressing oozed out of Elder Douglas's corned beef special and onto the paper plate. Frowning, he scooped it up with an index finger and stuck it in his mouth. His table manners were atrocious, but that's not why Brooke wanted to get rid of him. She needed him out of the way so she could speak privately to Elder Bolton.

The red-haired elder solved the problem by wolfing down his sandwich and excusing himself to go to the men's room. At most, he'd be gone a few minutes, hardly enough time to coax information out of Elder Bolton. Brooke needed to take a direct approach if she hoped to learn anything, but before she could launch an opening salvo, the missionary leaned across the table. "We need to talk. Are you free later this afternoon?"

The question took her by surprise. "I suppose so, but…"

"Elder Douglas has a dentist appointment this afternoon," he interrupted. "Meet me at two in the circle at the center of Easton. Pretend you're looking at your phone, and when I stop to talk, act like we've never met before. Pretend I'm a complete stranger sharing information about the Mormon faith. And whatever you do, don't let Elder Douglas know about it." He shoved a couple of brochures at Brooke. "Look at these and when he returns, act like we've been discussing them."

▼ ▼ ▼

Brooke arrived early at the designated meeting place, and Elder Bolton showed up a few minutes later. She pretended not to notice him until he approached and introduced himself as Elder Bolton from the Church of Jesus Christ of Latter-Day Saints.

"If you've got a few minutes," he said, his eyes bright and eager, "I'd love to talk to you about our beliefs and answer any questions you might have."

When Brooke agreed, he reached into his tote bag and brought out copies of the same brochures they'd looked at in the deli. "In case anyone's watching," he whispered as he sat down beside her, "we'll look at the brochures and act like we're talking about them."

He glanced around, as though checking out the people walking by. "Thanks for meeting with me. I'm desperate to talk to someone, and you showed up just when I couldn't bear it anymore."

Brooke's heart went out to the poor kid. How old was he. Nineteen? Twenty?

"Jenna phoned me around 11:30 the night before she died," he said. "She begged me to come over because she was scared to be alone. I told her I couldn't—missionaries take an oath saying we won't be alone with members of the opposite sex. By then she was crying and saying she was in danger and needed somebody to protect her. So what could I do— I couldn't leave her alone like that. By then it was nearly midnight, and since Elder Douglas was asleep, I sneaked out of the apartment and walked the ten blocks to the Beacon Arms."

He paused to point out something in the brochure and then resumed his story. "Jenna told me that late last winter, she was trying to get money together to expand her business. The banks wouldn't help because she didn't have any collateral and there was no one willing to cosign for a loan. Out of the blue, she hooked up with an organization that said they'd pay her a bunch of money to..." His voice trailed off and he glanced around as though worried that someone might be listening to the conversation.

"Basically," he continued, "she told me they were going to pay her to have an embryo implanted so it could grow for three months and then be aborted."

"What?"

"You heard me. She accepted the first payment when the embryo was implanted, but as the weeks went by, she began hating herself for what she'd promised to do. She kept thinking about how her birthmother had given her life, and she decided she'd do the same for the child she was carrying. When she told the people involved that she wanted out of the contract, they started threatening her."

By now Elder Bolton had stopped referring to the brochure and showing it to Brooke. Instead, he held it limply in one hand, his gaze fixed not on the words or the photographs, but on the ground.

"Jenna said I was the only one who knew her secret," he continued. "She said that talking to me that night helped her decide to do the right thing. She'd go to the police, tell them everything and ask for protection. I left her apartment feeling upset and confused about what she told me, but also proud and thankful that I'd helped her decide to do the right thing. But the next thing I knew, she was dead."

Brooke stared at the cars making their way around the circle. *Unholy*—Jenna had told Anita that her child was unholy. And no wonder. Jenna'd agreed to participate in what appeared to be a freakish genetic experiment. What was the nature of the implanted embryo, and why was it supposed to be harvested for study after three months. Was this what was going on in that house in the woods, and were the women in the limousine participants in the same sorts of experiments? If so, had they arrived there yesterday for implantations or for abortions? And if Jenna carried the child to term, what freak of nature would she have brought forth?

"Have you told the police about this?" she asked.

Elder Bolton shook his head. "Missionaries are supposed to do everything in twos. I was afraid if the missionary board found out I was alone with Jenna that night, they'd relieve me of my mission and send me home in disgrace. Do you have any idea what that would do to my parents? But now that I've waited so long, I'm afraid I'll be arrested for withholding evidence."

He slumped forward, his head in his hands. He no longer looked like a stalwart defender of his faith. He looked like a scared kid, lost at sea and trying to keep from drowning. It was safe to assume that nothing in his weeks of missionary training had prepared him for anything like this.

"How's this for an idea?" Brooke spoke up. "I'll contact the detectives, but I won't mention your name unless they promise to speak privately with you like we're doing now. And I'll tell them your concerns about the missionary board and your concerns about breaking the rules. Are you good with that?"

His face brightened somewhat. "Thank you. The truth has to come out one way or another. Otherwise, I won't be able to live with myself."

With that he rose to his feet, and as he shook Brooke's hand, he reconstituted his missionary persona. "Nice talking to you Brooke. If you have any questions about the Church of Jesus Christ of Latter-day Saints, please check our website. And if you'd like to talk to someone in person, feel free to call the number on the back of the brochure."

Thirty-nine

"I can't believe the weather forecast," Ashley said, her eyes on her cell as Ted steered the Jeep up her parents' steep driveway. Looking away from the screen, she glanced out the window at huge white clouds sailing like blimps across a clear blue sky. "Saturday and Sunday are supposed to be complete washouts. Since I can't stand driving long distances in the rain, I guess I'll have to go back to Pittsburgh tomorrow."

She looked over at him, her eyes as blue as the sky. "I wondered about this earlier, but I was hoping the forecast would change. I didn't mention it because I didn't want to spoil our day."

As far as Ted was concerned, the day had been spoiled from the get-go. The tense words exchanged at breakfast had cast a cloud over the visit to the Penn Museum and lessened his appreciation for Queen Puabi and her funerary ensemble. A late lunch in Old City Philadelphia had done nothing to lighten the mood.

But he didn't say as much. Instead, he reminded her that all was not lost—he'd be visiting her in Pittsburgh just six weeks from now.

She didn't seem overly thrilled at the thought of seeing him again, and to be honest, he wasn't overly thrilled at the thought of driving all that distance only to be mired down in petty arguments like the ones they'd endured today. But was he being fair? After yesterday's near-death experience, he'd had little patience for Ashley's chatter about bloodlines and family history and the correct way to serve tea to the upper classes during the Revolutionary War. Furthermore, he'd been distracted and anxious and way off his game—hardly the witty, raconteur she'd been accustomed to.

They parted with a kiss at the door and by the time Ted was back on the road, thoughts of Ashley had vanished from his mind. He placed a call to Brooke and was disappointed when her voicemail answered. Was she refusing to take his call? Was she ticked off because of what he'd said about God rescuing them from the hounds from hell? Or was she ticked because he'd nearly gotten her killed? Or was it worse than that? Had Tillman's minions closed in on her and was her life in danger?

He arrived back home and was annoyed to see a blue Prius parked in his usual spot. No big deal— this was a public street, and people were free to park where they wished. He found a spot further down the block and as he walked back to his house, he noticed that the Prius was occupied—a woman sat behind the wheel, and she appeared to be watching him. Ignoring her, he climbed the steps to the porch, and as he turned the key, the Prius door opened and slammed shut.

"Ted Roslyn?" the woman called out.

He stiffened as she called his name. Was this a set up? Was he about to step into a trap?

Turning around, he saw an attractive older woman with silvery hair. For some reason she looked familiar—and then it hit him. She was Tillman's wife. Eleanor. Her face had been all over the news. Was she here to do her husband's dirty work?

She didn't look the type to do anyone's dirty work. Her face was kind and intelligent, and she seemed completely non-threatening as she walked up the porch steps and extended her hand. "I'm Eleanor Tillman," she said. "I found your address on my phone, but until I asked one of your neighbors, I didn't know your name. Can we have a word in private?"

When he hesitated, she continued talking. "If it makes any difference, my husband has no idea I'm here. And that's how I want it to stay."

He wasn't sure he believed her, but even so, it seemed unlikely that she was here to kill him. Not when she'd asked a neighbor for his name—the connection would be way too obvious. His curiosity aroused, he invited her inside. When he offered her a seat, she said she preferred standing. She had only a few questions and then she'd be on her way.

Reaching into her pocket, she brought out a rectangular black object and held it out for him to see. "Is this yours?"

It looked like his tracker, but to be make certain, he asked for the last three digits of the serial number.

Turning it over, she read aloud. "Zero-one-two. Sound familiar?"

He nodded.

"Well," she said, "that's one mystery solved. Let's see how well we do with the others. You see, I've been curious as to where my husband goes when he leaves home for hours at a time. Last night, I went outside to plant a tracker on his car, and imagine my surprise when I found this one inside the wheel well. This morning, I checked the app on my phone and realized that the device I planted last night somehow made its way from Stony Vale to this house in Allentown before ending up inside Lehigh Valley International Airport? Care to explain?"

When he didn't answer, she continued as though understanding his hesitancy, "You see, I desperately want to know where my husband goes when he takes off for the day. At the moment he's out there somewhere, and if you hadn't removed the tracker, I'd know where he is." She looked at Ted with pleading eyes. "He was out all day yesterday and I have very good reasons for mistrusting the story he told. If you know where he went, I would like you to tell me"

"You sure you don't want to sit down?" Ted asked. "It might take a while."

Once she was seated, he began by telling her about the woman in the restaurant in Princeton. After that, he described the flash-drive exchange in the Walmart parking lot and ended up with a description of the house in the woods. She seemed particularly interested when he told her about the women in the limo, the bald guy with the mustache, and the frantic chase through the storm with wild dogs baying at his heels.

"It's worse than I thought," she murmured once he'd finished. He waited for her to explain, but she didn't. Instead, she asked for the address of the house in the woods, made a note of it and with a brief word of thanks, headed back to her car.

Forty

The drive seemed endless, and with Prescott due back at any minute, Eleanor had to hurry. When she got back to the house, she ignored the Corgis, raced up the stairs to the bedroom and emerged twenty minutes later with the room in disarray. She dashed back down the stairs and had just finished stashing things in the backseat when Prescott pulled into the driveway.

He got out of the Mercedes, a bouquet of pink roses in his hand. "Dinner will arrive in a few minutes," he said, smiling as she took the roses and brought them to her nose to breathe in the sweet fragrance. "While you arrange the flowers, I'll set the table, choose the music and select a bottle of wine from the cellar. It will be a special evening for the two of us. A time to heal our wounds and look forward to the future."

When they went inside, she found a vase, hastily arranged the roses and went upstairs to freshen up—or so she said. Instead, she put things in order, closed the dresser drawers and went into the bathroom to touch up her lipstick and blush. *Act naturally*, she told herself, her worried eyes looking back at her from the bathroom mirror. *Keep calm and follow the conversation where it leads.*

A heavenly aroma told her that dinner had arrived. Down in the dining room, she made a fuss over the elegant tablescape as Prescott poured wine into a crystal glass and handed it to her to sample. When she nodded her approval, he filled it the rest of the way and plated the meal—a luscious-looking bouillabaisse brimming with fish, lobster and scallops.

"I've been thinking," he said as he sat down. "It might be nice to get away for a while."

Eleanor watched his face. The remark was light-hearted, but the smile that went with it seemed forced. "Would that be for business," she asked, "or for pleasure?"

"For pleasure of course. We've been through a trying ordeal, and I thought it would be nice to get away for a while. Someplace different, like Andorra in the Pyrenees Mountains between France and Spain. Or if you prefer, we could make an extended visit to Russia. We felt rushed the last time we were there. This time we could rent an apartment in St. Petersburg and get to know the city and its treasures."

She swirled a sip of wine in her mouth. Did Andorra and Russia have extradition treaties with the United States? Had Prescott chosen those countries as places of refuge to avoid being charged with Jenna's murder and a host of other crimes? Is that what this was all about?

She searched his face for cracks in the smooth façade. Seeing none, she continued probing. "There's a murder investigation underway. Do you really think this is the time to flee the country?"

"Flee? The thought never occurred to me." Putting his fork down, he reached across the table and stroked her hand. "I don't want to live this way, Eleanor. We moved to Stony Vale to be anonymous—just an everyday retired couple. But since the murder, we can't even go to a grocery store, a library or a restaurant without being the subject of conversation. We're trapped like rats, and under these circumstances, we deserve an extended vacation. Six months to a year would allow us to blend in with the natives and get to know an entirely different way of life."

"And the commitments we've made?" she asked. "How would it look if the hometown hero abandoned the village he promised to revive?"

Prescott took a sip of wine and considered the question. "I'm beginning to think our work here is done. Think of it, Eleanor. Because of our efforts, there's a functioning historical society, an upcoming summer festival and a genealogy conference that will carry on for years after we're gone."

She didn't answer. Instead, she studied his face, and if she were reading him correctly, he was studying hers as well.

He set his wine glass down. "Listen. Whatever accusations the press has made, I had nothing to do with Jenna Henley's death."

Thoughts of a former president flooded Eleanor's mind. *I did not have sexual relations with that woman.* Prescott's denial had the same hollow ring to it.

"The police have to hang this crime on someone," he continued. "Given that Jenna Henley ended up in our pond, it's only natural to assume I had something do with it. I didn't, of course, but…" he hesitated. "There's a slight possibility that certain individuals and organizations with which I'm associated might be dragged into the investigation. If that should happen, I want to assure that…"

She cut him off. "Why would individuals and organizations with which you're associated be dragged into the investigation? Are you telling me that some unnamed colleague of yours came to our patio to murder Jenna and toss her in our pond?"

"Of course not. But if the investigation proceeds in that direction, there's a chance my name could be dragged in with theirs."

The wine turned sour in Eleanor's mouth. "Who are these individuals and organizations?"

"I'm not at liberty to discuss that."

She set her glass down on the table. She'd had it with this game of cat and mouse. It was time to show her hand and live with the consequences. "Let me take a guess as to who these individuals and organizations might be. In all likelihood they're connected to international biolabs conducting illegal genetic experiments in remote locations around the globe. Locally, they might be linked to a house in the woods not far from here. I don't know how Jenna Henley fits into the narrative, but perhaps in time the answer will become clear."

Prescott narrowed his eyes and she felt herself trembling beneath his steely glare. The organizations she'd referred to had tentacles reaching all over the planet. Would one of those tentacles wrap itself around her until she couldn't breathe?

"Let me assure you," he said, his words slow and measured. "Neither I nor my colleagues had anything to do with Jenna Henley's death. We're as mystified about what happened as anyone else."

"I want to believe you," Eleanor said, "but the facts paint a different picture. Fact one. You first encountered Jenna Henley last fall at a 24-hour veterinary clinic. Fact two. You spoke to her over the holidays at the casino in Bethlehem. Fact three. You lied to the detectives when you said you didn't know her. And fact four. You lied again when you told the detectives you'd been listening to the keynote address when, in fact, you were really back here at the house. So what conclusions do you expect me to draw?"

Prescott slammed his fist on the table. "You have no idea what you're talking about."

"Don't I?" She pushed back her chair and rose from the table. "As far as your earlier question is concerned, I have no desire to join you for an extended vacation. Not in Andorra or Russia or any other place where the law can't touch you. But I fully intend to take a nice long vacation—by myself. So, wish me bon voyage, Prescott, and I'll wish you the same."

She left him in the dining room with the wine, the candles, the roses and the music. Her luggage, purse and laptop were already in the Prius. She'd be staying with her sister until she could make other arrangements.

Forty-one

Brooke watched the detectives board the elevator and disappear from view. How would they handle the information she'd just shared? She'd omitted Ted's name when describing the visit to the house in the woods, but they'd assumed it based on recollections of past investigations. At first, Burleigh had downplayed her story about the women in the limo, saying they had their own reasons for being there that were none of her business. Furthermore, he claimed she and Ted were out of line for disregarding the no-trespassing signs. By doing so, they'd put themselves at risk and were lucky they didn't end up in the hospital. His attitude changed when she described her conversation with Elder Bolton.

At the end of the story, Burleigh gave her a no-nonsense stare—an expression she'd seen too often in the last year-and-a-half. *"Listen to me and listen good,"* he'd snarled. *"I don't want you telling a soul what you just told us. And by a soul, I mean that goofy yellow-haired friend of yours and that religious nut who dragged you into this mess. The last thing we need are amateurs screwing up the investigation. Do I make myself clear?*

Detective Radley echoed his boss's concerns, but even so, Brooke sensed that he'd gotten a kick out of the things she'd said. And why not? He probably didn't hear stories like this one every day.

She walked over to the window and looked down at the dumpster in the alley. How would things play out from here? Would SWAT teams storm the house in the woods, weapons drawn and police dogs tugging at their leashes? She imagined a dog war—Dobermans and German shepherds in a bloody battle, while inside the house, people rushed around frantically destroying evidence.

Her thoughts shifted to Ted. If she contacted him, he'd start asking questions, and she'd start answering them. But she'd been sworn to secrecy, and with the stakes so high, she had to follow orders—to do otherwise would jeopardize police operations. And yet Ted had been texting her all day. He was worried, and the least she could do was let him know she was all right.

"*I'm doing fine,*" she responded to his most recent text. "*I can't talk now. Maybe in a few days.*"

He got back in an instant asking for details. Was she in danger? Was she mad at him? Were Tillman's people following her? Or was it even worse than that?

She assured him she that she meant what she'd said—she was doing just fine. She longed to say more, but she forced herself to follow orders, as difficult as that was.

Later that night, she lay awake, her thoughts consumed by questions about Jenna and the fetus she'd carried. What does a creature become when it's part human and part something else? She'd heard about scientists implanting human stem cells into animal embryos with the goal of creating transplantable organs. But what happens when the order's reversed? What would be the result if animal stem cells were implanted in human embryos. Would monsters emerge? Would these traits be transmissible to the next generation? If so, what were the implications for the human gene pool?

She pictured the human-animal hybrids in the myths and legends she'd enjoyed as a child. There was Anubis, the jackal-headed god of the dead. Sobek with the face of a crocodile. Ra, the falcon-headed sun god crowned with the solar disk. She pictured Ganesh, the elephant-headed god of the Hindus. Cernunnos the horned god of the Celts. And lesser beings like satyrs, centaurs and fauns. Like the minotaur raging in his labyrinth or pale-faced harpies with their savage wings, or Medusa, the snake-haired gorgon facing off against the demi-god Perseus or Melusine, a water spirit who was half woman, half fish.

Melusine? Why hadn't Brooke thought of that before? The symbolism had been staring her in the face this entire time, but until this moment, the significance had bypassed her entirely. Like Melusine, Jenna's child was part human and part something else, and the secrets Melusine sought to hide had been bequeathed, not to Jenna, but to her unborn child.

Unholy. Jenna had described her child as unholy.

The thought kept Brooke awake late into the night. On Friday, she dragged herself out of bed and spent the day alternating between a search for news about Tillman and research into the implications of CRISPR gene-editing technologies. What she found was deeply disturbing—things were far more advanced than she'd imagined. In the wrong hands, these technologies threatened to wreak havoc on a gullible human population who'd grown accustomed to accepting whatever the so-called experts proclaimed to be true.

Saturday morning brought a continued dearth of information about Tillman, but perhaps there was a reason for that. Perhaps the operation was being kept under wraps. If so, she'd have to be patient and wait for the outcome.

The big story, however was a Nor'easter storming up the

eastern seaboard. Frantic broadcasters pointed to maps of the storm's progress, charts of expected rainfall, graphs showing windspeeds, images of damage wrought so far by this behemoth, and footage of people storming grocery stores for batteries and other necessities. Brooke already had these necessities, and as she glanced out the window at the dark, angry sky, someone knocked on the door.

"Open up. It's me—Maggie. "I've got some amazing news."

Brooke had amazing news as well—none of which she was allowed to share.

"I can't talk long," Maggie said when Brooke invited her in. "I have to get to work, but wait until you hear this. Nora Murphy came in the store yesterday, and as we were talking, she mentioned that her mom said there used to be a Gilbert family in Stony Vale, and they attended the Center for Spiritual Growth. Gilbert was Katherine Strauss's maiden name—remember? Nora's wondering if the Gilberts from Stony Vale were related to Katherine. If that's the case, Derrick might have visited Stony Vale as a kid, and he would have known his way around. And that's how he was able to come up with a plan for killing Jenna."

At the point, Brooke knew too much to take the idea seriously. "Too bad Derrick and Geoff had alibis for the time of both deaths," she said.

Maggie scoffed at the suggestion. "Don't tell me you're buying that story. Detective Burleigh tried to tell me as much, but I know better. And here's why. Derrick and Geoff own a super successful lumber business that employs bunches of people. Add to that, a resort and conference center that'll soon bring lots of money to the area. The local police aren't about to bite the hand that feeds the whole community, and that's the reason they bought into Derrick and Geoff's trumped-up alibi.

"But anyway," Maggie said with a quick glance at her watch, "Nora's going to the Center to check through the records to see what she can find out about this Gilbert family. And if they turn out to be related to Kathryn, it just might change everything about the investigation.

"And on a related note," she added, as she walked over to the door. "Seth and Nora seem to be patching things up. She told me they're having dinner together tonight."

With that, Maggie headed off to the Emporium, leaving Brooke to focus on work and news updates. There was plenty of work and zero updates—just continued coverage of the storm by reporters who acted like they'd never seen rain until now.

Brooke wasted huge chunks of time trying to find out about the Tillman situation and went to bed Saturday night vowing that on tomorrow she'd ignore the news and focus on her work. Her efforts were fruitful, and around five Sunday afternoon, she sent off a newsletter she'd edited for a nonprofit organization and turned her attention to dinner. Afterward, she called Uncle Nelson to see how he was doing.

His voice when he answered was subdued. "It's hard, to believe, isn't it?" he remarked. "How can so many terrible things keep happening in a tiny village like Stony Vale?"

The question was bewildering. "What are you talking about?" she asked.

"You mean you haven't heard?"

"Heard what? I've been working all day."

"Oh, my dear," he said. "I'm afraid this will come as a terrible shock." He hesitated. "It's nearly six. Turn on the local news and call me when it's over."

Brooke felt a thrill of excitement as she picked up the remote and gave it a click. *This is it*, she told herself. *Finally, I'll hear the news I've been waiting for.*

The broadcast began by announcing breaking news. But instead of showing a SWAT team storming the house in the woods as Brooke expected, the camera focused on a smug individual with graying hair and wire-rimmed glasses. "The charges linking my client, Dr. Prescott Tillman, to a criminal conspiracy to murder Jenna Henley are completely unfounded," he asserted. "Dr. Tillman is innocent, and I look forward to proving it in court."

Before Brooke could savor this long-awaited moment, the focus shifted to yet another breaking story. This one began with a reporter and an elderly woman huddled beneath an umbrella.

"This morning when I let my dog out," the woman said, "I noticed my neighbor's back door hanging open. I phoned to let her know, and when she didn't answer, I pulled on my rain jacket and went over to close it for her. That's how we are in Stony Vale—we look out for each other. I shouted her name through the door, and when she didn't answer, I went inside. The kitchen was a mess with chairs knocked over, and there on the floor…" The woman brought a hand to her lips and stifled a sob. "I tried to revive her but…"

The scene shifted to a reporter outside a popular Easton restaurant. "Video producer, Seth Walker," he said, "has been detained in connection with Nora Murphy's murder."

"Nora!" Brooke screamed into the silence. How was this possible? And Seth? She thought back to his gentle words and kind expression as they'd stood together on the pedestrian bridge with the Delaware River flowing southward beneath their feet. This couldn't be happening—could it?

The camera segued to a middle-aged man who introduced himself as the restaurant's maître d. "The couple started arguing, and when the racket disturbed our customers, I went to the table and asked them to tone it down. Instead of apologizing, the woman swore at me and ran out in tears. The gentleman kindly apologized for both of them, settled the bill and followed her."

Brooke sank back against the sofa cushions. She'd expected the news about Tillman, but Seth killing Nora? It didn't seem possible.

Once the shock eased a bit, she called her uncle. He didn't feel much like talking, so they cut the conversation short after a few words.

Later, she lay awake, thinking about Nora. She pictured her alone in the basement of the Center for Spiritual Growth, sifting through files in hopes of finding something to tie Kathryn Gilbert Strauss to Stony Vale. Hours later, Nora was dead. Was there a connection? Was it possible Seth was taking the fall for someone else?

The answer to those questions might be hidden in some long-lost document in the Center's filing cabinet. If she handed the matter over to the detectives, precious time would be lost as they scrambled to get a warrant to search the place, and in that time, evidence could be destroyed. There was only one solution. Someone who didn't need a warrant had to visit the Center as soon as possible. At the moment, the only person she could think of was herself.

Forty-two

"We're devastated," Doris said when Brooke called the next morning. "The news is just too terrible to believe. Nora—murdered? And Seth—such a kind, thoughtful man—how could he do such a thing? And Prescott—our dear friend. Conspiracy to commit murder? How is any of this possible?

Doris continued for some time in that vein before Brooke could explain the reason for her call. Not her real reason, but a story she'd made up. She claimed to need access to the Center's files to verify information for a piece she was editing about life along the Delaware Canal.

"Normally that wouldn't be a problem," Doris said when Brooke finished. "But yesterday, Heather and Ryan moved documents out of the Center and into the house so they could finish computerizing the records. They hope to complete the job before we leave for Wyoming—that way they can hand things over in good shape to whoever replaces us. At the moment, stacks of folders are all over the floor in Ryan's study, and I can't imagine anyone being able to make sense of them. And besides that, no one will be here. Heather's scheduled to work at the organic farm where she volunteers, and Ryan and I are driving Ralph to the adult daycare center and taking the children out for the day—they're terribly shaken by everything that's happened."

"I understand," Brooke said. "It's just that I'm on deadline and I was hoping to get this settled."

Doris hesitated a moment. "I guess there's no harm in your being here alone. After all, you're Nelson Roberts' niece, so of course I trust you. Here's what I'll do. I'll leave the key under the mat by the kitchen door. Make yourself at home, and feel free to use the copy machine."

Brooke thanked her and then, on impulse, she called Detective Burleigh in hopes of filling him in on her plans. "On Saturday," she began, "Nora Murphy went to the Center in Stony Vale to search for information about a Gilbert family who once lived in the area. Nora was murdered a few hours later, and I can't help wondering if it was related to something she'd learned that provided a link Kathryn Gilbert Strauss's death and Jenna's murder. If true, it would open up a whole new angle in the investigation into Jenna's death. Yesterday the files were moved into Ryan's study so they could be digitized. I've decided to check them out." She hesitated. "Unless you'd rather handle it yourself."

Burleigh let out a laugh. "You don't quit coming up with theories, do you? But at this point, it hardly matters. We found Walker's fingerprints in Nora's house and he admitted to being there briefly after their argument. The Tillman case is out of our hands, but the FBI has it pretty much wrapped up. In other words, both cases are closed, so if it makes you happy, go over to Stony Vale and make a nuisance of yourself to your heart's content."

When the call ended, Brooke glared at the phone. The information she'd shared was compelling. Why couldn't Burleigh see it?

▾ ▾ ▾

In spite of lingering drizzle, Stony Vale was buzzing with activity when Brooke rolled into town. News vans lined the block outside the Tillman's home, and reporters crowded the sidewalk, umbrellas open and microphones raised like bayonets.

Leaving them to their business, she hurried to the Stevensons' house and found the key under the mat at the back door. Once inside, she locked the door behind her and headed through the kitchen into the dining room. As she entered the living room, a shiver worked its way up her spine. She was here alone, and other than Detective Burleigh and Doris Stevenson, no one knew where she was.

Shaking off the momentary anxiety, she went into the foyer where the goddess Aurora stood guard outside Ryan's study. Brooke paused to take a look at this work of art that loomed so powerfully over the space. Was it solid marble, she wondered. Tapping it, she heard a hollow sound. Definitely not solid marble as it appeared—just plaster with a faux finish.

Ryan's study was every bit as messy as Doris had indicated. After picking her way through an obstacle course of file folders, Brooke sat on the rug in front of the desk and chose a stack at random. Weak light through the stained-glass window behind her cast pastel ribbons across the manilla folders as she started her search. The contents weren't much to see—just a bunch of hand-written financial records dating back years. A second pile contained old programs listing guest speakers, workshop leaders and special activities through the decades. Next up was a solitary folder that contained the Center's founding documents.

The next stack consisted of alphabetized lists of members through the years. To Brooke's great disappointment there was nothing in the G folder about a Gilbert family. Was that because there'd never been a Gilbert family at the Center, or had someone found the information and removed it—perhaps after Nora's visit? If so, who had a reason to keep that information quiet?

The next stack was made up of folders containing bimonthly newsletters dating to the Center's inception. Brooke flipped through dozens of issues filled with metaphysical musings, quotes from sacred texts and descriptions of activities and upcoming events. After paging through several years-worth, her eyes began to glaze over, but she kept at it until a headline from thirty-two years ago jumped from the page. *Hats off to Kathy Gilbert for a Great Summer Retreat* it said. The article spoke about a grad student named Kathy Gilbert who worked summers at the campground where the retreat was held. The author praised her for working with the center to arrange activities that made the event a huge success.

Brooke looked closely at the photo accompanying the article. In showed a young, handsome Ralph Stevenson standing next to a fair-haired beauty in shorts and a tee-shirt. Ralph and Kathy Gilbert were surrounded by a crowd of smiling people who appeared to be enjoying the great outdoors on a sunny, summer day. Was this the same person who became Dr. Kathryn Gilbert Strauss?

Brooke got up from the floor, amused at the thought of Burleigh's reaction when she'd hand him a copy of the article and photo. But would he be impressed by the evidence she was about to present, or would he brush it aside as a coincidence that proved nothing.

As the machine spit out a copy, her attention was diverted to a bookshelf lined with scrapbooks. Doris Stevenson was an avid scrapbooker—did the albums contain additional photos of Kathy Gilbert? Should she take the time to find out?

She didn't have a choice. While Burleigh might consider one photo a coincidence, multiple photos would force his hand. Once he reopened the investigation into Nora's death, he'd have to reopen the investigation into Kathryn's and Jenna's as well.

The first scrapbook Brooke selected contained a collection of pedigree charts—family trees arranged sideways to provide more information than could be contained in a typical family tree. The first page began with Doris. Her maiden name was Billings and her grandmother's maiden name was Allen, and her great grandmother's maiden name was...

Brooke had to look twice to make sure she wasn't mistaken. No—Doris's great, grandmother was a woman named Laura Gilbert. Did that meant that Kathy Gilbert wasn't just a random grad student who'd overseen a successful retreat, but a distant relative of Doris Stevenson?

Brooke set the pedigree charts aside and grabbed a scrapbook from the shelf. It was all about Ryan as a little kid, and the second scrapbook was a work in progress showing images of Stony Vale through the decades. The third was a more likely target—it featured photos of Doris's side of the family. Brooke flipped through the pages, the captions blurring into one another, and then stopped—her gaze riveted to a series of photos of a family reunion in a wooded picnic grove.

A photo at the bottom of the page showed a youthful, handsome, muscular Ralph Stevenson helping a cute young thing in shorts and a halter top reel in a huge fish. He stood behind her, one arm around her waist and the other helping her steady the fishing rod. There was a sense of intimacy in the way their bodies meshed together and a hint of shared interests and shared pleasure as they stood together in those rushing waters. And the caption? *Kathy Gilbert Gets the Catch of the Day.*

A wild thought struck Brooke as she stared at that photo. Kathryn was Jenna's birthmother—by now, everyone knew that. But her father? Could it be Ralph Stevenson? No—that wasn't possible—he was a doddering old man. But according to the photo, he hadn't always been that way.

The phone rang on Ryan's desk, shattering the stillness in the study. At the same time, Brooke heard it ringing in the living room as well. She recalled Doris mentioning that the phone was hooked up in three spots—the study, the living room and the office in the Center. Was it possible that without knowing of his condition, Kathryn had called Ralph to tell him about her upcoming reunion with Jenna? Did she say she intended to tell Jenna he was her biological father? Ralph would have forgotten all about the conversation once it ended, but if Ryan listened in, he certainly wouldn't have forgotten.

Now that Brooke thought of it, Tillman wasn't the only person who'd been late to dinner on the Monday Kathryn fell to her death. Heather Stevenson had been late as well. Did she take a detour to Wellsboro on her way home from the Conference at Penn State? Did she and Ryan conspire together to murder Jenna and Kathryn in an attempt to protect Ryan's inheritance from the claims an illegitimate sister—Jenna— might make on the estate? Were she and Ryan afraid that if Jenna demanded a share of Ralph's money, there wouldn't be enough to make their dream of a ranch in Wyoming come true?

Brooke's cell vibrated in her pocket, startling her from her thoughts.

"I can't talk now," she whispered to Ted. Whispering wasn't necessary—there was no one to hear her, but the choice was instinctive. "I'm alone in the Stevensons' house with photos that could upend the Jenna Henley murder investigation," she told him. "I'll call back once I'm safely out of here."

She put the scrapbook on the copier, pressed the button, and as the copy slid into the tray, the front door opened and footsteps echoed in the foyer.

Forty-three

Things were hectic at police headquarters following yesterday's arrests—Seth Walker by the locals and Prescott Tillman by the FBI. To escape the racket, Radley and the boss slipped into the boss's office to discuss the evidence in the Nora Murphy case—evidence that tied Seth Walker to the crime scene. They'd found his prints in Nora's living room and kitchen as well as bits of his hair on Nora's clothes and on the floor. When confronted, Walker said he'd broken up with her and she wasn't taking it well. "She came at me like a banshee," he' said. "But I didn't retaliate. It's not my style to hit a woman let alone kill her."

That, of course, is what they all said.

"By the way," the boss said as he slid the Walker file in a desk drawer. "I had a call this morning from Brooke Roberts. Can you believe she had the audacity to suggest that the Murphy case should be reopened? Something about information Nora uncovered while snooping around the Center in Stony Vale."

Radley didn't say anything. The boss had a chip on his

shoulder when it came to Brooke. After all, she'd upstaged him on two separate occasions—both of which were high-profile cases. The first involved her husband's death eighteen months ago, and the second involved a murder a year later at an upscale private school called Sussex Academy. The boss was legitimately concerned for her safety and for the integrity of his investigations, but it didn't take much in the way of brains to see other forces at play. But perhaps Radley shouldn't be critical? How would he like it if 30 years from now he was facing retirement only to have an upstart like Brooke steal his thunder. He wouldn't like it one bit, but even so, he liked to think that he wouldn't let his emotions cloud his reasoning. That concept was drilled into a cop from the first day of training right on up to the last day on the job. No, as far as Radley was concerned, if Brooke had something to tell them, it deserved a respectful hearing.

"The evidence against Walker is plain as day," Burleigh continued, "but somehow Brooke got it in her head that Nora Murphy was murdered because she found evidence linking Jenna's birthmother to Stony Vale. As we speak, Brooke's at the Stevensons' house, tearing the place up and trying to solve a mystery that doesn't exist."

Radley shifted uncomfortably in his seat. "I'd like to know what Nora found, wouldn't you?"

The question earned a scoff. "What's the point? We've got our man and the FBI's got theirs. No, my friend—it's time to close the books and move on."

Burleigh grinned as he gazed at Radley from across the desk. "I know what your problem is. You're sweet on Brooke, and I can't say I blame you. But take some advice from an old pro. The last thing a detective needs is a love interest meddling in his work. Take my wife for instance. She's content to do her job at the bank and let me do mine. It's better that way."

"I'm not sweet on Brooke," Radley argued although the

thought had crossed his mind. Especially back in those days following her husband's death when she was all weepy and vulnerable and spooked by powerful forces she had every right to be spooked by. "All I'm saying is that if Brooke stumbled onto something, it might be a good idea to provide backup. In case you've forgotten, three people are dead."

"Correct. And those three people are dead for unrelated reasons."

Radley was about to challenge the remark when Burleigh's phone rang. He glanced at caller ID and gave Radley one of his condescending smirks. "It's Wellsboro—probably calling to say that Katheryn Strauss's death was a slip and fall. Case closed."

He snapped up the phone and after listening for a few seconds, the smirk faded. "Are you sure?" he said into the mouthpiece. "You're saying you have evidence that Kathryn Strauss and Doris Stevenson are distant relatives?" He listened for a few more seconds. "I understand, but at this point the FBI's handling the Jenna Henley murder. It's no longer our case, and it will be difficult to…" He paused to listen.

"What's that?" he continued. "A witness came forward saying she saw a person in a hooded rain jacket exiting Kathryn's house on the day of her death."

Before Burleigh could finish, Radley was on his feet and headed for the door. "FBI or no FBI, I'm going to Stony Vale to provide backup. Are you coming with me?" he shouted. "Or do I have to go there by myself?"

Forty-four

Brooke huddled behind Ryan's desk, hardly daring to breathe. The footsteps in the foyer grew louder, and then a shadow fell over the open doorway. Heart pounding, she waited for Ryan to enter, but it wasn't Ryan. Instead, Heather stood outside the study, a derringer in her hand. Brooke recognized the model right away—the Snake Slayer— the weapon she and Karl used to take on camping trips.

Two shots, she told herself. If she could get Heather to waste both of them, she'd be safe. Sort of. She'd still have to contend with Heather's height and strength advantage, but at least she wouldn't die from a bullet to the brain.

"I know you're somewhere in this house," Heather called out, her voice echoing in the stillness. "I heard you talking to Doris on the phone, and I saw your car in the parking lot." Entering the study, her gaze came to rest on the scrapbook Brooke left on the copy machine. "I never thought of Doris's scrapbooks," she muttered to herself, her back to Brooke as she crossed the room, grabbed the copy from the tray and stared at it. "How could I have been so stupid?"

If Brooke intended to evade the Snake Slayer's bullets, this was the time to act—while Heather was distracted. Her only hope was to surprise her from behind and wrest the gun from her hand.

Taking a deep breath, she lunged at Heather from behind the desk and grabbed at the gun. Heather let out a shriek and yanked the derringer away, but before she could aim, Brooke grabbed her wrist and dug her nails into the skin to force her to release it. But Heather wasn't about to give up so easily. As they struggled for control, the derringer pointed toward the floor, the ceiling, the desk, the copy machine, the scrapbooks and then…

A shot rang out, and on the other side of the room, the stained-glass window exploded into shards of multi-colored shrapnel. Brooke felt the sting of glass against the back of her neck, but she couldn't worry about that now. She'd easily survive a few bloody scratches, but not the single bullet that waited for her in the gun.

Cursing, Heather brought a hand to her forehead and wiped away blood that ran down her face and into her mouth. The taste of it seemed to ignite something within her, and with the fury of an Amazon warrior, she yanked her wrist free from Brooke's grasp. As she raised the gun to fire, her foot slipped on a manilla file folder and she stumbled backward against the desk. The impact sent the gun hurtling into the air and crash-landing on the rug. In an instant, Brooke grabbed it and darted into the foyer.

She'd only gone a few steps when Heather came at her from behind, tackling her and bringing them both crashing to the ceramic tile floor. Brooke's hand—the one that held the gun—was crushed beneath her, while next to her, blood from Heather's forehead dripped like rose petals on the clean white tiles.

The pressure eased a bit when Heather shifted her weight,

but when Brooke tried to break free, Heather forced a knee against the nape of her neck, driving the glassy splinters deeper into the flesh.

"Don't do this, Heather," Brooke begged, gasping for air. "You and Ryan are in enough trouble already."

"Ryan had nothing to do with this," Heather snarled. "I listened in on a phone call and found out that Kathryn was planning to tell Jenna that Ralph was her father. I couldn't let that happen—if Ryan knew he had a half-sister, he'd have taken pity on her and cut her a share of his parents' money. I had to do something to protect our inheritance, so I bought a burner phone, made up an alias and contacted Jenna to say I had information about her biological father I'd share if she met Saturday at nine on the Tillman's patio. I pretended to leave early for the conference at Penn State, and then I parked a mile away from the house, walked back along the canal path and hid in the woods until Jenna showed up on the patio. I fooled Kathryn the same way—I called and said I had information she needed to know before she met Jenna. The stupid fool welcomed me into her house, and I assumed that the nasty business was over and done until Nora told me about information she'd found at the Center about a Gilbert family from years back. After I silenced her, I purged the records but I never gave a thought to Doris's scrapbooks."

Brooke couldn't comment—not with Heather's knee pressing on her neck and stifling the flow of air. Her lungs screamed for mercy, and she was too weak to resist when Heather reached beneath her and took the gun. As Heather stood up, air flooded into Brooke's lungs, but with the derringer aimed at her head, there didn't seem to be any way to avoid certain death.

I'll claim self-defense," Heather said, her voice quivering as blood dripped from the gash in her forehead. "I'll say I found an intruder in the house and fired before I realized who it was."

"It won't work," Brooke told her. "They'll see the broken window and they'll see the blood, and they'll realize that there's more to the story than you're telling."

"I'll figure out a way to explain it," she said. "But first…"

A ferocious desire to live forced Brooke to take the only option left. She grabbed at Heather's ankle with enough force to throw her off balance and send her staggering backward into the goddess Aurora. The impact broke off a wing that crashed against the back of Heather's head, pitching her forward. In the chaos, she accidentally fired off the second bullet while at the same moment, the door flew open and Burleigh and his partner appeared in the opening. A sudden, anguished cry escaped Burleigh's lips as the bullet struck his leg, and as he dropped to his knees, Jason Radley knelt to assist him.

In the aftermath of the gunshot, Heather lay moaning on the floor, the wind knocked out of her by the collision with Aurora's broken wing. Radley hastily abandoned his fallen comrade, and rushed over to force Heather's hands behind her back and clamp on the cuffs. Meanwhile, Brooke struggled to her knees, intent on assisting Detective Burleigh while at the same time, the lop-sided, one-winged Aurora teetered on her pedestal and with a lurch, succumbed to gravity. The statue knocked Brooke back to the floor and sent shockwaves of pain coursing through her skull as her head struck the hard, ceramic floor. From what seemed like a very great distance, she heard Jason Radley asking if she was okay.

Forty-five

Ted hadn't bothered waiting for a return call from Brooke. Instead, he'd climbed in his Jeep and broken every speed limit between Allentown and Stony Vale. To his surprise, Main Street was eerily quiet when he arrived. He'd expected to see reporters outside the Tillman's house, but while news vans lined the block, there were no other signs of life.

That changed when he pulled into the parking lot next to the Spiritual Center. Reporters swarmed the exterior of the Stevenson's house, but they weren't alone. There were cops—lots of them. And terrifyingly—three ambulances.

Ted emerged from his Jeep and elbowed his way through the crowd. "What happened?" he shouted.

"Gunshots," a reporter said. "Three people down—two women and a cop."

"I heard one of the women died," another reporter spoke up.

"That hasn't been confirmed," said another.

"The women," Ted asked. "Who are they?"

"No word on that yet," someone answered.

Without waiting for details, he broke away from the mob and fought his way toward a pair of cops guarding the front door.

"A friend of mine is inside the house," he said. "I've got to make sure she's all right."

"I don't care if your mother's in there," one of the cops snarled. "You can't go inside."

"You don't understand. My friend called and said…"

"Listen, buddy. Everybody has a story about why they should be allowed to enter. Why would I believe you?"

The second cop was more reasonable. "This is a crime scene, sir. We need you to stand back there with the others."

"You don't understand," Ted argued. "Brooke called me. She's in danger and I want to make sure she's…"

Before he could finish his sentence, a third cop emerged from the house and elbowed Ted aside as he raised a megaphone to his lips. "Clear a path between the door and the ambulances. First responders coming through."

Ted craned his neck to see who was on the stretchers, but it was no use, not with cops and medical personnel gathered around. He watched, helpless as the ambulances swallowed up the victims. And then, sirens wailing, the ambulances left the parking lot and sped away.

Forty-six

Aglow in the distance grew brighter. Was this the proverbial tunnel of light Brooke had heard so much about—the one connecting this world to the next?

Her eyes fluttered open and she gazed into a muted light directly over her head. Not the tunnel of light after all. She was still in this world, not the next.

Memories flooded her mind as she lay there. Heather. A derringer. Detective Burleigh. The goddess Aurora. It seemed like a long time ago.

Shifting her gaze, she watched a woman in lavender scrubs enter something into a tablet. She tried to sit up, but hammers pounding inside her skull drove her back against the pillow.

The woman glanced in her direction. "Lie still," she said. "Now that you're back among the living, I'll get a doctor to speak to you."

Eventually a physician arrived. She informed Brooke that she'd suffered a grade-three concussion as well as multiple contusions and lacerations. While she was expected to be fine, she'd be staying overnight for observation. She could expect to feel sleepy, nauseous and headachy for about a week.

The doctor exited, and after a long wait, an orderly showed up and wheeled her off for an MRI. The pounding and banging were the perfect accompaniment for the pounding in her head, and once the ordeal was over, the orderly deposited her in a private room where she spent the rest of the day dozing. Occasionally a nurse roused her, but mostly she slept.

She emerged from her slumbers late in the afternoon and found a bouquet of pink roses on the bedside table. Looking around, she saw Uncle Nelson in a chair at the foot of the bed.

"You brought roses—they're lovely,"

"As lovely as you, my dear."

She tried to smile. "I don't feel very lovely at the moment. My head's throbbing, I'm dizzy and my stomach's churning." Falling silent, she reflected on the events that had brought her here. "It all happened so fast," she recalled. "No sooner had I begun to figure things out than Heather appeared in the doorway with a gun."

"So far, the details are rather murky," Uncle Nelson said. "According to news reports, Ralph Stevenson was Jenna's biological father, and Heather didn't want Jenna cashing in on her in-laws' assets. As you can imagine, Ryan and Doris are devastated, Ralph is bewildered and confused, and I can't begin to think how this will affect the children. Heather, on the other hand, is facing a lifetime in prison."

He shook his head sadly. "It's a tragic situation. At this point, the only winners are Malcolm Mackenzie, Seth Walker and Prescott Tillman. All three can relax now that the cloud of suspicion's been lifted."

"What's being reported about Jenna's baby?" Brooke asked.

"Nothing as far as I've heard. The pregnancy's unrelated to the murder, so I assume the authorities will opt to protect the father's identity."

"The father's identity isn't the issue," Brooke said angrily.

"There isn't a father, not in the usual sense. The issue is Tillman and his creepy genetic experiments."

Uncle Nelson raised an eyebrow. "Creepy genetic experiments?"

"That's right. By now the media must be going wild with stories about his experiments with genetically altered human embryos."

Her uncle's look of concern deepened. "There was a bit of a kerfuffle about a fertility clinic Prescott was involved with, but the accusations didn't amount to anything. Are you sure you weren't…"

"Dreaming? No. I was there at that house in the woods. I saw the women getting out of the limo. I got chased by savage dogs, and the next day a Mormon missionary told me what was really going on. By now, it should be a huge international scandal."

"I've followed the news throughout the day," Uncle Nelson told her. "The only mention of anything related to genetics was an FBI investigation into a private clinic that offers reproductive and genetic services. Concerns about irregularities vanished when those in charge provided licenses, financial records and paperwork to prove that their services are aboveboard."

Brooke was astounded. "You're saying that paying women to have embryos implanted and harvested after three months is aboveboard? The documents they showed the FBI were fake— I'd bet my life on it."

"I'd advise against it," her uncle said. "You've already made too many bets with your life." His gaze was tender as he looked at her. "Perhaps this is a conversation for another time. For now, you need your rest."

He was right. This exchange had taken a toll on her, and by now her head was pounding, not just from her injuries, but from the thought of Tillman getting away with his crimes. And then a thought flashed into her mind. "Detective Burleigh!"

she cried. "Is he all right?"

"He'll be fine," her uncle assured her. "Jason Radley stopped by to check on you a short time ago. He said the bullet splintered Detective Burleigh's femur, and while the injury's a challenging one, he's expected to make a full recovery.

"I wonder what brought him to the Stevenson's house," Brooke mused. "He didn't think much of my concerns when I called him earlier this morning."

"Detective Radley mentioned that as well. He said they were responding to a tip alleging that Kathryn Strauss was a distant relative of Doris Stevenson. A second tip came from a neighbor of Kathryn's who claimed to have seen a tall woman in a hooded rain jacket leaving Kathryn's house on the afternoon of her death. Knowing you were alone in the Stevenson's house, the detectives responded immediately."

She nodded, but didn't say anything. She felt all talked out, something which her uncle seemed to understand.

"You need your rest, my dear," he said, his expression tender. "But before I say goodbye, a nurse asked me to give you this."

He handed her a bag with a logo from a gift shop at a nearby nature center. "She said a visitor stopped by earlier, and when he realized you were asleep, he asked the nurse to give you this. She passed it on to me."

Brooke eyed the bag warily. "Is it safe to open?"

"I had the same concern," her uncle said, "and so I took a look. The gift strikes me as odd, but perfectly safe."

"Okay then." Pulling out the decorative tissue paper, she reached inside and felt the soft plush of a stuffed animal. Not an animal exactly, she realized as she removed it from the bag and saw the red crest and pointed head of the pileated woodpecker. A tag on its neck said "press here for the authentic call." When she did, a loud cuk-cuk-cuk filled the room.

For a moment she was speechless. Anyone else would have

sent flowers, but Ted? He'd thought of something special—
something that would amuse her while at the same time lasting
long after flowers wilted. The gift was personal and thoughtful,
and she felt a momentary pang of envy at the thought of Ashley
reeling in a guy like Ted.

"I'm assuming the gift means something to you," her uncle
said.

"Indeed, it does."

"And it's related to the story you'll soon be telling me?"

She nodded.

"Wonderful. Until then, you need to rest, but before I
leave, can I convince you to stay at my apartment for a few days
once you're discharged?"

She thought of what awaited her at the Beacon Arms. Reporters. Nosy neighbors. Endless questions. And then she
thought of what awaited her at her uncle's. Earl Grey tea.
Scones with marmalade. A Bach concerto playing in the background.

"I wouldn't have it any other way," she told him, and she
meant it.

Epilogue

A week later, Brooke looked into Ted's eyes across a candlelit table. It was strange seeing him in a restaurant instead of a coffeeshop, and stranger still to see him duded up in a tweed blazer instead of a hoodie. He looked different—savvy and professional in a way she found appealing—as much as she hated to admit it.

Over appetizers, she filled him in on her meeting with Elder Bolton and listened as he described a mix-up involving tracking devices that ended in an unexpected visit from Eleanor Tillman.

From there the conversation moved on to more recent events. In the last 48 hours, the Tillmans had put their house on the market, Eleanor had gone off somewhere with the Corgis—ostensibly to finish her book—and Tillman had departed for an extended vacation to parts unknown.

Ted reached for his phone, scrolled around and handed it to Brooke across the table. "Tillman's not the only one unloading his house. How about this—look familiar?"

On the screen was a real estate ad featuring the white

stucco house in the woods. The price tag? Six-point-four million. Subsequent pictures showed the interior—spacious rooms now vacant.

Brooke handed the phone back. "It kills me to think they're getting away with it—all because of fake documents their lawyers designed to fool the authorities."

Ted paused to wipe his lips with a linen napkin. "It's a drag, but face it—that's how the world works. Powerful people in powerful positions know how to guard their secrets."

"And that puts us in a tricky position," Brooke remarked. "We know too much. Do you think Tillman's got people watching us?"

"Possibly, but I doubt they'll come after us, not when the authorities have a record of the things you told them—the timing would draw attention. I suspect Tillman's people will wait a year or so, and if we've kept quiet all that time, they'll leave us alone."

"And if we haven't kept quiet? If instead we decide to dig in deeper?"

He looked at her from across the table, the candlelight reflected in his eyes. "Are you saying you'd like to dig in deeper? And did I hear you say 'if we decide to dig in deeper' as in you're contemplating a joint venture?"

She met his gaze. Was he challenging her? Or was she challenging him? Either way, she hated to let Tillman get away with his crimes.

"All I'm saying," she said, choosing her words carefully, "is that I don't appreciate being gaslighted, and I don't like being told I didn't see what I saw, and I don't like being told I don't know what I know I know."

"You and me both," Ted agreed. "I've spent my whole life prying into the secrets of people and organizations that don't want their secrets known. I'm in it this far, and at this point, there's no turning back. But what about you?"

The server showed up to remove the first-course plates, giving her time to think of a response.

"Let's just say," she mused aloud, "that my curiosity's aroused. For now, I'll leave it at that."

"Fair enough. So, while you're thinking about where to go from here, there's a matter I'd like to discuss with you. After years of researching and hosting my own podcast, I decided it's time to write a book. The first draft's nearly done, and I'll soon be looking for an editor to go over the manuscript and give me an honest opinion. I'm looking for someone who will call BS if my arguments aren't sound. Someone who's insightful and curious and willing to follow an argument to its logical conclusion. Interested?"

The question took her by surprise. "Assuming I fit that description, what about your lady love? Won't Ashley be jealous if we're working together?"

Ted responded with a shrug. "Things have changed a bit in that department. Late last week I got a text saying it's over. To be honest, I was expecting it. It was just a matter of which one of us made the first move."

The news was startling. The only reason Brooke had agreed to have dinner with Ted was the knowledge that he and Ashley were a couple. Ashley was a safety net assuring that Brooke could spend time with Ted without running the risk of emotional complications. Without Ashley in Ted's life, that safety net was in tatters.

When Brooke didn't respond, Ted spoke up. "Maybe we should discuss your rates. I'm prepared to pay whatever you think is appropriate."

Rates? That was the least of Brooke's concerns. Instead, she was worrying about what she'd be walking into if she agreed to work with Ted on a lengthy project. "Rates aren't an issue," she said. "Eighteen months ago, you saved my life and the lives of two other people. I've never had a chance to pay you back."

"Don't be crazy. Paybacks aren't necessary."

She shook her head. "I mean it. I couldn't ask a penny from you."

"So, you're saying you'll take the assignment?"

Brooke fell silent. Without realizing it, she'd made it sound like she was agreeing to the arrangement when that wasn't the case at all. She looked away, and there in the glow of candlelight, something shifted inside her. If anything, Ashley had given her the space to recalibrate and realize how much she wanted Ted in her life. Should she take the risk and see where it led?

"Of course, I'll edit your book. The sooner we get started, the better."

Acknowledgments

Thanks so much to Sandra Carey Cody, Carol Billman and Marielena Zuniga for reading and commenting on various iterations of *Face Down in the Gene Pool*. Special thanks to Mike Gerow for his thoughtful critique and to editorial consultant Melissa Sullivan for her in-depth analysis. Kudos to Jon Labs for managing my website and endless thanks to my multi-talented husband, Wayne, for sharing his expertise in all facets of editing and publishing.

About the Author

Nancy Labs lives with her husband, tech editor, author and fine arts photographer, Wayne Labs, in Bucks County Pennsylvania.

The Brooke Roberts Mystery/Suspense Series springs from a lifetime fascination with historical puzzles, contemporary enigmas, theological conundrums and things that go bump in the night. *Face Down in the Gene Pool* is the third novel in the series.

You can visit her website: www.NancyLabs.com or contact her by email at BOOKS@Nancylabs.com.

Wishing You Harm

Artist Karl Erikson hasn't been himself in the days before his death. He's been anxious. Fearful. Obsessively religious. Odd for someone who's been a lifelong atheist. His house is broken into six weeks after the funeral. The investigator asks his widow: Is there anyone who wishes you harm? Brooke can't think of a soul who wishes her harm, but how else to explain the break-in? Drawers emptied onto the floor. Upholstery slashed. Valuables left untouched. Did Karl hide a treasure somewhere in the house? Did the intruder find it, or will he be back to search again?

Brooke's search for answers leads her into a dark world of secret societies, coded symbols, ancient prophecies and spiritual warfare. She soon realizes that high-tech security cameras, motion detectors and alarms can't protect her from those who are out there in the night, watching, waiting, and wishing her harm.

Undead All Over

The first rehearsal of Dracula goes off without a hitch—except for a corpse staring up at Brooke from a closet floor

It's not just any corpse. The victim is Nina Powell, a stunningly beautiful African American feminist and an art instructor at an elite academy for the progeny of the rich and powerful. The grief-stricken students thought Nina was amazing. Their parents, the school board and the cops—not so much.

Outraged by rumors that the police are intentionally bungling the investigation, Brooke decides to do some investigating of her own. Before long she's face-to-face with a white supremacist hate group, a bombastic radio talk show host and a vampire cult engaged in mysterious midnight rituals. Meanwhile, the killer is out there in the night, and like Dracula, he, she or it is thirsty for blood.